LITTLE EDENS

March 2004

For Lynn,

*who is bringing
wonderful energy
and ideas to
Annapolis.
Thank you
for being such a*

*wonderful support.
I'm so grateful
you're here.*

Barbara

LITTLE
EDENS

Stories

BARBARA KLEIN MOSS

Barbara Klein Moss

W. W. NORTON
& COMPANY

New York London

For information about permission to reproduce selections from this book, write to Permissions, W. W. Norton & Company, Inc., 500 Fifth Avenue, New York, NY 10110

Manufacturing by Quebecor World, Fairfield Inc.
Book design by Barbara M. Bachman
Production manager: Anna Oler

Library of Congress Cataloging-in-Publication Data

Moss, Barbara Klein.
    Little Edens : stories / Barbara Klein Moss.—1st ed.
        p. cm.
    ISBN 0-393-05712-7 (hardcover)
    1. Psychological fiction, American. 2. Loss (Psychology)—
Fiction. 3. Paradise—Fiction. I. Title.
    PS3613.O7795L57 2004
    813'.6—dc22   2003018196

W. W. Norton & Company, Inc.
500 Fifth Avenue, New York, N.Y. 10110
www.wwnorton.com

W. W. Norton & Company Ltd.
Castle House, 75/76 Wells Street, London W1T 3QT

1 2 3 4 5 6 7 8 9 0

For Stewart and Sara

and in memory of my mother and father

Lillian and Frank Klein

Contents

. . . Here all is distance;

there it was breath. After that first home,

the second seems ambiguous and drafty.

—RAINER MARIA RILKE,

EIGHTH DUINO ELEGY

(Translated by Stephen Mitchell)

LITTLE EDENS

Rug Weaver

His *daughter-in-law* is always wheedling him to leave his rooms over the garage and join her on the patio, but when Ebrahim Nahavendi hears her knocking on the door, his eyelids drop involuntarily. It is not just the Southern California sun that makes him squint—this he attributes to his months in a dark cell as a guest of the Revolution—but the sight of so much unabashed skin, so casually displayed. Years of gazing at shrouded women have permanently dulled his eyes. Like the receiver of tablets before him, he doesn't dare to look upon naked glory.

Today she is wearing a cut-off T-shirt and tiny shorts. The long length of her is damp from her daily run, her yellow hair sticking to her neck and shoulders. "A Persian treat is waiting for you," she says. "I stopped at Trader Joe's after dropping the girls off and raided the place for dried fruits— peaches, apricots, plums, dates, figs. The catch is, you're not allowed to eat them in this smoky *cave*." She brushes by him and moves with mock exasperation through the kitchenette into his bed/sitting room, raising blinds, opening windows, extinguishing his cigarette in the ashtray balanced on the arm of the couch.

"As soon as you leave, I'll make it dark again," he says. But she is so soft and diffused in her blondness, so much like light herself as she passes through the room that he allows himself to be swept into her orbit and led outside.

She insists that he sit in the chaise while she showers, and again he complies, although he dislikes looking at his stretched-out legs in their somber trousers. His feet, too, are overdressed, a pair of immigrant dandies in silk socks and braided sandals. For her sake he tries to adjust his back to the slump of the chair. He hopes she won't tell him to relax. He has no natural talent for it, and ends up contorting himself in postures of exaggerated ease like the boneless princes in Persian miniatures.

"We *live* out here," she had said, showing him around for the first time. Over the last month, he has seen that this is true. The patio is as lush as the interior of the house is spare, filled with green plants, potted flowers, and menacing cacti that she calls succulents—an oddly sensual word for such bristly growths. Toys and games are scattered on the redwood table; the children's bathing suits dry on the backs of rustic chairs. Against the stucco wall is the imposing gas grill, an altar on which, most nights, his son Yousef burns an offering. His daughter-in-law will eat no meat; it pollutes the system, she says. He has imagined with pleasure the sunny corridor of her insides: peach-colored, moistened with delicate washes of herbal tea.

She reappears in one of Yousef's shirts and an ankle

bracelet, carrying a large silver tray heaped with fruits, which she sets on the low table at his side. He takes an apricot from the tray—it is a Seder plate that belonged to Mina, his dead wife, and the apricots have been carefully arranged in the gully meant for the roasted egg—and holds it briefly on his tongue before shifting it to the pouch of his cheek.

"Is it good?" she asks. "Is it like the old country?"

"Dried fruit is dried fruit, here or in Iran." The words, flatter than he intended, measurably dim her luster. When you are that fair, he thinks, the slightest pressure leaves marks. "Very nice," he says repentantly, and bites down on the softened apricot, the sour sweetness flooding his mouth at just the moment that he says her foolish, long-limbed, gawky deer of a name. "Very nice . . . Kimberly."

Back in his apartment, he does the usual search for his cigarettes, finding them this time in the empty flour canister. Day after day she performs this infant's trick, apparently believing that if an object is out of sight he'll stop wanting it. Her persistence annoys him, but he senses that for her it is a kind of game. A flirtation, even. If she can't convert him to her creed of eternal health, she'll settle for provoking him.

The window in the dining alcove is the only one that suits his purposes. If he shuts the vertical blinds, then opens them so that slivers of light slant in, he can get the effect of bars in the reflection on the opposite wall. He doesn't really need this; it is only, he tells himself, a device for meditation, something to stare at while he focuses his mind. He lights a cigarette and settles back in his chair, feeling the slight vibration under his feet as the station wagon pulls into the garage beneath him. The high voices of the little girls float up in a brief clamor before the kitchen door slams shut. Sucking in smoke, he begins to weave.

First, strands of light teased until they stretch the length of the wall, the thread skeleton flickering like a home movie, reminding him of how humbly he began. Then color rising like mist, uncertain and quivering, the reds mixing with blues and blacks, and out of this chaos the first suggestion of swirling forms. Always this is the moment he fears to lose it all. The pattern assaults him all at once, the shapes he labored over singly bearing down on him in a tangled mass. Panicking, he fixes on a five-pointed star—or a moss rose or a bird on a branch, whatever surfaces first to his eye—and the pattern slows and stills, the whole design bows in submission. He is still the rug's master.

Its servant, too. Without it, how would he have survived those days in the cell, contemplating a death like Mina's father's?

The old man was taken first, dragged by Revolutionary Guards through the swinging doors of the carpet emporium he had modeled on a Paris department store, an ornament of the Shah's new Teheran. Three days later, they learned that Moses had been condemned as a Zionist agent and shot, along with the refined young Baha'i who assisted in the showroom.

Almost as an afterthought, it seemed, the Revolution came for Ebrahim. One guard held a machine gun to his head while the other—a wild-haired boy young enough to be his son—tore through the files in his small office and ravaged his shelves, flinging to the floor the books of carpet lore he had collected for years. Moses, having recruited Ebrahim as employee and son-in-law chiefly to reap the benefits of his fluent English and educated eye, had liked to indulge him with rare illustrated volumes. As the guards herded him out, they stomped conscientiously on the splayed pages of priceless rugs.

For the first two days he was locked in a room with many others. Amid the terror and confusion, men were removed in the night in a dreamlike constant shifting and others brought in to replace them. Then, inexplicably, he was transferred to his own small cell. He waited, huddled on the foam rubber slab in his English suit, to be taken for interrogation, or worse. But no one came except the guard who brought him food twice a day.

A solitary man, Ebrahim had always recoiled from enforced intimacy, but now he longed for the desperate camaraderie of the other prisoners. He discovered in himself a horror of dying alone, anonymous against a wall, without the sheltering ceremonies of his faith. The son of a Talmudic scholar, even in the realm of business he had retained an otherworldly aura that hinted at a preoccupation with higher things. For this also Moses had wooed him.

When Ebrahim thought of Mina, her fear infiltrated him like a virus. He saw her as he had left her, sedated on a couch, her hands still clutching the handkerchief she had been wringing moments before. Her bumbling brothers would have to organize the mourning for the father who had all but disowned them; his own sons, thank God, were at school in Paris, living with an uncle. Although Ebrahim had never loved Mina, his whole office as a husband was to hold her together. He imagined her emerging from drugged sleep, resting for a moment in the dimness of the curtained room before the awful knowledge descended on her. Moaning, she would run from room to room, tearing at her hair and clothes, the servants chattering after her like crows.

He remembered how she had first looked to him when Moses brought him to the house—as solid as Mother Earth, a buxom, deep-eyed young woman who lit the Sabbath candles before dinner and spoke the blessing with a slight lisp. As they ate Western-style at a gleaming oval table, she kept her eyes on her plate, but Ebrahim caught her glancing at him from beneath her heavy brows. She was in good health, Moses informed him later, pressing his thick fingertips together as if cradling an egg, but a little nervous owing to the early loss of her mother; she had been a dutiful daughter too long and needed the stability of her own household. Ebrahim knew he was being gulled. She was already twenty-six, the only daughter of a rich man and not yet married. Still, the comfort and opulence of the house seduced him, its brocade drapes and polished silver and massive furniture seeming to embody his dreams of France. Mina was a little heavy for his taste, though not unattractive. "And she has business sense," Moses said. "More than my useless sons. A scholar like you needs a woman who can take care of practical matters."

There, at least, Moses had spoken truly. Mina proved to be a shrewd bargainer, with Moses' feral instinct for quality. She trafficked with importers to furnish the house Moses gave them as a wedding gift; then, having feathered her nest in the finest European style, hid herself within its walls. In Ebrahim's presence she was soft-spoken and eager to please, but emotion billowed up in her. Any minor thing might unleash it—a lost key or the blunt reply of a servant. His own

words, at first soothing and then accusatory, had little effect.
Yet Ebrahim saw that she would like to oblige him. With
birdlike cries she tried to stand against the gale rising within
her, clutching at her skirt with small, futile gestures as if to
keep it from flying in her face. But always the storm carried
her away.

In spite of these eruptions, the life of the household
took on a shape, if only because there was such a handsome
house to contain it. Mina took a voyeur's pleasure in the
domestic arts. However unsettled her week, she appeared each
Friday evening to preside over the Sabbath meal at the baro-
nial dining table that she had ordered from Belgium. She
was always beautifully dressed and coiffed for these occasions. Moses, damp-eyed, murmured about her mother
coming to life again. The other relatives beamed on her and
nodded their heads. It was, Ebrahim thought, as if she struggled for six days to subdue her oozing clay, emerging on the
seventh as a fully formed ceremonial wife.

Their restrained lovemaking—neither of them, he realized, wanted to risk stirring her feelings—produced two
sons. Yousef was born when they had been married little
more than a year, a large, red-faced infant as hairy and
demanding as the biblical Esau, and Sami two years later,
after a precarious pregnancy spent mostly in bed. Mina
never really got up again after the second birth. The children
were tangible reminders of the fragility of the world: the delicate Sami, in particular, drove her into fits of hysterical
anxiety that left her prostrate. Servants were sent from
Moses' house to raise the boys.

At the end of the working day, having dealt with the
crises that awaited his homecoming, Ebrahim would retreat

to his study, where he ignored the comforts of his walnut desk and leather club chair to sit cross-legged on the carpet, lost in the words of the sages and mystics. He learned the numerical values of letters of the alphabet and meditated on God's garden: its vanished perfumes, its lost light that allowed Adam to see from one end of the world to the other.

Fragments of the texts he'd read came back to him as he waited in the solitude of his cell—odd bits of Kabbalah or Midrash that floated to the surface of his mind like black spots sailing across his field of vision. He took to speaking them aloud, finding they had an incantatory power that calmed him. One morning he awoke early, nudged out of sleep by the pinkish light drizzling through the bars in the window, and heard, "Paradise is present in our own time, but concealed." The voice was his father's, which, since childhood, Ebrahim had identified with the voice of God. He repeated the words in a whisper, lying on his back with the light seeping into his half-opened lids. Immediately, he was filled with a sense of well-being.

As the day wore on, the feeling faded. No revelation, it seemed, could survive the tedium of endless empty hours. Even his fear of death was blunted into something close and stale, a tumor whose dull ache he had grown used to bearing. He tried to remember the origin of the phrase that had come to him at dawn. It was probably some mystical reference to the hidden meaning of the Torah; the words seemed both concrete and maddeningly elusive, as, no doubt, their author had intended. When Ebrahim spoke them now, he heard a taunt, a challenge to the uninitiated. "Where should

I look, then?" he said to the spectral rabbi who mocked him. "If paradise is a state of mind, it can be found anywhere, even here. Shall I check the corners?"

His eye swept over the tiny cell, settling at last on the single window. They had taken his watch when they arrested him, but he could tell by the angle of the sun slanting in that it must be late afternoon. He was struck by how the light appeared at this hour, solid yet delicate, like a bolt of fine fabric stretched across the room. The sun had gnawed at the thickness of the iron bars, reducing them until they appeared as slender and tensile as ropes. In their rectangular frame, they made him think of the looms set against mud-brick walls in the mountain village he had visited with Moses. Ebrahim had liked the half-finished rugs best: the vertical threads of the warp, shot through with sun, seemed as beautiful to him as the ornate pattern creeping upward. "I wish I were the weaver and not the seller," he had said to his father-in-law, as they sat between two towering looms on the earthen floor of a hut, sharing the midday meal. "You'd be bored," Moses told him. "This is no work for intellectuals. These people have the designs in their fingers, from generation to generation. You think they sit around dreaming up symbols?"

Ebrahim had said nothing at the time, but now he argued back. So, Moses, here is the little scholar you bought all those years ago, locked in his cubicle, ready to spin thoughts into gold. Who is left to interrupt me?

He closed his eyes and, with a voluptuous sinking, traced in his head the motions of the Persian knot, passing like a skywriter under one warp thread and around the other, snaring both strands in one loop. When his eyes opened, the bars of the window were threaded with light.

"Come to the store tomorrow," Yousef says. "I could use some help organizing the Labor Day sale."

The air has cooled so quickly after dinner that they have been forced into the living room. Already the days are getting shorter. Ebrahim sighs and shifts in his soft chair. The rugs are on sale continuously, the store in a perpetual state of liquidation. Banners line the windows, announcing 30 percent off, 40 percent on holidays and during the slow season.

"What do I know about sales?" he says. "In all the years I worked for Moses, we never had one. We sold quality, people paid for it. Those who wanted bargains went to the bazaars."

"I'm telling you, it's a different attitude here. Class has nothing to do with it. You take your big-spending tourists or your wealthy retirees, money can be falling out of their pockets but they have to believe they're getting a deal. They have to be seduced."

Directly above Yousef's head, on the wall over the couch, is a large bronze disk that reminds Ebrahim of a rayless sun. It is the room's only ornament, apart from photographs of Kimberly and the children. Yousef has told him that his eyes ache from looking at patterns all day. When he comes home, he wants the simplicity of neutral walls.

Ebrahim fixes his glance on the disk. "If you need me, I don't mind coming. At least I can make myself useful in the office."

"We'll go to Harry's for breakfast. A little celebration. Nahavendi and Son." Yousef extends his arms along the back of the couch, visibly pleased to have won this small battle. He has been pushing Ebrahim to work at the store part-time. "It's healthier for you to be active. Kim is worried you're not adjusting. You stay in all day thinking about the past, you'll get depressed."

"Why do you assume I live in the past? Maybe I'm thinking about what I read in the newspaper. Maybe I'm thinking about you."

"Come on, Baba," Yousef says, grinning. "Since when did you waste time thinking about me?"

His son, Ebrahim reflects, is like Mina without the nerves, Moses without the sly intelligence. A purely physical being. Whatever he is feeling stands out on him like sweat. Just over forty, already he carries the heft of Mina's side of the family. But he is tolerant of his flesh, makes no attempt to contain it. His shirts are always half open, a dark, curly fleece bursting out. His thighs strain at the flimsy cotton of his shorts. Watching him eat, you know exactly how he makes love—the pagan gusto, the avid tongue and lips. Ebrahim would like not to think of it, but sometimes, on sleepless nights, as he lies on his sofa bed listening to muffled noises from the house, he does.

Morgan and Sydney run in, wrapped in Disney towels after their Jacuzzi bath, their wet hair swirled in peaks on top of their heads. Blondes, both of them, although the seven-year-old has Yousef's wavy hair and a duskier skin tone. In one generation the Semitic strain has been all but effaced, laundered out in a kind of New World ethnic cleansing. It is possible—Ebrahim has learned to be unsurprised by such things—that they were conceived in the hot tub, Yousef leaning back with his eyes closed, his manhood submerged in tepid water, while Kimberly, the energetic, efficient American, commanded him to relax.

The children head straight for Yousef, who sweeps them into his lap and begins to nuzzle their hair. They never come to Ebrahim unless ordered to do so. When he first arrived, they'd been shyly curious; he had been advertised as the grandfather, the only one they had, since Kimberly's father was dead. Speaking to them quietly in his formal English, he had presented them with costumed dolls before bending to kiss their soft, averted cheeks. For a few days they stood at a little distance, staring at him solemnly as he ate or read the newspaper. If he reached out his hand, they giggled and ran. Now he has become a part of their landscape, no more noticeable than the monumental couches that crouch like sphinxes in the bare expanse of the living room. He doesn't mind. They are alien to him, with their blue eyes and bird bones and English gentleman's names. Yet he marvels at the fact of them. He would like to send a photograph of them to Mina in the afterlife, where, he imagines, she still tosses restlessly: Be still, be at peace, all our struggles have come to this.

"Bedtime for mermaids," his daughter-in-law announces, bringing a bowl of cherries. She is wearing a short, sea-colored robe and smells pungently of piney shampoo. "Did you say goodnight to Pop-Pop?"

As always, she is vigilant on Ebrahim's behalf. She reaches for the children, but Yousef grabs her and pulls her to him, encircling all three of them in his meaty arms.

"Look what you're doing!" With one hand she clutches

the ends of her robe—suddenly modest, Ebrahim notices, because he is watching—and with the other tries to balance the bowl. Fruit spills over their tangle of tanned limbs.

Yousef laughs. "What do you think, Baba?" he says. "How do you like my bouquet of girls?"

After the first exhilaration, the childish acrobatics of his eye, there was nothing for hours. The window was only a window, a frame for the prison yard's harsh spotlights, which pierced the blackness of his cell. Still, he stared at the bars, alert and unmoving, his exhaustion congealed into a leaden attention. Toward morning the thought occurred to him—appearing prosaically, like an equation scratched on a blackboard—that he should begin as God began, by separating light from dark.

So he made a sun. A simple sun such as a child might draw, a round golden plate surrounded by corkscrew rays. He had underestimated the difficulty of transferring it from his head to the lower left corner of the window; it required an effort of imagination that he felt too weak to make, a spasm that was almost physical, as if the object were lodged literally behind his eyes and he had to tear it loose. When, after hours of focused thought, he could see it before him, he set about refining his sun, buffing the color until a reddish tint surfaced and unifying the rays so that their golden tips pointed in one direction. Once he had the pattern, the labor of dreaming came more easily to him. By the time the guard brought his food, he had made a whole row.

After eating, Ebrahim fell into a deep sleep, awakening early the next morning with a sense of anticipation, as if some good news had been revealed to him in the night. Still, he had to compose himself before daring to turn his con-

centration to the window. He shut his eyes, letting the picture form in his mind, and when he opened them the suns
were standing at attention like soldiers. He set to work
immediately, weaving above them a border of blue with black
arabesques, an intricate darkness like the night sky. By late
afternoon he was finishing his first moonface, whose blown-
out cheeks and sated smile he had seen in his night dreams.

As his confidence increased, he became more playful. It
gave him pleasure to enlarge an herb until its branches
twined with those of a fruit tree, or to alternate birds with
fish, teasing out the symmetry of wings and fins to make a
witty rabbinical commentary on two forms of floating. The
herd animals refused to come alive for him until he remembered the fragment of the Pazyryk carpet, mounted horses
marching around its borders. With these ancient beasts as a
model, his sheep and goats and cattle took on motion,
reverberating with incipient rhythm like lines of musical
notes.

The rug revealed itself to him gradually. He could not
admit that he was replicating the grand design of God; his
own arrogance appalled him, as if he had dared to speak the
holy name. His father's face came to him, as stern as any
mullah's, the brows meeting in a disapproval so pure that it
was almost impersonal, and he felt again the awe and fear he
had known as a child. To free his mind, he had to turn into
a Kabbalist, concealing his deeper purposes from himself.
Each morning he labored like the humblest craftsman,
sweating over the curve of a ram's horn or the arrangement
of scales on a fish, refusing to see further than the task of the
day. Not until evening did he allow himself what any weaver
took for granted: a look at the pattern as it grew on the loom.

And when he saw what he had made—how the images in their orderly rows leaped out at him; how the colors radiated separately and yet submitted to each other; how, even at this early stage, the figures made an abstraction that was greater than their parts—he exulted shamelessly.

"Idiots," Yousef mutters. "A pair of idiots."

Ebrahim isn't sure whether he is referring to the sleek but weathered couple who have wandered in from the pink hotel across the street, or to his nephews, Amir and Faraz, who are showing them a carpet. Sons of Mina's brother, they have worked at the store for two years without acquiring any skills; "Good for nothing but eating my money," is Yousef's standard complaint. But Ebrahim has to admire their flair as they unfurl the rug, a dance of servility and style that jogs his memory of an apprentice waiter in Paris spooning sauce over a plateful of fish.

He has spent a few hours in the office wrestling with the computer, and allowing Yousef to show off some treasures and elicit his opinion on the latest auction finds. Ebrahim does his best to appear involved, but the business holds no interest for him now. The rugs are only commodities, their beauty a whore's finery. They will end up on their backs in the houses of balding executives like this one, pierced by the spike heels of lacquered women like his wife, who is now complaining about the busy pattern on a handsome old Kerman while her husband waits vacantly until it is time to do battle over the price.

Ebrahim turns away from Yousef's earnest sales pitch and wanders over to the window. He had planned to plead a headache and take the bus home, a ride he likes for its companionable solitude and views of the cove. But Kimberly is due any minute to take him to lunch at Balboa Park. The children are spending the day with friends and she has insisted on giving him her free afternoon. Staring at the strip of street between the giant sales signs, his mind on nothing but the weight of the morning's pancakes in his stomach, he sees at first only a girl in a white linen shift, her long American stride sanctified by the flash of sun on her gold sandals. Although he has been expecting her, he gets a pleasurable frisson of surprise when she swings through the door.

"I'd take it on approval," the woman customer is saying. "But if it doesn't work, will you cover the cost of shipping it back from Denver?"

Yousef doesn't answer because he is staring at his wife with the same dazzled awe he wore when he introduced her to Ebrahim. The woman looks, too, a brief, assessing glance that takes in her companion, whose alertness has visibly quickened. Behind them, the nephews offer white-toothed smiles above the backup rug, a Tabriz whose corners they elevate with delicate distraction, like attendants lifting the train of a bridal veil. Ebrahim sees it all in a tableau, as he has trained himself to see.

"You got all dressed up for a walk in the park?" Yousef excuses himself and walks over to Kimberly. "You're as bad as my father, with his suit and tie."

"I didn't want my distinguished escort to be ashamed of me. He's always staring at me like he can't believe the way I go around." Kimberly tosses her hair, as if to shrug off the seriousness of this.

"Not true, not at all true," Ebrahim stumbles. "But you

look especially charming today. Very Greek. Like a goddess."
Immediately he repents of his banality, but before turning
his eyes away, he sees that once again he has left his mark on
her. A faint flush this time.

Yousef puts his hand to the heightened color on her
cheek and rubs it with his thumb. "You have to watch out
for the old man," he says. "You think he's contemplating the
meaning of heaven and earth, but all the time he's watching
you out of lizard eyes." He looks over his shoulder at the customer, who, ignoring the rug and her husband, is chatting
vivaciously with Amir and Faraz. "I'd go with you, but if I
leave, no business gets done. Take him to the Hacienda for a
nice lunch, maybe a margarita. A *small* margarita for a Jewish
monk." He reaches into his pocket. "You have money?"

The park on this bright Wednesday is uncrowded, populated
with a scattering of tourists, some aimless-looking locals,
and groups of schoolchildren who are being herded in
ragged lines between the stucco palaces that house the city's
small museums. Along the main thoroughfare where they are
walking, mimes, magicians, and street musicians compete
for sparse audiences.

"Everyone must be at the zoo," Kimberly says. "We have
the place to ourselves."

Ebrahim knows that the Moorish buildings with their
elaborate wedding-cake ornamentation are not really old;
Yousef has explained that they were constructed for an international exposition in 1915. But the lush greenery kindles
his old fascination with France. As a boy he had smuggled
French novels into his room, reading them at night when he
should have been studying Torah. Gradually there grew in

his mind a landscape of broad avenues lined with stately houses and tall, thin trees that bowed in the wind like the consumptive aristocrats he read about. He had stared at one illustration so obsessively that he half believed he could pass through the page and join the promenade past the busy café (*Glace* lightly sketched on its striped awning), at his side the wasp-waisted woman with red lips whose hat brim cast a slanted shadow across her face. In the streets of his dream Paris—he smiles now, remembering it—horse-drawn carriages coexisted seamlessly with the latest racing cars.

"What are you thinking about?" Kimberly asks. "You have this look on your face like you're in a different world. Are you thinking about Iran?"

Her flat tones jar him, but at least she didn't say "the old country." She seems to have in her mind some orientalized version of the scrubbed hearths of her own Dutch ancestors, toward which she assumes he is always helplessly longing.

"I was thinking of the romantic idea of France that I had when I was young. In my mind, it was the opposite of what I saw around me. The hills around Teheran were bare and parched, so Paris had to be like one big garden, flowers everywhere. This place reminds me of it."

"But you *lived* in Paris, didn't you?"

In her voice he can hear her amazement that he would waste time mooning over an imaginary city when he had experienced the real thing.

"Yes, yes. After my release. For three years. But, you understand, it was not my fantasy. We had lost everything and were living in an Algerian neighborhood. Yousef had left school by that time and was working with me at a furniture store; Sami had just started university. My wife—in a strange place, she became more . . . confused. We did the best we could for her, but in the end, I had to send her away. A private place, an old convent, very refined. In six months she was dead. No one knew why. Her heart just stopped. It will always be on my conscience." He reaches for the pack of cigarettes in his breast pocket, remembers, and drops his hand. "But you must have heard all this."

"Yousef has told me. I can't get over how much you went through." She takes his arm, squeezes it. Looking into his eyes, she smiles as if to reassure him that the old, bad days are over.

He has a perverse desire to cloud her forehead by telling her about his visits to the asylum—about the French nuns, oddly familiar in their dark habits, and the way Mina pleaded with him, each time he came, to save her from the "revolutionaries" and take her home for Shabbat. Instead he says, "We did the usual tourist things, of course. The Louvre. The Tour Eiffel. The Tuileries."

"Oh, those names sound gorgeous coming out of your mouth! Did you know I took French all four years in high school? My best friend and I had this plan that we would be flight attendants and have an apartment in Paris and find fabulous French boyfriends. I was halfway through the training when I met Yousef. And then I got pregnant. So I never got to fly the happy skies and see the world." She laughs. "I guess France was my dream, too. I almost forgot I had one."

With a gentle pressure, she leads him into a cloistered walkway that fronts one of the baroque facades. In the sudden shadow, half-blinded, he is acutely aware of the weight of her arm on his, of the tanned smoothness and the little golden hairs, the idea of them prickling his skin inside his jacket sleeve.

A carved door opens, not into the room he expected but a sunlit courtyard with a fountain in the center. "*Voilà!*" she says.

His first impression of open space alters: the place is crowded, the tables along the walls filled with guests who have the alert, hectic look of tourists, their faces momentarily eclipsed by enormous glass globes from which they sip reverently.

"This fountain is perhaps the Fountain of Youth?" he says to Kimberly. "These people are taking the waters of life?"

But his wit is lost on her. "Don't worry," she tells him, heading for the maître d'. "I made a reservation."

An arbor of fat red blossoms overhangs their table. Leafy shadows play over her face as she scans the menu. Watching her, he wonders how long it has been since he sat across from a woman. A Jewish monk, Yousef called him, but he has had his moments: hurried encounters in Paris, intense for all their brevity, and even in Iran, after his return, hints from the wives of friends (veiled, of course, like the bright, clinging dresses beneath the chadors). His good looks have brought him some privileges. He could have the Malaysian student of linguistics; he could grind his sorrows out in her coolly and quickly, and be back in time to make dinner for his sons. What he has not had is this simple being-with, this normalcy, this face to face.

Would he take the same pleasure if the face were not so purely oval, the eyelids round as a sculpted angel's? There is, he thinks, a certain restfulness about spending time with her. She has no ideas, no real conversation, no demands except the no-smoking variety. All that is required is to take in the way her hair grazes her cheekbones. The humor does not escape him: he who has spent his life excavating hidden meanings finds out in his dotage that the surface is enough.

"You must try a margarita," she urges. "I promised Yousef. It's the national drink around here." When the waiter sets his down—the same size as hers, he notes—he cradles the globe in both hands and brings the salted rim to his lips. The pale liquid slides into his mouth, silvery, elusive. Even after swallowing, he isn't sure what he has tasted.

Kimberly licks the rime from her upper lip. "Tell me more about Paris. I hate that I've never been anywhere."

"Why not get Yousef to go with you? You could stay with Sami; it's about time you met him. Although who knows how he lives? On air, I think. Air and poetry."

"Are you kidding? Yousef would never leave the business. He's obsessed. I swear it's all he thinks about, apart from us. And his beloved California. Why travel if you're living in paradise? Besides"—she glances briefly at her nails—"I shouldn't tell you this, but he really resents Sami. Thinks he's a leech, the way he sits at his desk all day and depends on your uncle for handouts. He's always felt that Sami is your favorite. The one who looks like you. The writer."

The liquor has hobbled Ebrahim's tongue. A graceful denial is called for, but he has lost the power to shape it.

"There is a park," he says, enunciating carefully, "not far from where I worked. By day it's just a nice place to sit. A few statues, beds of flowers, old trees, a pond. But you come there at dusk, at the moment the sun is setting, and the shadows deepen in such a way that you would think you have stepped out of time. As if you had lived all your life in a flat world and suddenly you are in three dimensions." He sighs and looks down at the table, where a bowl of red sauce shimmers, untouched. "Maybe I'll take you myself."

"Do you mean it? That's a great idea!" Her skin suffuses with the thought, the color rising so quickly to the surface that she seems, actually, to glow. "We could go during spring vacation. April in Paris, right? We could do all the things you missed the first time around." She reaches across the table to grab his hand. "It could still be our dream."

How like her, he thinks, to assume that two weeks in her radiant company will wipe away his past. Once the light fades the park is drab, he wants to tell her, not a place a girl like you would walk at night. Paris when you live there is just another city, a place to work and sleep and bear your troubles. But he is stirred in spite of himself, shaken by how quickly the enchantment comes back to him, all its colors intact, a page of a book not opened for fifty years. His hand with its raised veins and brown spots lies in hers like a dead leaf. He is grateful for the distraction of the plates arriving.

Kimberly attacks her ethereal salad, spearing lettuce as she spins out plans. The girls will stay with her mother. Yousef's cholesterol level will have to be monitored from afar. If Sami has no room for them, they'll stay at a pension or maybe do a house exchange with one of those well-preserved Frenchwomen, who'll make *bifteck* for Yousef, he'd like that, wouldn't he? Ebrahim listens with one ear, his thoughts racing. Why not? It would be the beginning of an education for her. They might get a few glances, but the French are accepting of such things.

"I'd want to see the real Paris," she says, putting down

her fork. "Not just the places tourists go. I'd want Sami to show us around. Maybe you could give me some names of poets to read, and we could practice talking about them so he won't think I'm too ignorant." She takes a miniature corn from her plate and dabbles it absently in the red sauce. "Yousef's mysterious brother. I've been curious about him forever. Does he really look so much like you? When you were young, I mean."

Kimberly is staring at him expectantly, her blue eyes fixed on his. As the moment extends, a faint line appears between her brows.

He tips his glass and takes a long drink of the margarita. Definitely an elixir, but not from the Tree of Life. The Tree of Knowledge, maybe. That fruit would have a little salt in it.

By the end of his second month in prison, he was ready to attempt the central field. Thoughts of it had been germinating in his mind while he worked on the borders. He wanted a garden, of course, but not the compartmentalized squares of the classic garden rugs, each plant penned in its own little plot. What was needed was more of a meadow, an ordered lushness, at once profuse and disciplined.

The first days were difficult. He had trained himself to repeat one or two figures in a straight line. Now he had to mimic spontaneity, planting narcissus here, china roses there, calculating the texture of the green between them. This was, he saw, a higher form of art, approximating more closely the handiwork of the Maker. As he struggled to reproduce every flower he could remember, and to invent what he could not recall, he began to wonder if God was finally taking revenge on him for his ambitions.

Often he was overcome by exhaustion. He woke each day resolved to make progress, but before long the object of his attention would blur and he would fall into a stupor. Not only had exhilaration left him; he lacked even the will to rouse himself. He would sit with his head in his hands, wanting only to lie down on the bed of green he was making and close his eyes. He could almost feel the buoyant cushion of leaves giving way beneath his weight, the mingled fragrances rising up around him.

While he was in this state, two guards came for him. It was midmorning, but he was as dazed as if he had been roused from a sound sleep. As he stumbled between them, one guard muttered to the other, "An old drunk." Ebrahim realized how he must look to them: bearded, filthy, red-eyed. All these weeks he had lived inside his head, giving no thought to his body. Now his natural fastidiousness reasserted itself, rising along with the terror he had tamed for so long. How could he maintain his dignity when he had been reduced to this?

He was pushed into a brightly lit room, bare except for a large metal desk covered with papers. The man behind the desk raised a long, sallow expanse of face whose blandness was disrupted by black-rimmed glasses and a patchy beard. He shuffled his papers, and, with the slight sigh of a bureaucrat interviewing yet another pensioner, said, "You handled overseas business for the firm of Moses Kashani and Company. You have been a key agent in his espionage operation. You are part of an international network of spies seeking to propagate Zionism." He leaned back in his chair as if he had completed his task.

The rote quality of the speech gave Ebrahim courage.

Every day of his working life he saw men who looked like this one: office workers scurrying through the business district in their cheap jackets, darting into a tea shop for a quick glass to get them through the afternoon. "I know nothing of espionage or international networks," he said. "I have no interest in Zionism—I have never been very political. I am a student of the Jewish sacred texts. My father was the scholar Yaghoub Nahavendi."

The man at the desk nodded as if taking in this information, and a guard stepped forward. Raising his arm in a leisurely manner, he struck Ebrahim across the mouth, sending him staggering across the room.

An hour later, nursing his bruises in his cell, Ebrahim wondered if invoking his father's name had saved him from a worse beating. The guards had roughed him up but had shown a lack of zeal. They'd hardly done more than blacken his skin. Had some secret signal restrained them, or were they holding back, keeping him intact for further interrogation? His father had been a personage in Teheran and beyond, a professor known as much for rectitude as for learning. In the shah's Persia, his spirituality and scorn for the material world had made him a misfit, the model of the Old World Jew. What irony, Ebrahim thought: if his father had lived, he would have been at home with the new austerity.

Ebrahim's body ached and his mouth still tasted of blood, but his mind was clear. The torpor of the last days had lifted, leaving him focused and eerily calm. He had no illusion that he would leave the prison alive. The long stasis was over and the procedure for his elimination had begun. He probed at the fact gently, as his fingers probed his damaged flesh, and found that it held little terror for him. His weeks in the cell had worked a purpose in him that was greater than his fear. He had been allotted space to create a paradise, to draw it out of its hiddenness and into the world. All that remained for him was to finish what he had started. Painfully he dropped to the floor and, crouching with his forehead on the ground like an Arab turned toward Mecca, cried out for time.

He saw where he had gone wrong as soon as he began to work. The garden, for all its beauty, was never meant to be more than a backdrop. "Always look for the essence," his father had taught him. "Think of the letter of the law as the honeycomb and the meaning beneath it as the honey." He had been guilty of the worst kind of legalism, reproducing flowers like a shortsighted botanist when he should have been orchestrating the primal drama.

As if his understanding had seeded it, a tree began to grow in the center of the field. It seemed to grow on its own, so rapidly and effortlessly that he felt almost like a passive observer, lending his faculties to a process that had already been set in motion. First, awkward roots appeared, large-knuckled fingers that clutched the bottom border, contrasting with the orderly parade of animals below. Then came the trunk, scarred and deeply furrowed, born old in the new world. He had completed a third of it when a knot on the trunk's side began to bulge as if it had a life of its own. He sat back calmly, waiting for the protuberance to reveal itself. Perhaps an hour passed before the diamond pattern came clear, barely decipherable at the tail but bolder as the body thickened. Ebrahim laughed out loud. The serpent, audacious as always, had materialized like a stowaway. There would be no finishing the rug without him.

The snake was red and black with glints of gold, a liberated border twisting round and round the darkness of the trunk. Ebrahim let it climb with him all the way up, but took care to leave it headless while he worked on the foliage and fruit. He made each branch separately, adding clusters of leaves from which golden orbs hung like small suns. Only then did the multicolored mosaic of the serpent's head push through the foliage: more pleasing to the eye than any fruit, and a fit repository for honeyed words.

The opening of the cell door broke his trance of concentration. He had worked all night, barely aware of the altering light. He stood, trying to gird himself for the bright room with the thought of what he had accomplished, but the guard set down his food as always and left. He wondered if his interrogator had decided he wasn't worth wasting muscle on. Whatever their plans for him, then, he hadn't much time left in the cell. Mechanically, he began to eat the rice, surprised to find himself hungry. His work was almost complete. He needed only to add the final symmetry: the figures of Adam and Eve on either side of the tree.

It had always been his opinion that the human form had no place in the pattern of a rug. "Too much like a painting or a medieval tapestry," he'd said, when Moses admired a rare old hunting carpet in a museum. "How can I appreciate the design if I'm watching the hunter stalk the deer?" Together they'd jeered at the portrait rugs that had appeared in the bazaars, immortalizing President Kennedy and the shah. But now, as he called up the rug for this final effort, he realized that his reservations went deeper than matters of taste. If, as his faith had taught him, it was a sin to imprison God in a form, how could Ebrahim think about duplicating the first pair made in His image? Until this moment he had believed that God would forgive him his ambitions. He had imagined the Holy One standing back like a connoisseur, withholding judgment out of respect for a fellow artist.

The rug had never looked so beautiful. Long ago it had grown beyond the window, and now the wall glittered with pulsing colors and intermingled patterns. I could stop here, he thought, and give no offense. But already images of Adam and Eve were passing through his mind, piling up like rejected sketches: a primitive, square-bodied couple whose pendulous parts gave them the look of fertility amulets; two refugees from a Flemish tapestry, pale and languid, the woman all but breastless with a starveling's swollen belly; a matched set of doe-eyed Persians of whom he was sure Mina would approve, tasteful as table lamps, flanking the tree.

None of them had any life. Archetypes, they were as flat as the dust of the ground before God breathed on it. Ebrahim shook his head and let them blow away. A rug is not a painting, he had told Moses, but he wanted his rug to do what a painting did, and more. He wanted the roundness of flesh, faces that spoke. He wanted the moment of fullness just before the Fall, the new world brimming like wine in a cup, ready to spill.

Ebrahim looked again at the window, where he had begun his work. The day that it framed was gray, streaked with a thin winter rain that was soothing to his eyes. He continued to look out, even as he heard the heavy footsteps of the guards, the door being unlocked behind him.

They marched him up one corridor and down another, passing the door he remembered as the interrogation room. He wondered whether they were taking him to the mock court for his trial or if they had decided to dispense with that formality. In the weeks after his father-in-law's death, Ebrahim had forced himself to imagine the details, believing that familiarity would neutralize the horror. But there was so much he didn't know. Had the shooting taken place in some hidden room or outside, against a wall? At the end of this wide hall was a gray door with a window, a patch of light that showed him Moses' fate and his own.

He was not aware of feeling afraid, but his legs gave way as if they were disconnected from the rest of his body. The guards, still clutching his arms, looked down at him.

"My wife," he said. "I haven't spoken to my wife."

"Don't worry, old man." The taller of the two hoisted Ebrahim up. "You'll be together with her soon enough."

So she's dead, he thought. Dead for being Moses' daughter.

He kept his eyes on the small window. He would go out looking at framed light. An odd fancy came to him of dropping to his knees and pleading for another week of life, time to finish his work. He almost smiled when he thought of explaining to them what his work was. He would have to use a euphemism, of course, something vague like "getting my affairs in order."

The door opened and the guards, as if at a secret signal, let go of him. He stood stupidly on the threshold until one of them pushed him into the yard. Instead of the wall he expected, there was a chain-link fence patrolled by a languid fellow who looked like a parking lot attendant, and beyond it a line of traffic passing with a serene indifference that he found hard to comprehend. "Maybe he's waiting for an umbrella," he heard the smaller guard say, and he was suddenly aware of the rain pelting down on him, much heavier than it had appeared from his window. All around him space gaped, vast and disorienting. He was possessed by his old illusion of stepping through the page into the picture, but the scene he had blundered into was strange to him.

"Old man!"

He forced himself to look around. The guards were standing in the doorway, laughing. The tall one said, "Go home, already. Go home to your wife that you love so much."

Ebrahim stared at them a moment, turned, and began to walk. So this is how they do it, he thought. In the back. They make a game of it. He tried to walk slowly, in a straight line, so it would be over quickly. But when he came to the fence, the attendant opened the gate.

He stumbled into the traffic, weaving like a sleepwalker in and out of the paths of wildly honking cars and trucks. When he reached the pavement, he turned again and looked back at the prison. The guards still stood in the doorway, rifles slung casually over their shoulders, blocking the entrance to his Eden.

Ebrahim walked for hours, driven by an inner compass pointing north to the suburbs where he lived, making a drunkard's path across the city. The sudden assault of noise and activity sloughed off him. He passed through the heart of Teheran as lightly as a ghost, arriving at his own door well after nightfall.

Within a week he and Mina were on a plane to Paris to join their sons. It had all been arranged—his release, too, he suspected—by his father's brother, a well-known rabbi who taught at the Sorbonne. As his sedated wife slept in the seat beside him, Ebrahim reflected that perhaps his mullah of a father had proven to be a benevolent spirit after all, guiding and protecting him each day of his imprisonment. But he could not conjure him up, not during the journey, nor in Paris, as he carved out a refugee's existence in the city of his fantasy, nor even when he returned to Iran three years later to pick up the pieces of his old world. In death, it seemed, Yaghoub Nahavendi preferred to disseminate his wisdom in the solitude of the cell.

What he feels for his daughter-in-law is not sexual, Ebrahim tells himself. Not *precisely* sexual.

He is watching her from his kitchen window as she stretches after returning from her run. She has extended one leg behind her in an exaggerated runner's pose, and she bounces rhythmically over the other, blond ponytail flopping as she massages her calf. He is fascinated, as always, by her rapt expression, her absorption in her body. If he feels a wisp of longing for her as she jogs, damp and panting, up the patio steps, it is kin to what the serpent must have felt for Eve: remote and mixed with a kind of pity for her heedless nakedness, for the innocence of her sweat, for the patch of freckled back she offers to his dry eye as she bends to flick an insect off a plant.

He taps a cigarette out of the pack and sits back in his chair. And if she is Eve, what does that make him? The twisted old knower, watching, always watching, from his leafy bower, contemplating the monotonies of a perfect patch of ground? He will woo her with words, tempt her with stories about the wide world. *Arise, my love, my fair one, and come away . . .*

He hears the slap of the sliding screen door. She has gone in to shower, and soon she'll be at his door, wet-haired and wearing some bright scrap of clothing, to invite him to sit outside on the patio while she cooks. Their afternoon has been extended. Yousef is working late and the girls have been invited to stay overnight, so they'll have dinner, as she puts it, *à deux*. She is making *polo* and, as a special concession to him, adding chicken to the casserole of rice, fruit, and nuts. In exchange, she's informed him, she expects to hear more about France. Does he think they can fit in a side trip to Provence?—she wants to get that book that everyone's reading. He never went anywhere near the south, but realizes that it makes no difference. He can invent what he doesn't know. A new thing will be seen on the earth: the sultan will tell stories to Scheherazade.

Ebrahim remembers how, in prison, he awoke once in the middle of the night, wondering what would happen after the rug was completed. Day by day, lost in the rigors of the work, he had avoided thinking about endings, his own or the carpet's. Subconsciously he must have imagined that both ends would come at once: he would tie the last knots—some infinitesimal refinement to please himself, a deepened shadow at a petal's root, or the sheen on a tailfeather—and the guards would arrive, and he would be marched off with the rug whole in his head. That night he had broken out in a cold sweat at the thought that he might survive. He imagined a long, lax afterlife in exile, Ebrahim the Carpet Peddler carrying his masterpiece around like a dead weight, its colors fading, its patterns sinking into the weave until it was only an idea of a rug. Perhaps this is why he has never attempted another Adam and Eve. Unfinished, the rug is always in process. He is still the weaver.

And now fate has brought him to this new land where his son, dense man of earth, tends shop and prunes prices, and his luminous daughter-in-law is more naked than she knows. Certainly he has no designs on their lives, no thought of interfering. Sanity has returned to him in the lucid half-light of his room. She will go to France, alone or with Yousef or not at all. He'll stay in his murky den and pique his senses with the old man's aphrodisiac, curiosity. Did God, he wonders, know how the tale He told would end, or did He keep it hidden from Himself? Did He allow Himself the luxury of suspense as Eve pondered the apple?

Without Ebrahim's noticing, the room has darkened around him. He draws deeply on his cigarette and holds the smoke in, feeling it curl around the cavity of his chest. Not since his months in confinement has he experienced such a sense of the fullness of time. As the smoke plumes out of him, he raises his eyes again to the window and waits for it to come to life.

Little Edens

The Calverts had been settled in San Rodrigo less than a week when the earth moved beneath them. At four in the morning their newly rented house began to rock to the sound of clashing cymbals. Myra, awakened from a rare night of unbroken sleep, thought immediately of the plates of the earth parting and butting, grinding against each other like metal-horned rams. Russell had instructed her about tremors. The two of them lurched across the bedroom to the doorway, where they stood with their sides touching, braced against the frame, until the shaking stopped. Afterward, staring at the ceiling while her husband snored beside her, Myra had two revelations: that the clatter had actually been caused by the mirrored closet doors slamming together; and that she had not been the least afraid, would never again fear any natural or man-made disaster, because the worst had already happened to her.

Six months before, she had lost her only son. The disease that swept over Andrew had uprooted him from his life as an architect in New York and deposited him, weak and disoriented, in the room of his boyhood. It became her business, then, to tame the tidal wave, to hold off the bear with her small chair. Her friends remarked on how strong she was. She could not explain to them the intimacy she had achieved with his illness, a closeness that cushioned shock, so that she sometimes felt—yes, she would dare to think it—like a partner. Each step that death advanced she stood prepared for, assimilating what she could not stop, taking back what was hers even as her son slipped away. Toward the end she thought of a dance: Death and the Matron, a stately minuet of ordained steps. So great was her control that she didn't even cry at the funeral. Russell cried—Russell, who had hovered on the margins of her caretaking like an apprentice waiter, hardly daring to insert his presence to ask if she needed help. He had leaned all his weight on her narrow shoulder and wept gouts of tears, as if some ruddy, palpitating optimism were pulsing out of him.

Not until the ceremonies were over, the expressions of sympathy acknowledged, her son's possessions given to charity, did she begin to crack. Her house became oppressive to her. Its square rooms and tiny leaded windows seemed as confining as the grave, and the ancient graffiti on the attic walls scraped her nerves like skeletal hands. The past, which had always held great attraction for her, had become a charnel house. She wondered how she had lived so happily with worm-eaten moldings and gently battered antiques, the leftovers of departed lives. "This house gets no light," she said to her husband, as if they were viewing it for the first time. "The dust! The maintenance! What do we need it for?" And she flung out her arms to take in the town they had moved up to by inches—an old and gracious suburb of Boston where Revolutionary battles had been fought and transcendentalists had strolled arm in arm, discoursing on nature and the universe.

So when Russell told her, half-joking, that he'd been offered the chance to supervise his company's new office in Southern California, she didn't laugh. "They want to send me downriver to a nice cushy retirement," he said. "In three years they'll call me a consultant and I can set up an office on the beach."

"You can't expect me to stay here!" she heard herself shrill, and he, sensing the direction of her need, set about in his methodical way to put the move in motion. It was, finally, something he could do.

Her friends all advised her not to make any decisions about the house for a year—two years, one said authoritatively, as if some government study had quantified the median length of the grieving period. But desperation made her reckless; she had just begun to feel that first frail surge of life that is almost like giddiness. Sell, she instructed Russell. Store everything, even the memorabilia of Andrew's childhood, the photo albums, favored toys, school papers. They could always have things shipped if they decided to settle out West.

Myra's first sight of San Rodrigo brought to mind a board game that she had played with the preschool Andrew. She didn't so much think the name as hear him croon it, full of vamped longing for the Oz of his infancy: *Candyland,* as they stood outside the airport in their winter jackets, blinking at the palm trees that shimmied against a cloudless sky; *Candy-*

land, as they glimpsed from the taxi window the sheen of turquoise sea, an amateur watercolor of an ocean compared to the Atlantic; *Candyland,* as they drove through coral gates banked in flowers into La Paloma, the planned community where Russell had sublet a house, sight unseen. Slowly the driver circled blocks of cream-colored stucco ranches fronted by garages. All the lawns were vividly green, clipped precisely according to pattern, varied only by the calculated spontaneity of flowering bushes and trees.

"There aren't any landmarks," Myra said, as they passed Caminito Ysabel for the fourth time. To herself she whispered, Stuck in vat of peppermint ice cream, go back six spaces, and imagined Andrew leaning over her shoulder, waiting to make his move.

Russell took out the small map that the realtor had sent. "I'll tell you what's going on," he said. It had been a constant source of comedy between Myra and Andrew that Russell always knew what was going on, what things were made of, how they worked. "We're way the heck out here in Seville when we ought to be in Barcelona. That's our subdivision. Barcelona."

And then Myra did hear her son's voice, the words deposited in her ear one by one like pennies in a child's bank. *Bar-thelona,* he said with a Castilian lisp. *All my life I longed to visit Barthelona.*

The interior of the house was cool and pale. Its white walls and carpets and large, spare furnishings gave an impression of abundant vacant space. Identical pastel sofas were stranded yards from each other at opposite ends of an enormous bleached-wood coffee table. "But this is huge!" Myra said, and saw at once that the living room stretched into the infinity of a mirrored wall. Mirrors were everywhere: on the ceiling of the dining alcove, doubling the splendor of the crystal-and-gold chandelier; in the shining cube of the master bath; on the doors of closets that took up an entire wall of the bedroom. The sight of herself and Russell reflected from multiple surfaces—sag-faced, weary, prim in their layers of clothing—made Myra laugh out loud. "New England Gothic," she said to his image in the glass.

He glanced at her nervously and tossed the keys onto the coffee table. "I don't know what Ted Metzler was thinking when he told me this place was in good taste. I wasn't expecting some goddamn Hollywood hotel lobby. Remember, this is just temporary, until we find a house."

"Well, it's certainly clean enough." Myra walked into the white-tiled kitchen and ran her hand lightly over a counter, opened a cupboard, and was surprised to see stacked dishes. There were pots and pans, a drawer full of silverware, everything of generic design, sleek and inoffensive. The whole house looked untouched, as if it had just been unwrapped from cellophane by a corps of silent workers wearing gloves. She expected that the refrigerator would be stocked with soft drinks, chocolate truffles, polished fruit, but inside was an elegant bareness relieved only by a bottle of champagne and two frosted glasses. A card dangling from a gold ribbon around the bottle's neck read, "Welcome to Paradise. Ted and the Beach Potatoes at Mortimer Keene."

After unpacking, they sat at the patio table in the small, enclosed yard, sipping champagne and watching hummingbirds dip into the bougainvillea that covered the walls.

"I feel as if I'm in a movie," Myra said, but actually, she felt as if she were watching one. Maybe it was the wine that kept her removed from the scene, an onlooker registering the stylized smiles of the couple at the table, checking the meter of their pleasure. Wasn't this the ultimate cliché of the good life—palm trees, flowers, blue sky, sun? After the rigors of a New England winter, how strange to be transported to the kingdom of leisure. *Lezh*-ure. The word seemed to encompass the soft fall of an overripe fruit, the slung bottom of a beach chair. *And once sunk in,* she heard, *there is the problem of rising up.*

Russell filled their glasses a second time. "No more winter. Tangerine trees in the backyard. And we don't have to go home in two weeks. I could get used to this." He stretched luxuriously and laced his fingers behind his head.

"*It's one thing to anticipate Paradise; another to have arrived.*" The phrase had materialized suddenly in Myra's mouth, and without thinking, she let it out.

"What's that supposed to mean?" Russell squinted at her, his face beginning to tense into familiar lines of puzzled suspicion. When she and Andrew played their word games, he had always suspected that he was the subject of their code.

"I don't know. I honestly don't." Myra began to laugh silently, her shoulders shaking so hard that she had to set down her champagne. Russell's look turned stricken. She knew that he thought she was weeping, but had no power to quench the frivolous lightness rising in her. She remembered with sudden clarity the first weeks of her pregnancy: the infinitesimal extra weight; the presence glowing in her like a shrouded light, invisible but distinct. Now, having borne and lost, she could almost believe she was carrying again. She saw clearly, as if Andrew were sketching one of his spiky visual puns while she watched, the cord that linked her to her dead son: a line of words flowing smoothly through a tube scalloped around the edges like a cartoon cloud. And perched on top of the cloud, the pair o'dice, stick legs dangling, the dots on their square faces so cleverly arranged that the features were unmistakable. When he was a boy, he was always bringing her pictures, asking her to guess the word from the drawings. Clearly, he was sending her a message. News from the front.

Russell came up behind her and started to knead her shoulders. "Don't mind me," she gasped. "I'm fine. It's just the bubbly."

Andrew didn't always choose to speak. Some mornings, as Myra walked the fitness trail through the greenbelt at the center of the colony, she might feel nothing but a quiet presence, another layer of her own thought. She might even begin to doubt that he was with her at all. Then she would glance at something quite ordinary—one of the Mexican gardeners, or a tanned retiree being pulled along by an exuberant dog—and she would feel a subtle heat that she recognized as the stirring of his attention. Soon she began to look for unfamiliar streets, seeking new sights that would stimulate him.

But she understood that she must step lightly, never manipulate, preserve at all costs the delicate give-and-take of their relationship. Even into his early teens, he had liked to go places with her. They would set aside a day for following his whim of the moment, his "Andrew thing," as she called it. There was never any pattern to his choices: alongside him she had hunted for mushrooms in damp woods, taken tap-dancing lessons, gone skeet-shooting at a range, sifted the soil under an old tavern for bones and glass, sat through *Parsifal.* They'd once spent an entire afternoon watching a stonecutter inscribe a name on a grave marker. After a while, she had developed an instinct for what would appeal to him. It helped, now, to think of her foraging expeditions as treats planned for his pleasure.

The Mormon Temple was her greatest coup. Its silhouette of gleaming white sandstone and sky-piercing spires loomed above the condominiums and shopping malls like a castle in a suburban fairy tale. Russell said that the structure was a technical marvel. "You can wave to Moroni from our shower," he claimed, and insisted on lifting her up to the window above the bathtub so she could see the golden angel poised on tiptoe on the highest steeple, aiming its trumpet at the heavens. On her walks Myra made it a point to pause in front of the Temple, taking in for Andrew the life behind its filigreed wrought-iron gates. Apparently only Mormons in good standing could gain access to the sanctum. Once inside, they were obliged to change to white robes; she thought of this as she watched the men in dark suits and the women in chaste dresses and heels, decked out for church even on weekdays.

One particularly hot morning, she let her eyes glide slowly up the facade to the spires shimmering in the sun. Against the sky's intense blue, the angel seemed to waver as if he were about to dissolve into pure spirit. *Molten Moroni,* she heard, a breathy whisper this time. *Just another Icarus. An aspiration to us all.*

Aspiration. Andrew and his puns. She'd teased him about them, called them the lowest form of language, but even she had to admit that his had flair. From the time he learned to speak, words were elastic for him, supple playthings that he could stretch and twist into odd shapes. Myra was only a couple of blocks from home, but to closet her exhilaration was unthinkable. Instead, she walked twice around the perimeter of the colony, canted backward like a woman in late pregnancy, letting the heavy air hold her up.

That night she dreamed they were having a picnic on the lawn of the Temple. Myra and Andrew were dressed in white, she in a picture hat and spreading skirts, he in a linen suit with his hair slicked back like a dandy from the twenties. He was very thin, as he had been in the last stages of his illness, but his cheeks were pink and he glowed with health. The atmosphere was permeated with mild satire, as though the two of them had dressed for a costume ball and were laughing at their transformed selves. Russell appeared, flushed and sweating in his business clothes, striding away from the guard's booth at the gate. "No picnicking allowed," he called out. "Only Mormons in good standing can eat on the grounds." Andrew watched him approach, turning on his father the familiar one-sided smile.

"You obviously haven't heard, Dad," he said, his eyes courting the amusement in hers. "When you die, you become an *honorary* Mormon."

He stretched out his hands toward her, and in the space between their reaching arms a white picnic cloth sailed down, landing on the grass with the precarious grace of a floating carpet.

In San Rodrigo, Myra hardly ever cooked a meal. "California is making me decadent," she told Russell, but he was happy to see her relax. In La Paloma's little shopping mall there were three restaurants, Greek, Mexican, and Japanese. The food at each was cheap and tasty; Russell theorized that the same Mexican cook serviced all three kitchens via underground tunnel. It became their habit, after drinks in the yard, to walk up through the greenbelt to the mall for dinner.

One of Russell's colleagues told him about a Thai place at Toscana, a colony about a mile away. They drove there on a Friday evening and found themselves strolling through a theme park of the Italian Renaissance, complete with bell tower (but the bell, Myra noticed, was tongueless) and arched *ponte* over a briskly flowing mini-Arno of recycled water. Pink town houses were clustered beneath roofs of terra-cotta tile. Under the setting sun, the whole scene took on the enhanced reality of a stage set after the house lights had dimmed. Not exactly Florence, Myra thought, but some midwestern banker's idea of Florence—and why not? She felt suddenly defensive about her new home. What was so wonderful about authenticity, that tired Yankee buzzword? Why should the past be remote and untouchable, preserved in amber? Hadn't someone done a study showing that most Americans preferred Disney's walk-through historical fantasies to the real thing?

"This is pretty," said Russell. "I could see living here, couldn't you?" Without looking at her, he took her hand.

After that night they began to seek out other colonies. They told each other they were looking for a house; a couple of times they contacted realtors, but this seriousness spoiled the game. The real pleasure lay in entering a strange land without passport or plan: driving through the gates, selecting a restaurant, assessing the efficiency of the shopping center—"You could live your whole life here and never have to leave," was Russell's highest compliment—and wandering through the parks. Myra was fascinated by the completeness of these miniature worlds. The green spaces, with their contrived brooks and waterfalls and groomed flower beds, seemed to her like little Edens. For all their crassness, there was an innocence about them, a feeling of optimism and fresh beginnings. The original Paradise had been new, too, she reminded herself. Did it matter that such abundance had sprung from the calculations of developers instead of the hand of God?

"Where are we traveling tonight?" Russell would say. "Italy? The south of France?" He had begun to affect a Mediterranean style and would often dress for dinner in an open-collared silk shirt and pastel jacket. In their circle at home, he had once passed for handsome in a burly American way, but he'd gained weight and gone jowly with age. This new exoticism suited him. Now that his thick gray hair was longer at the top and back, and his neck freed from its starched collar, he looked leaner and looser. Catching him patting aftershave into his temples one evening, she told him, "You're beginning to remind me of an Italian movie star."

"Call me Marcello." He glanced at her quickly and mumbled, "Do you like it?" She was more touched than amused to see that he blushed.

A gallantry had sprung up in him, stoked by their weekly excursions. To her surprise, she found herself responding. When he took her arm, as he always did while they were strolling, it seemed natural to lean into his side. After dinner they would choose a bench—the stone one at Toscana or the wrought-iron at Lisboa—and sit like lovers, his arm around her shoulders, inventing lives for the people passing by. That leathery runner with the beeper hooked to his shorts and the tall young brunette by his side—was he a CEO exercising with his daughter or a plastic surgeon showing off his latest trophy wife? The old Asian man solemnly rotating a stroller around the park—did he resent his modern children for forcing him to do woman's work? They had never found the same things funny. Here, at least, they could be silly together, trying to top one another's wild speculations.

Anyone glancing at the couple on the bench would see the silvery patina of long devotion, Myra thought. It was mostly sham, of course. The two of them had married right out of college, with only the shallowest knowledge of each other, and had lived for years in separate spheres. Russell buried himself in his work, relaxing on weekends with golf. Myra volunteered at the museum and concentrated on her son. But in this place of appearances, it was easy to mime the girl she had been: dreamy and sensual, quietly flirtatious.

Andrew was amused by the romance. Myra was certain of it, and even indulged in a fantasy that he had played matchmaker, arranging this new intimacy to compensate for his absence. But as soon as the thought entered her head, she felt a folding-up of his presence. As a child he had punished her by turning his face to the wall, withdrawing because she had failed to understand him. In the old days she had pleaded with him to talk to her, but now she knew the nature of her sin. She was playing the game too earnestly, losing the irony that they had retreated into like a private room from the time he was a small boy.

"I wish Daddy wouldn't come home yet," he'd said that time he had the flu, the two of them cozy in front of the fire. She'd gently rebuked him, but hadn't she known how it would be when Russell blew in, smelling of the outdoors, wanting to know what they'd done all day? The look that passed between Myra and her son then had grown into a kind of culture, with its own language and traditions, its secret signals. Like their day trips, it was an extension of Andrew himself—his singularity, his odd humor, his skewed, Martian way of looking at life. When the boy turned twelve, Russell, having foreseen that he would not make a football player, took him golfing. "You try and push this little *ball* into this little *hole*," was the way Andrew described the experience to Myra. That phrase became their code for Russell's point of view. It made perfect sense to her that Andrew would first be drawn to architecture after discovering Gaudí's eccentric buildings. Those curvy facades covered with dollops of wedding-cake frosting. Those leaning Mad Hatter towers topped with broken teacups. What better way to rebel against Russell's right-angled world? No wonder, she thought now, tickled at the revelation. No wonder he had wanted to go to Barcelona!

"Andrew, you always said your father had no interests outside of work, so you'll be glad to know he's acquired a hobby," Myra said aloud, after Russell left for the office. Her voice echoed foolishly, but she felt a low simmer of attention. "Our recreation has become his passion. He spends all his spare time researching planned communities for our weekend trysts. He even keeps a calendar! Next year's anniversary is going to be spent in the lap of luxury at Persian Gardens, which I gather is a cross between Xanadu and Shangri-la. The only problem is, the place hasn't been built yet."

She was rewarded with a slight fizzing heat in her inner parts, as if her organs were outlined in phosphorescence.

Leonie Bledsoe, their English neighbor, came to Myra's door one morning to warn her to keep her cats in. She was a small, spry woman with tinted red hair, who transfixed Myra with her birdlike gaze and constant smile. When Myra told her that they had no pets, she was undaunted. "Really, dear? I took you for a cat person. A coyote's on the prowl again, and last night he got Mrs. Hollander's tabby. Well, they're like the Indians, aren't they? They were here first. I wouldn't even let Reg out, big fellow that he is. You must come over to meet my drooly-man and see my roses."

Myra steeled herself for a senile husband, but was introduced to the roses first, individually, by name. Red, peach, and several shades of pink, they grew so thickly over the walls of the yard that she thought of the sinister enchanted hedges in fairy tales. Experimentally she touched her finger to the point of a thorn, half-expecting to feel a languor steal over her, instant passage to the land of stopped time. "That's *Queen Anne*," Leonie said. "My Gerald's favorite. English to the core, just like he was, poor lamb. This is going to give you goose pimples, dear, but she started to wither the very week he passed. I brought *her* back, but he dropped not a foot from where you're standing and I couldn't do a thing for him. Well, we mustn't dwell on the past, must we, life is for the living, Gerald always said, and what would he think of me letting the sun bite you when you could be enjoying a nice, cool drink?" Like a captive maiden, Myra followed her into the house.

All the light in the shrouded living room seemed to be concentrated in the TV screen, where a wedding was taking place. "I leave it on all the time," Leonie told her. "Fools the burglars, you know, and Reg likes it." As Myra's eyes got used to the darkness, she could just make out the bulldog crumpled like a collapsed pillow in the middle of the couch. When she settled herself on one end of the flowered chintz, the dog let out a low, dyspeptic growl. Together they watched the couple proceed up the aisle toward the altar: the young man bald and expressionless in Navy dress whites, his bride a porcelain blonde whose small features were blurred by an old-fashioned veil.

"Now isn't this just serendipity?" Leonie said, bringing in glasses of iced tea on a tray. "These two beautiful young people won a contest to be married on national television—he has a brain tumor, you see, and she wrote the most touching letter about love being eternal, they read it last week—and you and I get to watch and have our visit, too. Who says we can't have our cake and eat it?"

Myra found it strangely restful to sip the sweetened tea and drift in and out of Leonie's conversation, which flowed on in an uninflected stream. With Andrew in mind, she let her thoughts swerve to the row of Staffordshire dogs sitting at attention above the adobe fireplace. The house was a duplicate of her own, but so crowded with knickknacks and furniture that its spaces were unrecognizable. Apparently Leonie had constructed, piece by piece, a model of prewar English coziness and transported it intact to this alien house in an alien land. *The yard is just another room*, Myra thought—or was it Andrew thinking?—and saw through his eyes the likeness of the clotted roses and heavy floral drapes.

". . . don't want to frighten you," Leonie was saying, "everything looks so safe and pretty, Paradise, really, ever so much cleaner than Spain, but what I'm telling you, dear, is, take a little care. Only last week Reg and I saw a homeless man sleeping on our favorite bench by the fountain, a beard as long as Jeremiah's and probably smelled to high heaven, we didn't linger to find out, did we, Reg? I'm as softhearted as the next person, but I can't quite sit there now, can I? And then there are the crazies! Have you seen the walking woman yet? Right on the side of the highway like a car with engine trouble, only the poor thing never stops, and no directionals, just marches on regardless . . ."

Myra felt a sudden warmth. On the way to Marbella one afternoon, she had noticed a stolid figure in cotton dress and hiking boots trudging purposefully along the breakdown lane. "I think we've seen that woman," she interrupted. "I have, I mean. Older? Gray hair in a bun? She seemed awfully dignified for a hitchhiker."

"A violinist," Leonie said. "Or so the story goes. Rumor has it there was some tragedy, a stillbirth or a love gone bad, Mrs. Hollander swears to an orchestra conductor who left her—someone famous, she says, though where she gets her information is beyond me. What does it matter, it was enough to snap the poor lady's mind, wasn't it? Too sensitive for this world. She's been walking as long as I've been here, and my house is the oldest one in La Paloma. A mystery, really."

The couple on the screen was taking their vows. For a

moment the skein of talk dropped as both women watched the exchange of rings. Then Leonie took it up again. "Don't let an old scaredy-cat like me make you nervous. I used to drive poor Gerald mad, making him seal up the windows and put extra locks on the doors. 'What have we got that's worth going to all this trouble?' he'd say. 'It's only things!' But if you take care of them, they last, don't they, dear?"

The Navy man lifted the veil from his new wife's face. A single tear, the shape of a pearl, traveled down the sculpted curve of her cheek.

A mystery, Leonie had called her, and Myra and Andrew had always loved mysteries. Myra began to take the car out in the afternoons. She had sensed lately a fading of her son's presence, a pallor almost. Her walks weren't providing enough sustenance for him; no matter how she tried to vary her route, each street offered the same condos and gardeners and ubiquitous joggers. So now she drove the eight miles to the chic seaside town of Marbella two or three times a week, hoping for a sighting. She scanned the breakdown lanes and stared at the faces of vagrants leaning on the lights at intersections—tanned, haggard men who held up cardboard signs saying, Vietnam Vet Will Work For Food. In defiance of Russell, she thrust dollar bills out the window. He had assured her that it was a scam; the men were too young to have fought in Vietnam and wouldn't take a job if they were offered one. He never failed to add that he could think of worse places than San Rodrigo to be homeless.

The cliffs and canyons that bordered the highway made Myra feel pleasantly ephemeral. She liked the idea of all the new buildings squatting so tentatively on this bleached rock where dinosaurs might have lumbered. History didn't haunt here—how could it, when it never took root? Driving along, she had a sense of life lived on the surface, of improvised civilizations that rose and fell soundlessly. What was it that Russell always said when he knocked on the walls of the house? Obsolescence built in.

Her well-being evaporated when she arrived in town. Andrew disappeared entirely, shunning Marbella's sleek affluence as he would have in life. Dutifully, she looked in the windows of upscale shops and nursed a latte at one of the cafés that dotted the main street. Then she walked slowly down to the cove, and, leaning over the railing, watched the seals sleeping on their boulder as the sad immensity of the ocean spread out around them. Sights that used to give her joy soured on her now, like milk left out in the sun.

She spotted the walking woman only once. Intent on getting home after staying later than usual in Marbella, she would have driven right past if she hadn't felt a sudden urge to look to the left. Myra hardly had time to glimpse the woman's face, but she formed a vivid impression of it from the set of the shoulders and the determined stride: broad and calm, with a carved quality to the cheekbones and chin, like the presidents on Mount Rushmore. "Our friend knows exactly where she's going, Andrew, I can tell you that," she said aloud, and then looked around to see if anyone in the other lane was watching. She was about to laugh at herself when she heard, breathed rather than spoken, *Our unravished bride of quietness,* and all the rest of the way she thought of the woman walking along, contained as a vase.

The hour in Marbella was what she talked about when Russell asked about her day. He was always so relieved that she was getting out. "Did you meet anyone?" he wanted to know. "Are you making friends?" He urged her to circulate her résumé at the art galleries, or to become a docent at one of the museums. His own work had escalated as September approached. She suspected that his grief was ebbing as he settled into the job; probably he felt guilty to leave the burden of bereavement to her. Lately he left the house before she was up and arrived home after seven, too tired for anything but a sandwich or a quick salad.

Although their mock trips were now confined to weekends, Russell was always full of stories about Persian Gardens. A high fence surrounded the construction site, but already there was talk of unrivaled opulence. Each unit would be unique, erected on terraced land to give the impression that the complex had developed like a city, over time. Ancient building materials were being replicated, buttressed by the newest miracle metals. A corps of landscape architects had planned a magnificent courtyard, with marble fountains and formal gardens as elaborate as the ones adorning the Taj Mahal. Arab oil money was said to be behind it all, but even at this stage, secrecy prevailed. No one was naming names. No one knew any.

"What I can't figure out," Russell said one night, "is why someone would take a risk like that when the economy is so shaky. Subdivisions are closing left and right. Remember all the hoo-ha about St. Tropez? It's going on the block next month."

"Maybe the sheik isn't building this pleasure palace for the public," said Myra. "Maybe he plans to live there by himself, with several hundred ladies from his harem."

They were sitting in bed watching the eleven o'clock

news. An enormous spotlight had been installed at a border checkpoint that day to make it harder for illegal aliens to slip into California. The mayor gave a speech. City officials and border police clapped as the switch was turned on for the first time.

Myra smiled, remembering how, even after he started school, Andrew would never go to sleep without his night-light standing sentinel, chasing the shadows away. Blinky, he called it. Only in this part of the world, she thought, could the powers-that-be come up with such a childlike solution to a national problem. A big light.

That night she lay on her back like a tomb figure, hands folded across her chest and eyes closed. It was soothing to think about all the hidden, silent life going on under cover of darkness. Instead of counting sheep she imagined coyotes slinking out of canyons, Mexicans tunneling under fences, the susurrus progress of snakes. Sometimes the movements were separate threads; sometimes they combined in a wave motion that undulated beneath her house and all the houses like it: a quiet, imperceptible tremor. Eventually she fell into a dreamless sleep. It seemed that her subconscious, too, needed to rest from its doubled labors.

The Santa Ana winds came in around mid-September, bringing hot, dry air from the desert. One Saturday, toward the end of the month, she and Russell went out for a late dinner of Spanish food. Sitting on the patio in the sluggish evening heat, they drank sangria as if it were water. "You can't get pickled on this fruity stuff," Russell assured her.

Around nine, a small band began to play tango music.

"Shall we?" he asked, and without waiting for an answer, swept her out of her seat and onto the floor. It was easy to submit to his dramatic dips; he had always been an excellent dancer. If there was any artfulness in his nature, it resided here. She remembered their first date at a club near the college. She had been reluctant to go out with a football player, but had been intrigued by how gracefully he carried his big body. This evening they were the only couple on the floor. They danced through an entire set, and when they walked back to their table, breathless, the other patrons clapped.

Myra stayed perfectly clearheaded on the drive home, but sank like a stone into bed. She was almost asleep when she became aware of Russell's hand on her breast. "It was nice holding you in my arms tonight," he murmured. Over the years their lovemaking had dwindled along with their dancing. She had put him off so often that he had stopped trying, but now she felt no inclination to resist. A lethargy had settled over her; her limbs were loose and pliable, only her skin awake to his hands and lips. The act itself was as awkward as the first time they made love—and almost as painful. "Sorry," he gasped. "Out of practice here. Sorry." And through it all she was aware, with an obscure shame, of the enormity of his relief. When it was over, she closed her eyes and fell into a thick sleep.

The child Andrew was running away from her, across the yard, and she was chasing after him, striving with great urgency but also being carried. Although he ran very fast, it seemed to her that she was gaining ground. She could see with tantalizing clarity his close-cropped head that seemed too big for the stem of his neck, the V of tanned skin between his sunsuit straps, the winglike blades sprouting from his shoulders, close enough to touch. "Andrew!" she called, reaching out to him, and woke without transition as if she had opened the door into another room. She was sitting bolt upright, her damp nightgown clinging coldly to her skin.

In the morning, Myra's head ached and her mouth was as dry as if it had been stuffed with cotton. Russell hovered over her with toast and coffee. "The trouble with you is, you lived in the land of the Puritans too long," he teased. "You're not used to the high life." She could see that he was in a good mood, buoyant from the intimacy of the night before. Tentatively he suggested an ocean walk, if she felt up to it, followed by lunch in Marbella. Everything about him grated on her today: his robustness, his cheerful solicitude that glided over her real needs. "I can't even *think* of food," she said, but in the end agreed to go.

Hang gliders dived from the cliffs above the pristine beach, circling like demented birds. Myra, walking hand in hand with Russell, tried to share his pleasure in the spectacle. Silently she chided herself for drinking so much; it had been foolish, adolescent, that much alcohol would give anyone nightmares. But she knew all the while that the wine was irrelevant. The dream—if it was a dream—had penetrated her inmost parts, as ink sinks into the crevices of a thumb. A piece of the past had come back to her with icy clarity as soon as she opened her eyes. Andrew had just turned four; she'd been putting in flowers and had let him plant a few seeds. He was absorbed in patting down the earth, carefully and tenderly, when the bee struck. The shock of the sting made him hysterical. Instead of coming to her for comfort, he had run wildly through the garden, flapping his hand as if to shake the pain away.

After lunch, Russell drove up a twisting road lined with gated pastel villas to the highest point in Marbella. Mount Serra, in spite of its name, was a modest ridge topped by a stone cross draped in unlit Christmas lights. From its peak all of Marbella and much of San Rodrigo could be seen, and beyond them, the new communities of identical houses that lay so lightly on the desert. Russell wanted to show her Persian Gardens from above. "See there." He pointed. "That big brown patch surrounded by fence. Look how fast it's going up. Someone's paying these suckers to work Sundays."

Like a scene out of the Bible, Myra thought. The construction site could have been the burial place of a king. From her height, the ant-sized workers resembled slaves laboring at some monumental pyramid whose final form they would never live to see. Even the steel girders seemed prematurely ancient: rust-colored and jagged, with the stripped elegance of ruins. Against this backdrop, the one completed building appeared shockingly new. It was whiter than the Mormon Temple, an aggressive, glittering white that stood out in stark relief from the beige earth around it.

"What on earth makes it shine that way?" she asked Russell.

"Mica is my guess." He began to gesture in the broad, expansive way he affected when explaining the mechanics of things. "Same as they put in sidewalks, only a lot more of it. What they've done is crush humongous quantities of the stuff in big grinders and mix it right in with the plaster. A stone as soft as that, they can get it fine as salt. It's like"—she could see that he was struggling toward metaphor, trying to paint a word picture for her—"it's like what our former fearless leader used to say. A thousand points of light."

"Very impressive," Myra said. "I imagine they'll decorate with painted statues. Aren't sheiks famous for that sort of thing?" It was a wispy enough remark, and she was not surprised at how quickly it faded into the air. The absence she had fought off all day gaped in her now. Her mind churned out antibodies: Russell's presence was intrusive, she was out of sorts from her strange night. One by one these pale excuses rallied and were overcome. With Persian Gardens gleaming beneath her and Russell still smiling at his turn of phrase, Myra understood that she was alone.

There had been other partings. Weren't there always, with children? She'd lobbied Russell to send Andrew to private high school, and he had found a group there for the first time in his life—bright, quirky outsiders like him. Myra hadn't minded that he pulled away from her; it was natural, wasn't it? She even became a sort of den mother to the little band of subversives, letting the boys assemble an alternative newspaper in her basement, defending them when the headmaster condemned some mildly scurrilous cartoons. That Andrew was gay was no surprise; she'd intuited it before she knew it in fact, but hadn't foreseen how enclosed his world would become. He left for college, and then New York, and never really came back until he was ill. What had moved Myra—sustained her—was how completely he returned to her, their communion as deep and effortless as when he was a child. In the midst of her anguish, she'd felt privileged to accompany him on this last excursion. She could see the circuitous route they had traveled, and when the time came, she could let him go.

All that grace fled from her now. After Russell left for

work on Monday, she roamed the house, stopping where she had felt Andrew's presence. But the walls gave back only her own image, a harried doppelgänger with uncombed hair and darting eyes. "It's these mirrors," she raged aloud. "These damn mirrors!" They left no privacy for the soul; they exposed all its scars and wrinkles. She imagined Andrew shrinking from the glass as he had from the crude light of the flashbulb that Russell was always aiming at him.

Myra remembered how, in the first days after his death, she had sat in the room where the two of them spent so many hours, wondering where he was. Up to the end he had remained himself. She'd had to lift his head to feed him but his eyes still snapped at her, challenging her to share his mockery of the thing that was gnawing at him. "Consume or be consumed," he said, trying and failing to swallow a spoonful of broth. When he was finally gone, she vowed to stare at the vacuum he left until it yielded to her understanding. She kept coming up with the same arid certainty: if he wasn't there, he must be somewhere. At last, weary of the logic that held her in like a whalebone corset, she'd thought of heaven. But it was impossible to imagine him walking on a cloud or floating in a sea of light. He had been too edgy for that: always the outsider looking in. If he were forced to spend eternity in such a place, he would be its court jester, standing on the fringes and aiming arrows of wit at the marshmallow cushions of the righteous. No, she thought now, his heaven would be a room, a cleverly designed room with everything he loved within reach. She saw in the mirror that the palms of her hands were spread over her womb.

Around midmorning, her thoughts drove her out of the

house. She walked rapidly along their old paths, stopping in front of the Mormon Temple, where she stood in a trance of staring while joggers detoured around her and passersby gave her second looks. The building had become an exercise in color, white on a blue wash of sky. It was as if the hollow in her had sucked roundness from the world. One of the Mormon women appeared in her line of sight, head poked forward in concern, carrying a large pocketbook over her forearm like Queen Elizabeth. Myra turned and stumbled off in the wrong direction.

By afternoon she was angry. "Why come back at all?" she harangued him, pacing back and forth from one end of the living room to another. "Wasn't one death enough? Do you enjoy making me go through this a second time?" Words poured out of her mouth that she'd heard from other mothers but vowed never to speak herself. "You're selfish. A tease. You've always taken what you needed and left when you felt like it. I don't deserve— You have no right—"

She went on like this for a long time, collapsing finally in the bedroom, spent. Then her anger softened into abjection. She reasoned with him, bargained, turning up the same frayed arguments again and again. "Andrew, are you punishing me? That night was just an accident, it was the alcohol, that's all. Your father is a good man, but you know how he is, he only sees a square inch of what's there. You and I had perspective. We could look at something and see the absurdity of it. Can you imagine the loneliness of having no one to laugh with?"

At the end of the day Myra felt as if she were living inside Russell's square inch. The walls of the clean, undemanding house pressed in on her. When he came home, she was sitting on one of the twin couches, gazing across the great divide at the other couch.

"It's late," he said. "Are you in the mood for burritos and a beer? We could try that new place at Lisboa, but I thought we'd save it for the weekend. No transatlantic trips on workdays."

"My God, isn't this fantasy beginning to wear a little thin?" She stood, folding her arms across her chest. "Fake countries, fake antiquity, fake food. Are we supposed to live out our lives in a theme park?"

He took off his jacket and slumped down on the couch across from her. "I thought you were happy here. You seemed so much better. So cheerful."

"Did you really think I could be happy in a white box like this? Look around you!" She was aware that her voice was rising but could not stop herself. "I can't even bear to go into that walled-up yard anymore. What's the point of living in the West if we can't have a view?"

"It isn't so easy to find furnished places," he said wearily. "The plan was, we'd look for a house when you were ready. When you'd . . . recovered enough."

"Recovered? I suppose you think it's like a virus. He was just a puzzle to you, wasn't he? A rogue gene, not the all-American boy you ordered. Why should you mourn now that he's gone?" She drilled the words into the white wall behind him. "How I envy your capacity for getting over grief. You're such a simple machine, Russell. A real one-celled organism."

Myra watched him stiffen as the words hit him. His face clenched, and for a second she thought he was going to lose control, as he had at the funeral. But when he spoke, his voice was calm. "Maybe I never had the rapport you did.

Maybe I never understood the way he was, the way he lived. But for your information, he was my son, too."

He got up, hooking his jacket over his shoulder in an incongruously jaunty gesture, and walked out.

She sat on the edge of the bed, facing away from her reflection in the closet doors. "I'm vile," she whispered, "I know I am. You see how it is, Andrew."

She had kept just one thing from his apartment in New York: a summer shirt of finely woven cotton that she'd folded into a tissue-lined box and put in the back of her closet. The box was on her lap now. All these months she hadn't opened it. Some taboo held her back, some potency she feared to unleash. Ashes in an urn would have been easier; they were only—that stilted term—the remains. But he had worn the shirt next to his skin, the cloth might hold the smell of him. Slowly she raised the lid and lifted the box to her face. There was a ghost of sweat, so faint that even as she breathed it in, she felt she was using it up. She covered the box and set it back on the shelf.

The room had turned dark. Her heart was beating quickly and she was very cold. She undressed, got into bed, and pulled the covers over her head; as a child, afraid of thunder, she had huddled under the comforter on stormy nights, her warm breath heating the cave. The next thing she was aware of was the slight shifting of weight as Russell lowered himself onto the mattress. The rigid line of his back, parallel to her own.

Myra woke early, but pretended to sleep until Russell left for work. When she got out of bed, her neck and shoulders were stiff. In the shower she turned on the hot water full force and raised her arms to the steam.

She made herself a convalescent's breakfast of a boiled egg, toast, and tea, and ate it slowly, skimming the entertainment section of the newspaper that Russell had left on the table. The day had to be structured. "You could go shopping in the morning," she suggested to herself, in the brisk voice of a sensible friend, "and go to a movie at the mall." Simple things were wanted: ordinary, time-filling things.

She carried her few dishes to the counter and began to wash them, looking through the window above the sink. The Chinese woman came out in business suit and sneakers to walk her terrier before work. Across the street a tree service was sawing off the diseased frond of a palm. The recycling truck rounded the corner, earlier than usual, and in the same instant that she noted it, a shutter seemed to click over her vision and she saw the back of Andrew's head, the parting that she'd made on the right side with his special soft brush and a little water, wisps of damp hair feathering away from the pinkness of the scalp. Then the cold came—or she had come back to herself and could feel it—and she froze in place, her soapy hands gripping a cup. Her heart thudded painfully and her thoughts veered like trapped moths.

Get out of the house, the sensible friend whispered. Go see someone. Myra ran upstairs and got her keys from her purse.

In the front yard she stood with her head to one side, as if listening for the direction of the wind. Who did she know here except Leonie? "That funny little woman," she always said, when Russell asked about the neighbors. "Do you think I'd volunteer to visit her?" But now she had a powerful urge to sit again in the cluttered parlor, a cup of tea in hand, and listen to the Englishwoman's chatter. Myra could bring up the subject subtly, never alluding to the personal: a discussion program on the radio, the dead communicating with the living, did Leonie believe in that sort of thing? Surely Leonie, with her talk-show wisdom, would have opinions, perhaps even experiences. Myra imagined the soothing anodyne of her voice going on about seeing Gerald by the rosebush, transforming death into a comfortably furnished sitting room that the deceased could leave when he wanted company.

She walked the few yards to Leonie's door and rang the bell. No one answered, but she could hear voices, a woman's and a man's. She jabbed the button again—three short, urgent buzzes. The female voice trilled girlishly. Myra pictured Leonie and the ghostly Gerald entangled on the flowered chintz couch, and thought without hope of how Andrew would have enjoyed the fantasy. On impulse she moved to the side of the house. Feeling the eyes of invisible neighbors on her, she rapped on the window. The voices dipped and rose, undisturbed. She thought she could make out the words ". . . but the alcohol in perfume can be irritating," and, pressing closer to the window, glimpsed between a gap in the drapes a sliver of the flickering television screen and a large slice of the dog, who lay with his jowls on his paws like an obese potentate watching a dancing girl.

Slowly she walked back to her own yard, the keys dangling from her hand. She sat at the patio table staring at the furled blue umbrella. She and Russell never used the table now; the novelty had worn off, and it had been weeks since they sat outside. The memory came back to her of their first afternoon in the house: drinks in the yard, Russell's pleasure in the sun and flowers, Andrew's words suddenly in her mouth. Here she was, only a few months later, in the same chair, surrounded by the same primary colors, anointed by the same sun, and the whole scene was dust in her eye.

When the chill took her, she began to weep. He had come to her with the waning sparks of his attention—all he had left—and she had tried to nurture him. But time had dulled the brilliant surfaces that he loved. The place had grown old for both of them, and she was a woman with no milk in her breasts, she had nothing left to give. Her grief had always been dry—too deep for the banality of tears. Now she cried with abandon, the sobs gushing out of her with a sweetness that was like sexual release. She stopped only because no liquid seemed to be left in her.

She let herself into the house and walked straight through the hall and laundry room to the garage, closing the door behind her. After the morning sun, the darkness was opaque, her car a hulking solidity. She got in and put her hand on the key. A few deep breaths and the slow spinning into sleep, not so different from a child drowsing in the back seat as its parents drove through the night. She turned on the engine. Her hand lifted in reflex to the button on the mirror and the garage door rolled up behind her.

She drove blindly, coming twice to the highway entrance and circling back before losing herself in a maze of residential streets, an older neighborhood that she'd somehow missed on her trips. The houses thinned out, along with the vegetation. She passed a lime-green motel and an apartment building, both with the low-slung hacienda look of the fifties. Because she could smell the ocean, she guessed that she must be on a back road to Marbella. A route older than the highways, for this was the desert before its forced flowering: dusty sidewalks, a few parched palms, the ghost-town air of an abandoned resort. The road narrowed, giving way to sand and scrub. Rounding a curve, she saw first the iridescent shimmer of the water and then, coming toward her, the woman. Without hesitating she pulled over to the thin lip at the side of the road, rolled down her window, and shouted, "Do you want a ride?"

The walking woman gave no sign of hearing. She moved along, placing one foot and then the other with flat deliberation. Her face was obscured by large sunglasses. Graying hair stood out around her head in frizzled strands, and she was heavier than Myra remembered, the bulk of her body straining at the beltless dress that fell just below her knees. Her legs, straight as logs between the hem of the dress and her hiking boots, were carrying her right past the car.

Myra jumped out and thrust herself in front of the woman. "Do you want a ride?" she said again. "It's no trouble."

The woman rocked back on her heels, absorbing arrested momentum. With one hand she raised the sunglasses to her forehead and blinked. Against the bronze of her face, wrinkled and inscrutable as a Mayan grandmother's, her blue eyes were very light. They seared Myra briefly before looking beyond her.

"Keep moving!" she bawled out. "Move along now!"

With a squared military step, she marched around Myra as if she were a rock in the path and continued up the road.

Russell wanted the apartment to be a surprise. He would tell her
only that he had found it by a stroke of luck, a client mentioning that the model condo in Marrakesh was for rent
because all the other units had sold. Top floor, fully furnished, with a Jacuzzi and a view. "I think you're going to
love this one," he said. "It's very tasteful. What was the word
the agent used? Aerie. A real aerie."

A Santa Ana blew in on the night before they were to
move, fanning canyon fires that had been raging in the east.
The air was foul and full of cinders, but Russell would not be
deterred. He packed Myra off in the morning as if she were
a box of china, insisting that she spend the day beneath the
sundome of a new mall. Although she'd resisted, the perfumed greenhouse atmosphere put her in a frivolous frame
of mind. She wandered in and out of shops, buying makeup,
a bathing suit, a robe of silky cotton, then lingered over
pasta at a trattoria under the atrium, marveling at the sleek-
ness of the shoppers around her. On a whim she decided to
have her hair done. Not until she was paying the woman at
the desk did she realize that the day had spent itself; already
it was after five. In the rush-hour traffic she took half an
hour to drive the three miles home.

The sweep of balconies up the tiled facade of the new
building made Myra think of a vertical Casbah. She would
have to ask Russell about the challenges of fortifying so many
levels against quakes. In the anteroom she stared at the rows
of names above the buttons, struck by the thought that the
apartment she was about to claim as home was as unknown to
her as any of these others. The space over their bell was

blank. Russell's voice crackled over the receiver: "Calvert residence. Mover and shaker speaking. Did you buy out the stores?" He buzzed, and she pushed through the door into the lobby. Abstract weavings and potted palms. For Southern California the decor was restrained, a western take on a New York high-rise. As the glass tube of the elevator carried her to the top floor, she felt a childish delight that she could see around her all the way up.

Sand-colored carpet swallowed her footsteps. Behind closed doors, the anonymous names lived their hushed lives. But her door was open and Russell was leaning out of it, wearing one of his silk shirts. He waved his drink at her. "Don't you look nice! If I wasn't slightly stewed I'd carry you over the threshold. . . . What do you think? Classy, isn't it? After that last place, we deserve a little elegance."

"Very Nick and Nora," she said. She noted low furniture, a color scheme of apricot and beige with bright pillows.

"I thought it looked like you." He was talking quickly, bearing down on his words the way he did when he had been drinking for a while. "The kitchen's small, but who the hell cooks anymore? The place has got *features*. Did you notice the arched doorways? I said to the agent, *that's* the kind of detail my wife will go for."

On the coffee table he had set out champagne in an ice bucket, containers of dip, a plateful of crackers. She saw that he had folded napkins and arranged them in an overlapping circle around the plate. The thought of his hands laboring at this small nicety abruptly twisted her heart.

"You've made everything so perfect," she said. "So civilized. I don't know how you managed to do it all in one day. We should have a toast."

He put the bottle between his knees. With exaggerated effort, as if poised for a golf swing, he pulled the cork out, then filled two glasses.

"Wait," he said. "I think the air is breathable now. We might as well go out on the balcony and enjoy your view."

San Rodrigo was presenting one of its post-inferno light shows. The sun had mixed with the smoldering haze of the brush fires and was melting to a scarlet line along the horizon. It blazed briefly on the polished marble walls around Persian Gardens before dropping into the darkness of the canyon.

"I actually went over there," Russell said, not looking at her. "Just to see what all the hype is about. In the unlikely event we ever wanted to move up, you know? I swear, the damn place is harder to get into than the Mormon Temple. Guy at the gate told me they're *interviewing* applicants, narrowing the pool before they show the condos. My bet is, in six months they'll invite the common folk to an open house."

In the smoky air that all but obliterated the surrounding ridges and canyons, the buildings of Persian Gardens shone with a diffused glow. The colony looked as if it were floating, Myra thought. Like a city of stars, rooted in nothing but space. The illusion was so strong that a wave of dizziness passed over her, and the platform they stood on seemed to shift. Instinctively, she reached for Russell's arm.

"To the future," he said. Together they raised their glasses to the million motes of glitter suspended at the level of their gaze, as near as next door, as distant as the last bright home of the white-robed dead.

Interpreters

The child is Thomas's, not his. She knows this, just as she knows it was Thomas she tempted, Thomas's seed she wooed that first night in the house.

She had answered the last of the visitors' questions at her door instead of leaving by way of the fields as the two of them usually did at closing. She had taken off her cap and let her hair flow down her back. She had sashayed up the empty road, swinging her hips like a trollop, and gone straight to the joinery, where he was planing the legs of a chair. "Be gone, woman, can ye not see I'm busy?" Thomas said, but he had come with her without too much coaxing, and taken off her clothes by the fire, and spread her hair over her shoulders like a cloak, and made love to her for an hour, while the chicken she'd roasted grew cold on the spit.

Not that Thomas didn't fight off the pleasure, or pretend to. Thomas is a man of scruples, and as the heat grew between them she could almost hear them crack, a slow giving-way like stones being crushed. "No, no, no," he'd moaned at the moment of surrender, crying wolf to the Devil. But all the time she knew that Thomas had planted the seed as surely as he drove a nail into wood.

She could feel it snag, feel its tiny shaking as it settled into its nest. And like the joiner's wife she had become, she thought, *Tongue-and-groove.*

They met her second year at the community college, in the endless registration line for American Civilization. He was standing behind her—a dark, fine-featured man she had noticed around campus, a little older than the average student—and he took her hair in his hands, just lifted it as if it were a length of yard goods or the sleeve of a shirt on a rack. So delicately, with such a sure, impersonal touch, that she wasn't even startled. "Is this color real?" he asked. Yes, she told him, that shade of copper ran in her family; her grandmother had been a redhead too. But not until a week later, when he saw her fiery thatch of pubic hair, did she think he truly believed her.

She went with him to the space he rented above the organ factory where he worked. There was nothing in it except a broken-down couch, a mattress, and a large wooden chest set in the center of the concrete floor where a table should have been. What looked like pieces of trash had been placed on the window ledges: a shoehorn; a milk bottle with a pinched neck to hold cream; rusted iron tongs; an egg carton, its lid propped up with a stick; two Coke bottles positioned to catch the light that struggled through the thick, pitted glass. The Coke bottles were forty years old, he said. He had been incredibly lucky to find them; they were from the Golden

Age, before the company changed the design, long before the descent to cans. As he took her around, she learned that even the most ordinary objects had had Golden Ages. The world had fallen not just once, as she'd been taught in Sunday school, but piece by piece, again and again. She wasn't sure why it mattered, but was certain that it did. No one had ever talked to her about such things before.

The chest was for tools, he told her, modeled after one he'd seen in an antiques store. He had squatted on the floor for half an hour, examining the construction of the compartments inside, turning the whole thing over on its back while the clerk glared; then he had gone out to find the wood. She didn't say a word when he led her to the mattress.

Their first time was very different from what she had known with her only other lover: the fevered groping in the back of the car, the quick, violent climax. He undressed her slowly, folding her clothes in a neat pile on the floor. He fanned her hair out on the pillow. He touched her all over, using every part of his hand: indenting her nipples with his thumbs, making a Saturn's ring around her navel with his pinkie, tracing the line of each rib with the tip of his forefinger as if he were drawing branches with a fine-pointed pen. At first she was giggly, fidgeting like a ticklish child, but then she closed her eyes and gave in to the fantasy that he was making her from scratch. She knew she should resent being treated like one of his objects, but was too excited to protest. She had seen how his fingers had caressed the dovetailed corners of the chest.

When he finally entered her, she felt chosen. She realizes it now. His eyes, which looked at the world and found it wanting, had lingered on her. His beautiful, long-fingered hands had passed over her, pressing, appraising, touching her as she imagined blind people touch the faces of strangers. Rising to meet him, she saw that he was staring at the wall above her, his face distant and perplexed. He moved hesitantly, without rhythm or urgency. After minutes of this, the desire she'd felt when he was exploring her began to ebb. It was his attention she needed; he seemed to have forgotten about her altogether. She had heard about women who faked orgasms. Experimentally, she began to thrash and moan—as much to remind him of her presence as to help him along. "Don't," he whispered. His coming was so gentle that she almost missed it. He threw his head back and let out a deep sigh, as if giving vent to some long-held irritation. Then he rolled off her and turned away.

She lay as he had left her, wondering whether her body or her inexperience had disappointed him. The room had darkened. She listened to his even breathing; probably he'd fallen asleep, now that he'd gotten what he wanted. Although it was warm, she wished for a blanket. The vacant space around her made her feel like a small animal crouching in the open. Factories had always struck her as sinister, even in daylight—the sort of places where bodies turned up in the mysteries she read. She didn't like being naked in one. Easing herself to the edge of the mattress, she kept her back to him as she felt for her clothes. In her mind she had already pushed open the heavy door, run down the back steps and into the street, made a beeline for a phone booth or a bus or a kindly stranger. Her painted tights—she'd bought them to wear with her mother's leather skirt from the sixties—ripped as she tugged them on. Tears came to her eyes. She'd worn them because they looked arty and retro, because she imagined him easing them down her hips.

"I don't blame you." He was propped up on one elbow, watching her with a disinterested pleasure that seemed to have nothing to do with his words. "I'd probably leave, too. That was lousy. Terrible. I have too much on my mind." He reached for the black-covered portfolio by the mattress, handing it to her as if it were an explanation. Inside, on loose sheets of paper, were drawings of furniture—precisely detailed, shadowed into roundness, so that they stood out on the page with the immediacy of flesh.

"They're almost like portraits," she said, and could not resist touching the slant of a desk where it slid away from the flat front of the bookcase above it.

He held a corner of a drawing between his thumb and forefinger. "Shitty quality. The paper, I mean. Not worth wasting a five-cent pencil on. I have a friend, Owen, who's studying Japanese techniques. He's supposed to show me how to make my own."

"I don't know why you have to live with the guy," her mother had said, after they'd had it out about her age. "He may be nice-looking, but he has a sour expression. He'll never bring you any happiness."

"*Happiness*," she had mocked, trying to put into the word all the contempt he had taught her for what was cheap, tinselly, easily won. At times, though—after he had left the organ factory because he couldn't stand to make small parts anymore, and the carpentry shop when the rednecks he worked with started to rag him; after he had kicked the wall, cursing, when his aunt, who had raised him, said she'd just as soon buy the night tables at the unfinished furniture place; after they had moved from the empty loft to the pipes-filled basement apartment to a couple of dim, underheated rooms in the house of a fireman's widow—she thought she would settle for a little of it.

"Leave, why don't you?" he told her more than once. "I interrupted your destiny. Go get that assistant manager job at the Gap. Go marry Douglas with the A.A. in computers and move to some nice new subdivision and have your mother over for dinner on Sundays. Please, go marry Doug." She wanted to walk out when he talked like that, but not into the future he prophesied for her. Doug. She could just see the crew cut, the earnest, lopsided grin, the softening middle, the puzzled line in the forehead. Once, such a life wouldn't have sounded half bad, but she knew too much now; he had taught her to want more. "Is that what you think of me?" she would say. "Is that all you think I'm fit for?" She had to stay, if only to prove to him that she wasn't some dime-store trinket, made not to last.

She had already cut her course load by half and begun to waitress evenings at a café in town. He was away all night, anyway, working as a security guard at the college. He had been putting himself through school, but now he no longer made a pretense of earning his degree. What was the point, he said, of getting a piece of paper from one mediocre institution so he could transfer to another? He would rather study on his own. If he didn't have the space to make his furniture, at least the job would give him time to build it in his mind.

He usually crawled into bed with her when he got home, and they would snuggle for an hour before she got up. For months now, this animal closeness had replaced making love. One morning she woke alone, chilled beneath the covers. Half-asleep, she staggered into the living room to find him sitting at the table with Owen, his friend from the organ factory. A pot of coffee was on the hot plate, and they were warming their hands around mugs, looking at brochures spread over the flowered oilcloth. It was a long time since she had seen him so relaxed.

"Hey, I just solved your life," Owen said. He was an Ivy League dropout, a doctor's son who had taken the two of them up, she thought, as a temporary pastime, along with papermaking. "Go ye to Winstead Village. The state's putting a lot of money into the place, trying to build it into a little Plymouth, and I happen to know they're looking for craftspeople. Since you're already living in primitive conditions, you might as well get paid for it."

Tightening the cord of her bathrobe, she sat down. The brochure nearest her showed a woman in a ruffled cap and apron setting down a platter of some sort of fowl on a rough wooden table while her husband and children waited, knives in hand. She could see from the way their faces gleamed that the room was lit only by candles.

"I was there once," she said. "In fifth grade. All these people were walking around in costumes, and we kept asking them where they went to the bathroom so they'd tell us in colonial."

Owen smiled. "With that old-fashioned face of yours, you'd fit right in. If you're going to sell yourselves as a couple, though, you might have to be married for real. Something to think about, anyway."

After Owen left, she waited for him to explain to her why it was impossible. Instead, he looked around the room almost tenderly, as if acknowledging for the first time the lamp with the ceramic fire-hat base and the colored glass Dutch girls her mother had brought to brighten up the narrow windows.

"The thing that amazes me about the seventeenth century," he said, "is the absence of crap. Even the stuff they thought of as crap was beautiful. By our standards, I mean."

A justice of the peace was all they could afford. Her mother, weeping, had offered a cut-rate wedding package at the local Holiday Inn; she'd been divorced for years and wanted her only child to be married in white. They had refused, of course, but on the morning of the ceremony she was teary herself as she put on her old Indian skirt, the only long thing she owned. "Soon you'll be dressing up all the time," he told her, and went to let Owen in.

They had joked about using a twisty or the neck of a bottle cap, but when the justice instructed him to present the ring, he reached into his pocket and brought out a circlet of cherry wood, thinned to translucence and polished until it shone like muted gold. It fit her finger perfectly.

The child will be a girl. It has already been recorded in the briefing material she reviews each night, and lived before that. Eliza, wife of Thomas Coates, joiner, had given birth after a day's travail to a daughter whose fine strands of hair were the same russet shade as its mother's. The infant's beauty must have been some compensation; Thomas had wished for a son for his firstborn, as any man would, but his trade had given him a weakness for beauty. Why else had he married a skinny-hipped flirt of a girl who wept at leaving her father's house and was caught—great-bellied and well into her sixth month—playing tag with her sisters in the street? The elders of the church frowned on his choice of a bride, as they frowned on the ivory inlays he inserted in the panels of his chests, with no more purpose than to beguile the eye. They conferred in whispers about the legs of his chairs, which departed so far from the straight path as to take on the pagan shapes of serpents and griffins. But his sure hand was seen as the outward sign of an inward grace, and no one questioned his rectitude. How could they when his manner was as stern and plain as the pegged stools in the colonists' cottages? He was a man of few words and quoted Scripture when he spoke at all. If he garnished his furniture with furbelows, he withheld them from his speech.

She wonders how soon she will begin to bulge beneath her apron. She knows the comments she'll get then: the women talking about how realistic it looks, a few actually asking her, "Is that a pillow, dear?" And again and again, the questions pregnant women answer in any age: "When is it due?" "Do you want a boy or a girl?" *God willing, I will be brought to bed in summer. I care not, so long as the child be well.* Eyes to the ground. A slight blush, if she can manage it.

She playacts at being Eliza, gets by on looks and charm and a few phrases and gestures. She can't manage the rural English accent at all; if she gets the words right, the cadence is off. The visitors love her anyway. The men flirt. The women are maternal. Yesterday a toddler ran to her and burrowed in her skirts. But she hardly ever sinks beneath the surface, and when it happens, she makes too much of it. "I swear, I didn't even know anyone was watching," she told him one afternoon. "I felt like I was in a snow globe with water all around me."

She still remembers the look he gave her. "We'll have to shake you up in the morning, get those fake flakes circulating," he said.

He doesn't have to play mind games. The past is his natural element, the air he breathes. The language flows from him as if he were born speaking it. Now that they're living at the Village, he is Thomas almost all the time—just as well, since he never wanted a child himself. It would be a crime to bring a kid into this world, he used to tell her. Besides, you never knew how they'd turn out. With kids, you had to take what you got.

Their first few days at Winstead, she'd thought nothing had changed. He kept to himself during orientation. At night he would invite Owen over and lampoon the other villagers, expecting her to take part when all she wanted was to fit in. The goodwives were an easy target. He set them in neat categories like chess pieces: stocky, red-cheeked wielders of trowels, recently sprung from organic farms; retired librarians with chapped cheeks and the glassy stare of zealots, dispensing advice along with recipes for pottage. He had only a little more tolerance for the cooper and the potter and the smith.

"Come on, man," Owen said. "There must be someone you can relate to. These people are artists like you."

"Are you kidding? They're a bunch of hobbyists, only they don't want to wait for Sunday afternoon. I defy you to find one who can do what I can with my hands."

His greatest scorn was reserved for the weekend warriors who spent their days off in wool coats and breeches, reenacting ancient battles. He mimed them shaking off sweat like wet dogs, panting with excitement as they charged across the field. "Like a game of goddamn paintball," he said. "Have you ever noticed how many of those guys are fat? They spend Saturdays waving their muskets and it improves their fantasy life." She thought he must be referring to the apothecary, a genial fellow whose gut hung over his breeches. "How be you, good mistress?" he would boom whenever he saw her. "'Tis ever a joy to see thy comely face."

The joinery made the difference, she thinks now. It was as if he had been Thomas all along, waiting to possess this dusky space, to lift the tools that had been laid out for him. He began to work right away, with such concentration that he never noticed her when she passed by, her basket on her arm. His silence seemed to spread to the visitors, who stood respectfully at the margins of the room. If a brave soul asked a question, he answered in measured tones, barely looking up. He was always courteous to those who grilled him about his techniques—even the know-it-alls who tried to impress him with their expertise. That was where she saw the change. Petulance seemed to have departed from him, cast out like a movie demon along with his tics and tremors, his rages, his nagging impatience. What was left was what she saw when she stood in the doorway: a man bent over his work, the dust-filled light from the single window trained on him like a high beam.

He made a table first, a delicate piece with legs like a deer's and little cloven hooves. "Shouldn't you be making something useful?" she said to him on the way home. But so many people asked about the table that Preston, the director, called him in and requested that he make another for the shop. Soon the villagers began stopping by. "In faith," the sawyer said, "I've not seen finer cabinetmaking in London!" He's getting a reputation, she thought with wifely pride. He had begun to read the Bible at night, a battered old King James version that had belonged to his grandfather. She looked in the concordance in back to find a phrase she remembered from Sunday school: "By their fruits ye shall know them."

Most of the interpreters wore their Village clothes home, but he preferred to change. She realized that he wanted to keep the house of the fireman's widow from mingling with the joinery, wanted to draw a line between them as if they were two separate countries on a map. So, each evening, after their walk through the fields, they would head for the office. The chopped-meat color of the new brick was always a shock after the earth tones of the compound. As soon as the building came in sight, her shoulders slumped, the heavy clothes hanging on her graceless as horse blankets. If they were lucky, there would be no goodwives inside the office door, chatting about what to stew in the kettle tomorrow, no potter talking football with the smith, no red-faced apothecary lingering around the front desk, apparently so he could wink at her. How did the apothecary know what was lacking in their lives? Did messing around with herbs give him special knowledge? Once, as she headed toward the bathroom, he had called after her, "Tell thy husband I have a potion for him, should he have the need."

"Decompression" was the word they came up with for the shedding of layers as the day fell away from them, the ascent into their outside life. He changed quickly, looking the other way as she removed her stained apron, overskirt, petticoats, bodice, collar. The cap was last of all. She shook her hair out and stood for a few seconds in her bra and panties, letting her skin breathe before submitting to the snugness of her jeans. "Remember, dear," Goodie Stubbs had counseled her when she put on Eliza's clothes for the first time, "no underwear even in cold weather. When you feel a draft down there, you know how *they* felt." For days she had been sure that her heresy was visible to the older woman's keen eyes.

The first few weeks, he did the driving. "All aboard for the Magical *His*-tory Tour!" he would trumpet into an imaginary megaphone. "Here's the scrubby beach where they came ashore, folks, and right across the road you'll see the Colonial Market, where they stocked up on bologna and spaghettiOs for that first terrible winter. . . ." She'd laugh, tickled that they were heading home like any young couple after a day's work, the evening stretching before them. She had started to collect recipes for one-dish meals she could make in the Crock-Pot—not that different from a kettle over the fire, really. So far he had refused to consider the TV her mother wanted to give them, but she thought he might soften in time. She pictured them curled up on the lumpy couch, watching an old movie and then making love afterward, easily and playfully, as if they'd never stopped. Once she'd awakened in a state of arousal after dreaming that she was sitting cross-legged in a field nursing a baby, her breasts overflowing with sweet milk. Maybe, she thought, he would soften about that, too.

One raw night, he stepped into the passenger side of the pickup. His eyes were hooded and he burrowed into his jacket. When she asked him if anything was wrong, he shook his head. Later he picked at the franks and beans that had been cooking all day. "If we're going to eat shit like this, we might as well open a can," he said. The unfairness of it made her cry, but after a few days, she realized that he was in a kind of limbo. He couldn't shuck Thomas along with his clothes, as she could Eliza; he was carrying him back to this peeling three-decker, to the fireman's widow taking revenge on the leaves in the front yard, to crowded rooms and an over-cooked dinner.

Each night, after eating, he sat at the table and read the Bible. She'd thought at first that he was studying seventeenth-century diction, but his absorption was too great for that. He was reading it from front to back, like a novel. She got used to the sight of his head bowed over the tiny print, his finger tracking each line in the glare of the overhead light. It was very lonely for her. She tried to read herself, but the magazines and books she picked up didn't hold her attention.

With the weekend ahead, she decided to distract him. On Friday she took special pains with dinner, preparing a chicken stew with herbs from a recipe she'd cut out of the paper, and splurging on a bottle of wine. He ate hungrily, chatting with her about the Village in an easy way. There was a rumor, he told her, that one of the larger houses was being readied for year-round occupancy. "They want to crank up the whole living-history thing with live-in colonials. Get away from the idea of the place as a museum."

"That would be interesting," she said carefully. "But weird, too. Not going home at the end of the day."

After the table was cleared, he took up his Bible again. It was already after ten. Quietly she went into the bedroom and

changed into her favorite nightgown, a white, angelic one
that he liked. Barefooted, she walked back to where he sat
and stood behind his chair. She tried to align her breathing
with his—something they had done in the early days before
having sex. He seemed not to notice, but she was certain that
he knew she was there. She lowered her head over him and
dangled the ends of her long hair over the page he was reading. He flicked the strands away as if a fly had crossed his
field of vision. She bent lower, letting the full weight of her
hair fall across the page; she had just brushed it, and it lay
across the blurred black and white like a piece of silk, unnat-
urally bright. "Come to bed, husband," she said.

"Will ye divert me from the Word of God, woman?" Her
hair was in his fist and he was wrapping it around his hand
like a bandage. It happened so quickly that she lost the
transition, her head suddenly level with the open book, the
reddish-gold edging of the pages wavering. Above her his face
loomed, hard as wood. Still clutching her hair, he dragged
her to the couch. Tears leaked out of her, but the pain was
distant, a molten rim on a spongy layer of shock. "The woman
that thou gavest me did tempt me," he kept saying. Her
nightgown tore like paper. Pinned beneath him, she felt his
slenderness as weight, sinewy and solid, as if hesitancy had
been leached from him. He knew what he must do and he
did it, all the while raining names down on her like pieces of
hail. It was Eliza who showed her that her weakness was her
strength; she must become the bawd, become the temptress,
bring him to release and earn her own. They came together,
which had never happened before. At the end he cried out
fragments of the Psalms—David exhorting God for help in
battle, pleading for strength to withstand his enemies. When

it was over, she couldn't stop trembling. Gently, he drew her ripped gown over her shoulder in a gesture from another life.

The next morning she examined herself in the bathroom mirror. Her cheeks were swollen, as they always were after she cried. Out of this mottled child's face her eyes stared, round and fixed, as if an accident she'd witnessed had been printed on them. She was sore, and there were a few bruises on her arms, but only her neck really hurt. A muscle must have been pulled, because each time she tried to straighten it, she felt a twinge. In the shower she let the hot water run over her for a long time, rehearsing lines in her head. *'Twas the weight of the water buckets. I must make me a poultice this noon.*

He was sitting at the table when she came out, looking boyish and peaceful in his collarless shirt. He had brewed coffee and set out a cup for her. The morning sun was so bright that he'd left the light off for once, and seeing him there, reading the paper in such an ordinary way, she felt the night lift from her like the remnants of a dream. It was Saturday. They had the weekend free. There was the toaster with its rounded flanks, there were the dented percolator, the rooster-and-hen salt and pepper shakers, the blue flowers on the oilcloth. She thought of the fireman's widow frying eggs and bacon for her husband day after day before he went out to fight the flames. It was not necessary to say anything, only to enter into this comforting drone of mornings, to take her place at the table and pick up her cup.

On Monday, driving to work, both of them were silent. He changed quickly and went off to the joinery, leaving her to put on Eliza's clothes alone. As soon as she picked up the rough cotton shift, she felt a kindling, a heat so faint that it seemed to hover just beneath the surface of her skin like a blush. She reached behind her to unhook her bra before slipping the shift over her head. The feeling of the coarse cloth against her breasts made her think of saints who punished their flesh with hair shirts. The nuns of her childhood had presented such chastenings as acts of sacrifice, but maybe, she thought, the saints enjoyed it in their way. Going about, leading their blameless lives, they might have been relieved to feel anything, even discomfort. She fastened the first petticoat around her waist. She pulled up the wool stockings, tied the garters below her knees. She put on the second petticoat, the overskirt, the waistcoat with its row of small buttons, the apron. With each layer, her body became more feverishly present to her, the memory of that night rising in an acrid glow. She hoped it didn't show. She imagined herself fluorescent like the living-room lights, casting a harsh glare as she passed among the meek grays and browns of the Village street.

All day she went out of her way to be charming and accessible. She chatted with the visitors while she cooked and cleaned, answering even the eternal hygiene questions with grace and, she hoped, a bit of flair. She gathered wood for the fire and made butter in the churn. When her neck and shoulder began to throb, she walked down the road to the apothecary to get some herbs for a poultice. What a ninny she was, she said with lowered eyes, to go out without her cloak; the chill wind had burrowed right down in her neck.

"Ah," said the apothecary. "Nought but a rubbing will help that. 'Tis a fortune thy goodman has such clever hands."

She kept her distance from the joinery. At closing time, having polished the kettle and scattered fresh straw on the

floor, she stood by the window in the waning light, waiting
for him to come home. Often he stayed late, finishing what
he was working on or readying the space for the next day, but
tonight he left the shop a few minutes early. She watched
him as he made his way through the modest crowd of visitors
heading for the exit. Was it the way he carried himself that
made him seem broader in the chest and shoulders, more of
a man? The visitors stepped aside to let him pass, as if roy-
alty were in their midst. He looked stern, she thought—not
exactly forbidding, but preoccupied. His eyes pointed
straight ahead, never looking to the left or right. That was in
the Bible, too, she remembered, and her skin flushed beneath
her shift.

The neatness of the cottage seemed to please him. He
greeted her with more warmth than usual and even took her
arm when they came out in the street. "Aren't they lovely?"
she heard a woman say, and for a moment she saw what the
woman saw, standing to the side like a guest at the wedding
she'd never had as the graceful young couple walked down
the aisle: the joiner and his helpmate, turned in toward each
other, one flesh. The early autumn sun was burnishing
them with an antique light, and she could feel the eyes on
them, feel the silence they left in their wake.

In the changing room, she was the one who was dreamy
and wordless. He had slipped out of character and was
talking rapidly, making jokes the way he used to. His eyes
were bright and there was an air of suppressed excitement
about him. She wasn't surprised when he took the wheel of
the truck. He drove slowly, one hand tapping out a rhythm
on the seat. "Preston came into the shop today," he said

when they were halfway home. "It seems people are talking about us."

"What do you mean?" She wasn't in a mood to be jangled. She wanted to keep the feeling she'd had in the street, wrap it around her like a soft shawl.

"We're a hit. A tourist attraction. The cute young colonials." He laughed, and she could hear the tension in it. "So they're thinking maybe we should be the ones to move in. Next month, in time for the holidays. There'd be some public relations stuff each season—dinner with the Indians and all that—but mostly we'd just live our lives."

They had come to the center of town. Soon they would pass the settlers' landing site in its Victorian iron fence, and a couple of blocks beyond that, the street where she had grown up. Her mother would be leaving the insurance office about now, heading for Quickmart to pick up a week's worth of solitary dinners. She had a sudden impulse to leap out at the next crosswalk and sprint home. Her mother would mount the porch steps wearily, arms slung with plastic bags, and she would fling open the door, grinning.

"How can they choose us?" she said. "There are people who've been there for years. They know tons more than we do."

"The old-timers'll be pissed—the few that are willing to leave their big houses in the suburbs. But what can we do? It's not our fault if they lack star quality. Like our fat pharmaceutical friend. He'll have to whack a few Brits to get over it." He was drumming on the steering wheel now, the old nervous dance. "Besides, what we know is not the point. Preston said it takes a special sense. An intuition. You could work there your whole life and not have it."

"Yeah, well, I hope intuition keeps us warm when it's no degrees out and we're huddling by the fire. People *died* over the winters." Now that she had said the words, she was genuinely cold. When the sun dropped, it had taken all the warmth with it, and the pullover she'd thrown on that morning was too thin.

He turned sharply onto their street. "Typical. I'm talking about a vision and you obsess about central heating. Do you think they'd let us freeze? You'll have your modern conveniences, cleverly disguised. There might be a privy in back, but it'll have a toilet and shower."

The fireman's widow was in the front yard. She paused, rake in hand, and peered at the truck through narrowed eyes, as if she had spotted a pair of varmints on the prairie.

"Look," he said, pulling up, "this is everything you ever wanted. The hardworking husband bringing home the steady paycheck. Your own house, a showplace, everything in it made by me. Maybe even a kid. I could see raising one there. A little joiner's apprentice, unpolluted by junk culture. Isn't it worth making a few sacrifices for a whole new life? The alternative—you're looking at the fucking alternative."

His voice had risen on the last word, almost cracking the way it used to when he was arguing with the world. She had learned to play the mother when he was like this, soothing, reassuring, pleading patience. Let's think it over for a day or two, she was about to tell him; let's write the pros and cons on a piece of paper and put it under our pillow, and in the morning we'll know what to do. But she never said a thing because his face was changing, an intensity gathering in the eyes and the set of the mouth that she recognized but could not name. He took her hand, turning it palm up as if he were reading the lines on it. He ran his thumb up and down the veins on the inside of her wrist.

"Personally," he said, "I could live without electricity. Candlelight is really nice on wood."

People died over the winters. Eliza had, and the child with her. "Wandered into the Wood at night," the parish register said, "in the Confusion of her Minde." The preacher built a sermon on it. The midwife recorded the facts in her diary. Goodwife Coates had been in the family way again, seven months gone and "Much Afflickted" with the troublesome urges that overtook a woman in this state. She had tried to run away in the autumn, but the joiner had pursued her and brought her back. Tied her to the bedstead by a long rope so she could look after the child, but only for a day or two, until her mind settled. This time she had waited until he was deep in sleep—slipped him a draught, some said—and crept out of the house with the little one wrapped in her cloak. She must have taken comfort in the softness of the falling snow as it covered her footsteps, hushed her passage through the village. By the time they found her the next day, snow lay over her like a feather quilt, and one might almost have thought it held the warmth in, for she looked so peaceful with her daughter's head against her breast. The child was still alive. Not until they removed her from the tight swaddling of her mother's garments did she start to slip away.

The joiner was two days and two nights making their common coffin, a thing of useless beauty and a rebuke to the earth that covered it—mahogany with mother-of-pearl flowers set in the lid. After the funeral he kept to himself, refusing the solicitude of the goodwives, the consolations of the church. A candle burned in his shop at all hours, and the sound of the lathe and saw could be heard through the night. It was rumored that he was furnishing his own house with pieces worthy of the governor's manse. A sideboard with signs of the zodiac set in the doors. A card table so intricately veneered that even an ardent gambler would pause before flipping back the lid to plain green baize. Chairs whose lacy backs, more air than wood, were fit to support only the pampered spines of gentry.

Who would enjoy these luxuries was a mystery, for certainly the joiner never entertained visitors. Customers learned quickly to make their needs known at the door, and even the governor's wife's maid was banished with a curt word, and not so much as a glimpse through the window to take back to her mistress. Nor did Thomas Coates marry again, as another man would who came home to an empty bed and all those surfaces to polish. His affection, it seemed, was reserved for his creations.

She's read the accounts so often that she can fill in the gaps. The snow, for instance, she knows about that. And the blue-marble look of Eliza's skin when they found her, and the way the child stirred just once and wrinkled up its face as if were about to cry and died instead. She takes out the briefing material in the evening, when he's absorbed in the Bible, and reviews it like a manual. "Haven't you got that in your head yet?" he asks her. Of course she does. It's not what happened then that she needs to rehearse, but what will happen next. She is plotting her escape, using Eliza's story as a springboard, and when the time comes for her to jump, she expects to be propelled all the way to the twenty-first century. She will know when to go. She is certain of that.

Not that she's ready yet. She has plenty of time; she's just begun to show. In many ways she has to admit that he was right, life at the Village is the best they've ever had it. They make a good team. It's a kind of game they play—the soft young wife working her wiles on the fortress of a husband. Even the visitors seem to sense the interesting friction. They ask so often about obedience and authority that she's perfected a certain look to go with her answer. *'Tis a wife's duty to submit to her mate. Has it not been so since Eve was led astray?* Eyes cast up. Lids hooded like Princess Diana's. A secret smile.

And the house is elegant. She has to pinch herself to believe she's living in such a place. A little museum of domesticity, and just when she thinks it is complete, he brings in another piece from the shop and places it just so, and it's as if it's been in that spot for centuries. "Like a Vermeer, American style," the photographer from *Colonial Homes and Gardens* had said, taking shots from every angle for next year's Thanksgiving issue. Hokey as it was posing at the table with pumpkins and gourds, she had felt part of something eternal, a work of art.

But as soon as they achieve this perfect picture, as soon as they become this still life that visitors hold in their minds—that is when things go wrong. She thinks it must be some wave she's sending out, although she sits as quietly as she can, reading or sewing or just dreaming. Dreaming is what she was doing the other night, after the magazine people left. She had lit all the candles for the photographs and couldn't bear to snuff them; the flickering light made the wood grains come alive, and with the fire blazing and the wind loud outside, the room radiated warmth. A few snowflakes had fallen that day, but it wasn't so cold that they needed to turn on the heat. He sat on one side of the hearth, reading as usual, and she across from him, leaning into the curved back of the chair he had made for her to nurse in. Her hands were folded over the small hill of her belly. She might have been smiling, she doesn't deny that, but not because the photographer had smoothed a wisp of hair that had fallen out of her cap and asked if she'd considered modeling. No, she was thinking of that Thanksgiving song they used to sing in grade school. *All is safely gathered in.* The two of them in the house. The baby inside her, a little, curled-up thing, only just formed.

What right did he have to call it "Devil's spawn," as if he'd had no part in making it? And then to be so rough with her, throwing her across the room and onto the bedding, breaking into the snug cottage she'd become. She had fought him with her teeth and nails, had screamed for the night watchman until he stopped her mouth with his hand. All the next day she was sick with worry, checking for blood every time she went to the privy.

He never said a word about what happened. He never does. But, after closing hours, he had insisted that she come with him to the shop and see what he was making: a cradle like no other, dark wood on the outside, honey-toned within, the angles of the cot rounded so the baby would nestle in it like a nut in a shell.

When she plans her getaway, it's not the actual leaving she thinks about. That's a blur, like Eliza's flight through snow. She'll just walk through the visitors' exit one day, as free as you please, and if he gives her any trouble, she'll get one of those restraining orders. He won't, though. Is he really going to follow her back to the fish-out-of-water life they left, to the misfit he was? She'll be as safe as if she stepped off the edge of the world.

She knows now that her talent is for the future. Already a new life has started to take shape in her thoughts. She has spent some time on practical details—her mother, the birth, finding work, resettling—but mostly she has been concentrating on a particular scene. It is summer, high tourist season, and she has come back to the Village with her daughter. The child is wearing a flowered sundress; her hair is done up in two ponytails, and she carries a doll by the leg. Her own outfit has evolved from a duplicate of this milkmaid look to something black and short, an understated city dress that shows off her hair and skin. She imagines that she lives in a city now—not necessarily the one next door, but a place of gray concrete, purposeful walkers, towers of glass that catch her colors as she rushes by. Probably she works in one of these towers, in the reception area of an office where stocks get bought and bonds traded. The buyers and traders like to hang around her desk and joke with her as they go in and out, and occasionally she dates one when she has the rare free night.

"Don't be born with red hair if you don't want to be noticed," her mother always said. People are certainly noticing them now as they walk up the dirt road, between the brown houses and the brown fences: she tall and willowy like Nicole Kidman—well, hadn't the photographer said so?—with that closed, distant look, her hair the only hint of what's inside; the child a small version of her, a little wild in a quaint way like Pearl in *The Scarlet Letter*. They get lots of glances, but the apothecary actually stops in his tracks and gawks. She steps right up to him, as if he weren't grinning foolishly and on the verge of breaking character, and says, "Pray, where be the joiner's in this town?" He gets hold of himself then and tucks his loose shirttails into his breeches. "Mistress, 'tis that low building four houses yonder. But why does a fair young woman like you wish to see that gloomy fellow? The day may be sunny, but Old Man Coates wears his own weather. You are not in the market for a coffin, I hope?"

The shop's window is shuttered. An overhanging copper beech casts such a wide shadow that the place really does seem to be in a different climate zone. A family descends the stairs as the two of them mount: the father lecturing about tools, the mother with a look of stunned patience, two boys in Pilgrim hats whining about lunch. When she pushes open the door, the child's grip tightens on her hand.

The interior is so dim that at first she can barely make him out. He is bent over a table, carving a piece of ivory for an inlay, his face almost level with his hands. Above him on a shelf, a single candle wavers. She and the child stand just inside the door, neither of them making a sound. The silence is palpable, thick with dust and wood chips, likely to go on forever until the child shatters it. "Let's go, Mama!" she shrills, and he looks up, turning.

No wonder the apothecary called him an old man. His hair that he used to keep so trim hangs over his brow and the lines in his face have deepened. His eyes are red and sunken from doing close work in poor light, the skin around them contracted in a permanent squint. He stares at her as if he doesn't know what she is.

She steps forward, her arm around the child. "I am looking to have a bed made for the little one. She has plain outgrown her cradle."

He opens his mouth, but no words come out. The sight of the child seems to have paralyzed him; she sees a recoiling in his eyes that looks almost like fear. "I don't make for children," he whispers at last.

"And why not?" Her voice is cool and clear. "It is customary, I believe. Have you no wife and child at home?"

"Dead these three winters." He is looking only at her now, his face filled with such naked longing that she stands before him as if framed in gilt, perfectly poised, perfectly still. She lets him look for a long time.

"Indeed, sir, 'tis a powerful misfortune. Truly, I am sorry for you." She takes a couple of steps back toward the door. "The ways of God be mysterious."

Sometimes she looks over her shoulder as she says this. Sometimes she sounds gentle, sometimes taunting, sometimes as light and high and trippingly cold as a soprano practicing scales. Sometimes—but only on difficult days—she replaces heavenly mystery with the wages of sin. The weather will get colder, her body will get heavier, and still she will carve new details, adding and omitting, polishing her lines and her outfit until the whole scene is as dense as life, as luminous as a vision. Eventually she will stop thinking about what follows. One minute she and the child will be standing in the doorway, ready to pass out of his sight, out of his reach, and the next they will have faded into the white vapor of the world to come.

December Birthday

T*his December 16*, as on nineteen others before it, the Luckscheins walked the five blocks from their apartment to Chez Pascal. Although it was Lotte's twenty-seventh birthday, she had taken, as usual, the child's place in the middle, linked to the arms of her mother and father.

"How cold it is this year!" said Mrs. Luckschein. She clutched the sleeve of Lotte's coat more tightly, patting it as if Lotte had complained of the weather.

"You say the same thing every year. Apparently," her father said, looking down his nose at Lotte, "we are entering another Ice Age."

Ize, he said, skating over the surface of the soft C, skimming it so lightly with his German tongue that Lotte thought not of the glassy patches on the sidewalk but of the vaporous mist of dry ice.

The restaurant had been old when her parents first moved to Cambridge. Although its fortunes had changed over the years, its appearance had not altered. The small

windows on either side of the door still sheltered lace curtains through which the pale ghosts of diners could just be
glimpsed, inclining toward one another somberly in the
amber light. Lotte was eight when they came for the first
time. She had been wistful about other children's birthday
parties, and her parents had meant the elegant dinner to be
a special surprise: not compensation, but a finer thing that
would cancel out her childish longing. In those days Chez
Pascal had been a distinguished place. She remembered her
mother's nervous primping as they approached the door,
her father's masked pride—"And so we are here!"—and her
own mixture of disappointment and curiosity as they were
ushered to their table.

"And so we are here!" Mr. Luckschein said now. In the
old days Pascal's mother would have greeted them, dressed in
black, lumbering painfully on swollen legs, the menus resting on her arm like a bride's bouquet. But she had died over
a decade ago, and now there was a new young woman every
year. As Mr. Luckschein often remarked, in tones of strained
reason, it was unrealistic to expect that *everything* remain the
same. Whenever he said this, Lotte and her mother always
looked at each other guiltily, as if they had been caught in the
act of demanding that time stand still.

It was early on Tuesday evening. Even during Christmas
season, the restaurant was never crowded on a weekday. A
scattering of elderly people—Chez Pascal's regulars, mostly
widows and singles from the neighborhood—had risked the
slippery streets for the pleasures of a warm dinner. The
hostess always seated these solitary diners against the faded
rose banquettes that lined the wall, where they ate staring out

at the rest of the room, as exposed as figures in a fresco. Lotte imagined the rich food radiating heat inside them as they walked through the cold back to their apartments.

The Luckscheins preferred a separate table. Lotte had told her friends Jane and Roberta how, each year, they sat in the same place, an equal distance from the flapping doors of the kitchen and the chill of the front entrance, and how her father would eulogize their seating by muttering, "Private but not obscure," and her mother, forever cupping his words in her own, warming them with her breath, would add, "Our own little nook."

Mr. Luckschein surveyed the ivory menu with one eyebrow raised, as if harboring a monocle. "Perhaps," he said, "I will attempt the sweetbreads this year." He waited for his wife's intake of breath, her tiny bleat of protest. A couple of years ago he had terrified her with kidneys, which had arrived intact, the burnished lobes glistening beneath a mustard sauce. "And you, my dear, what will you have?"

"Old friends are the best friends," said Mrs. Luckschein.

Her father winked at Lotte across the table. It was an abiding joke between them that Lotte's mother ordered *coq au vin* every year. He and Lotte were the adventurous ones, trying to outdo each other with daring choices—a challenge, since Pascal's menu was as fixed and weighty as statuary.

Shall I say something now, Lotte was thinking behind the mask of the menu, or wait until after the main course? She had plotted the words so often that they had gone stale before she could speak them, stillbirths of false cheer like the bell-ringing of streetcorner Santas. *My friends at work had an interesting idea.*

"The restaurant is their temple," she is telling Jane and Roberta, "and I am the living sacrifice." It is too cold to eat in the yard behind the Fogg, so they are taking their lunch break in the windowless slide room that Jane calls the Catacombs. Once again, Lotte is conscious of dramatizing her life for them, sculpting its formless clay into anecdotes for their amusement. She feels guilty about her rhetoric, but what other coin can she offer to repay their interest in her?

Jane laughs her cackling laugh and rakes her hair back with maroon fingernails. "No wonder you're still a virgin," she says. "They have to keep you pure or spring won't come."

Roberta puts her hand on Lotte's arm, quick, as always, to soften Jane's hard edge. "Just wait till she moves in with the Vestals. Soon she'll be as perverted as the rest of us. Won't you, Lotte?"

Lotte smiles, but says nothing. At such moments she inhabits their certainty as if it were a room in their house.

After the waiter left, Lotte and her parents were free to enjoy the restaurant's discreet holiday garnishes. Mrs. Luckschein drew their attention to the tree on its little table, glimmering so tastefully with tiny starlike lights. And had they noticed the sprigs of holly in the vase along with the usual rose?—a nice touch, one red offsetting the other. Mrs. Luckschein sighed, took a sip of water, squinted at the gold numerals on the small, round face of her watch. "In an hour and six minutes it will be twenty-seven years. Can you believe it?" It was time for her to begin the annual telling of the tale that, from early childhood, Lotte had thought of as the Christmas story.

". . . The snow came down like rain, in white sheets, you couldn't even see between the flakes. The windshield of the taxi was covered as soon as it was wiped. And the traffic! You can imagine, a few days before Christmas. Your father had to tell the driver"—Lotte could hear, through her mother's fluting tones, his dry, lecturing voice—'We must get there without delay. My wife is about to give birth.' "

Her mother looked well, Lotte thought. From year to year she hardly seemed to change. Her hair was still more blond than gray, though no longer folded into a French twist; she'd had to cut it short when it began to thin. She was wearing her mauve dress with the high collar, and on the gathered bodice a spray of pearl-and-amethyst flowers that Lotte and Mr. Luckschein had given her for her sixtieth birthday. The sleeves were, as always, long and full, smokescreens for fey, elusive gestures. So artful was she that Lotte had only glimpsed the numbers a few times, or had perhaps learned not to look. She remembered sitting in the bath, her mother's white arm in the water, the surprise of blurred blue arithmetic on pale flesh. She must have been learning to count, for when she began to name the numbers in alphabet singsong, her mother had snatched the arm away and wrapped it in a towel as if she had cut herself. Lotte wept. She had expected to be praised for her cleverness.

". . . and the nurse brought you to me, all wrapped in a blanket. You were not even red like most babies. Just a little flushed, like a pink rose." Mrs. Luckschein had reached the triumphant conclusion of her narrative. She smiled down modestly upon her bread plate. Lotte smiled, too, realizing that she had daydreamed through the heart of the drama, the short but savage labor.

The waiter came with the wine. Deftly, he removed the cork and poured from the swathed bottle into Mr. Luckschein's glass. Lotte's father sniffed the wine, beetling his eyebrows over it as if he disapproved of it on principle. He drew his lips together and took a small sip, patted his mustache with the white napkin, dipped his head slightly. As a child Lotte had believed that the waiter must be grateful for her father's approval, for after receiving the signal he always let the wine flow so freely, righting the bottle abruptly when the glasses were half-full, as if, in his relief, he had forgotten himself.

"To Lotte," Mr. Luckschein said, raising his glass.

"To our beloved daughter," said Mrs. Luckschein.

"And so," her father said, "we go on for another year."

"Did your parents actually meet in the camp?" Roberta asks.

At work they have been drawing her out, pulling her from her envelope of containment—she feels it almost physically—toward their looseness, their relaxed sprawl. Already she is learning to play to what intrigues them. Her background, she has been realizing with slow amazement, makes her exotic. She must use the few facts that she knows as other women use makeup or a scarf, to hide her dullness and show herself in a good light.

"In the transport train. He noticed her right away. He said she reminded him of a porcelain shepherdess—she was so delicate, and she was carrying a little round vanity case instead of the heavy suitcases that everyone else was lugging. When they arrived, the men and women were separated, but he managed to keep track of her. It was the end of the war. The camp was in chaos; some of the soldiers had already deserted and the work details were falling apart. There were rumors that all the prisoners would be killed before the Allies came. He would slip her an extra crust of bread when he could, and once he bribed a guard for a turnip."

Roberta's eyes never leave Lotte's face. She is the sensitive one;

Jane is more direct and curious. "Do they talk a lot about what went on there?" *she asks.*

"Hardly at all. Once in a while my father will say something when the two of us are alone, but it's as if he's talking to himself. My mother, never. All she'll say is that they both managed to stay alive until the Americans arrived. And they've been together ever since."

🍂

Over the years Lotte had pieced the rest of the story together from scraps. Even now there were great patches of black that would never be filled in. Her parents had relocated first to Palestine, but "we were not born to be pioneers," Lotte's father said. With the help of a cousin of his, he had been able to arrange passage to New York and a job as a floorwalker in a department store. Lotte liked to imagine him with hair slicked back, mustache immaculately trimmed above his small, pinched mouth, an impertinent little bow tie instead of the ascots he favored now, a carnation in his buttonhole. After standing all day, he would take the subway back to Brooklyn, hanging on a strap for an hour before climbing four flights of stairs to the dark little flat where his wife waited, sitting at a table that had been set since noon.

It was not an easy life for an educated man like Lotte's father, who had distinguished himself at Heidelberg in medieval philosophy. "*Highly* educated," her mother said, the first word arching like a minaret over the second. After a year of teasing out obscure connections, a job finally materialized at a small teacher's college in a suburb of Boston. True, it was only a beginning position, teaching introductory philosophy to gum-snapping girls from the mill towns. But the great University was so near. They could see the red-brick towers from the windows of their apartment, two bedrooms and a closet-sized study in a building that had once been a residential hotel for the elderly, not far from the Cambridge Common. "As soon as I came through the front door," Lotte's mother repeated often, "I said to myself, 'Here at last is a place of civilization. Here, we are at home.'"

They were still at home there. Mr. Luckschein continued to teach at the small college, although he had been forced to supplement his stipend with tutoring after his course was reduced to an elective. Mrs. Luckschein took care of the apartment, polishing the few good pieces of furniture that she had managed to collect over the years, brushing the quiet, styleless, well-made clothes that hung in their closets, cooking scientifically balanced meals according to the dictates of a Swiss doctor who had died before the First World War. And there had been, after several miscarriages, after hours spent in the waiting rooms of cynical physicians, after rationing hope from year to year and finally running out, a child.

"*Perhaps we should* do without dessert," said Lotte's mother. "The streets will be slippery, and we don't want to miss the angel."

Each year, after dinner, the Luckscheins went to a marionette theater to see a medieval miracle play of the Nativity. Mr. Luckschein had a scholarly interest in medieval drama, nurtured in his student days, and, as he told his wife and daughter, such plays were pure entertainment: the public had not flocked to the original performances to be instructed in holiness, but because they craved amusement. The puppets had become part of the spectacle of the season

for the Luckscheins, a pleasure they could slip into effortlessly, like the holiday itself. They had no religion. The pale
wash of Jewishness that they had inherited from assimilated
families had worn off in Palestine, a terrain all too suited to
the rantings of a rough and irrational Jehovah. For the faith
of their oppressors, with its fables of divine benevolence,
they had only contempt. But the annual pageant charmed
them—the colored lights, the spangled storefronts, the
stained and broken world dressed up. It was all foolishness,
Lotte's father said dismissively, indulgently—"but such *pretty*
foolishness," amended his wife. And, in truth, the Holy
Family's flight from Herod struck chords in them; its happy
consummation stirred them more than they would say.

"We have still an hour and a half! I am not going to leave
the cake. It is a birthday, after all." Mr. Luckschein had little patience with his wife's perennial anxiety about time.

Pascal brought in Lotte's slice himself, the candle
spindly in layers of puff pastry. After greeting the elder
Luckscheins, he turned to Lotte with a grave, half-satirical
little bow, as he had done since she was a child. "And how is
Miss?" he asked. "Without the plaits I don't recognize you."

"They had to come off sometime," she said. She had
never had her hair cut, except for a half-inch off the bottom
twice a year. When she grew too old for pigtails, her mother
wound the braids around her head in a coronet. Last summer, during lunch hour, Jane had marched her to the hair-
dresser and given orders while she sat meekly in the chair,
robed in plastic. All the way home she kept tossing her head
to feel the lightness, the freed curls. Her mother had opened
the door, gasped, and stepped back silently, hand to her
mouth.

"Just tell them!" Jane says. "You're not joining the Peace Corps. You're not even moving to another city. It's only a few blocks away, for God's sake."

"You don't understand." Lotte puts down her half-eaten sandwich and leans back against the wooden booth. She has been through this before. "My parents hate change. It makes them nervous. More than nervous. You know that story of the man who runs to the next town to escape Death and finds Him waiting there on a street corner? Well, they've already escaped once. They think that if we just stay put and make do with what we have and enjoy our little pleasures without calling attention to ourselves, death won't find them again."

And, as much to divert her friends as to placate them, she describes the nightly ritual: how, an hour before bedtime, her mother cuts three slices of bread and paints them thinly with butter from crust to crust and sprinkles brown sugar on top, and how they have the bread with hot milk served in their own special cups, and how her mother always says, after she sets out their plates, "Now, what do we lack?"

She does not tell them how, on nights when she can't sleep, she sometimes creeps into the kitchen and sneaks a roll or a hunk of bread and eats it in the dark over the sink so she can wash the crumbs away.

"If I have coffee I will have to visit the bathroom, and there is not the time!" Mrs. Luckschein had chosen to do without, and now she was forced to watch Lotte bolt the steaming brew too quickly while her husband performed a pantomime of leisure, arranging his mustache over the cup with each sip. She touched Lotte's forehead. "You look pale," she said. "It is not good, this rushing from the cold to the heat and back again. Perhaps you are too tired? We should have waited until Friday."

"I hope they are not working you too hard," said Mr. Luckschein. "We mustn't let them take advantage."

"Not at all. And actually, I have a little—well, it isn't really news."

"Don't tell me they have raised your salary. I have always been under the impression"—this was one of Lotte's father's favorite lines and he paused, widening his eyes in comic astonishment, to prepare them for the climax—"that you are working at Harvard for the honor of it!"

"No," she said too quickly, forgetting to smile, forgetting to prolong the moment with the verbal fencing that he liked. "It's just that my friends at work have asked me to move in with them."

In the silence, Lotte remembered holding out a pair of panties to her mother, folded to cradle the shock of bright blood. "*Mutti, I have a little—*" Her mother's hand had flown to her mouth. "*Ja,*" she said, the syllable swallowed like an aborted cry. And then, in a sharper voice, "Now it begins." Lotte had felt vaguely accused. She waited for her mother to say what she always said when Lotte ran too fast or played too vigorously: "It will end in tears." But nothing more was spoken. Her mother had taken her to the bathroom and shown her what to do. Afterward she put Lotte to bed, tucking her up in quilts, with a hot water bottle over her stomach and a cup of sweet tea.

Lotte's father patted his lips with his napkin. For a wild moment, Lotte wondered if she had only thought the words instead of speaking them. "You are referring, I think, to those young ladies living *la vie bohème* off Central Square," he said. "Of course they would like you to move in. You are a person of quality. And one must assume the rent check would not be unwelcome."

"So thoughtless," Mrs. Luckschein murmured. "Expect-

ing you to give away your small wages when you have already
a nice home." She looked at Lotte almost pleadingly. "But I
suppose they are quite fond of you?"

"Oh, yes, yes. We have lunch together every day, we've
become very close. At work, they've practically adopted
me. . . ."

Lotte let the words trail off. Her mother was very still,
but the pin on her bosom trembled slightly. Her father's
eyes were half-hooded, a distant smile on his face, as if he
were ruminating a chess move.

"What I mean is," she said, stumbling, "you've always
been so generous, so kind, taking care of all my needs and
never thinking about yourselves, but here I am, almost
thirty. I can't keep imposing on you forever."

"Imposing?" Mrs. Luckschein's voice was firm, but so
high and thin that it reached Lotte's ear as a kind of hauteur.
"In a family, is it correct to speak of *imposing*?"

Before Lotte could answer, Mr. Luckschein tapped his
spoon against his cup with a ceremonial clink to signify the
end of the meal. "Now is not the time to bring such things
up," he said. "Perhaps this discussion can wait until after?"
He glanced blandly at his wife. "I think, given the state of the
sidewalks, that we must consider a taxi."

*Jane and Roberta live in the center of Cambridge in a working-
class neighborhood that is slowly being overtaken by students. The
house is a faceless woodframe like all the others on the block, but
freshly painted. Lotte has heard all about the Italian landlord and the
various housemates, the two who will stay and the one who is leaving.*

*"Caroline's a slob," Jane said. "And she never shuts up. It's like
having the TV on all day. That's why we're drafting you."*

But Lotte knows she is their project. For months they have been working on her, teasing and prodding, treating her like a prodigy when she laughs, alchemizing her careful remarks into a brand of wit they call "Austenlike." If there is condescension in it, she doesn't mind. She likes the self that she has created for them, this quaint and clever Lotte, this caretaker of fragile survivors, this interesting artifact that needs only a little polishing before it can find an honored place in their home.

Inside, the house reminds her of a bazaar, with each of the bedrooms a separate booth. Jane's is draped with paisley and batik, every surface busy with prints as big and lush as Jane herself. Roberta's is the cell of a Buddhist monk, a covered mattress on the floor and a celadon vase on a low table. When they knock on the door of Dolores's room, a man's voice answers. Dolores and Mark are lounging on the bed half-dressed, feeding each other ice cream out of a container. "So this is the famous Lotte," Dolores says, and as if taking a cue, Lotte stammers apologies and retreats, blushing, into the hall. "Don't mind us," Mark calls after her. "We're having dessert first."

The room they call hers is in the back of the house, overlooking the little square of yard. Caroline's clothes and shoes are piled in heaps, from the closet to the suitcases open on the floor; her dresser is littered with limp bras, makeup, and perfume.

"The spillover of an untidy mind," says Jane.

"It's really a nice space," Roberta says. "You have to imagine it without the debris."

But there is something about the intimacy of Caroline's mess that allows Lotte to possess the room. The clothes thrown over the back of the chair are hers, only they are soft and boneless, not the narrow fitted suits and belted dresses that hang in a strict line in her closet at home. Like a visionary she transforms whatever she looks upon, seeding the clutter with pillows and hanging plants, arrangements of fruit in pottery bowls, all of this largesse bright but blurred like the background in a watercolor. It occurs to her that the bed might leave with Caroline. She claims it anyway for its luxurious width, but leaves it unmade, covering the tangled sheets with a flowery quilt.

"Look at her, she's having impure thoughts," Jane says, and Lotte is suddenly aware that the two of them have been staring right into her Matisse harem, have seen her sprawled like an odalisque across the bed, Chinese robe slipping off one shoulder. For a moment the enchantment recedes. Something about their paired smiles across the room reminds her of her parents' long watchfulness, their earnest whispered consultations about her moods, her complexion, the regularity of her bowels, the rising heat of her forehead.

They eat on the floor of the living room, kneeling on pillows around a large, low table. Amina, the Indian student, is cooking tonight—mashed lentils, rice with spiced vegetables that burn Lotte's mouth pleasantly, cooling mango with yogurt for dessert. People drift in and out. It is impossible for Lotte to tell who is visiting whom; everyone seems to know everyone else. She imagines what it would be like to live like this all the time, to have this easy intimacy, this constant bubbling in a common pot. After dinner, they sip tea from blue mugs and watch the sun recede from the uncurtained window.

Lotte is transfixed with desire. She, who has been told that she wants for nothing, wants this. The longing is not secret, like the wolfish hunger that rises in her some nights as she lies on her bed in the overheated room, her nightgown thrown up above her breasts and her breathing so harsh that the sound of it must disturb the fitful sleep of her parents next door. What she feels now is open and public, part of the charmed disarray of the house. A door will open and she will be behind it, flushed and tousled like Dolores. She will reach for her life and take it, as casually as the others are reaching for rose-

water sweets on a plate. A coppery lust teases the back of her throat. Her mouth is so dry she has to ask for more tea.

Precisely at 9:00, her father appears at the door.

The fact of him standing in the hall in his homburg and carefully knotted scarf is more than she can take in. Roberta introduces herself, and he bows and smiles his small smile, raising his brows as if to appraise not only the house and its occupants but the anomaly of Lotte herself in the midst of them.

"Why are you here?" she blurts. "I told you I would take a taxi!"

"I thought to save you some money," he says mildly. "If it is not convenient, I will come back later."

How old he looks, Lotte thinks. She is seeing him as she imagines Roberta sees him, with drooping cheeks and broken veins in his nose, the nostrils reddened from his perennial autumn cold.

"Really, Mr. Luckschein, I'd be happy to drive Lotte home," Roberta says. "It's still so early."

"Why should you bother? Lotte and I often take evening walks."

He waits in the hall while she gathers her things, twirling his hat in his hands like a nervous suitor.

For ten minutes they walk in silence. "Mutti insisted on getting bread and milk ready," he says suddenly. "I told her you would not be hungry."

Entering the theater was like paying a visit to a private home. No sign marred the facade of the old town house, only a small engraved plate above the knob on the red door. It was always a shock to open to a roomful of milling people, the adults chatting familiarly as if they were members of a club, the children in velvets and bow ties. The box office was a Victorian gazebo with a Harlequin puppet in one window and a flesh-and-blood vendor in the other. Mr. Luckschein waved his tickets at the plainer human visage; he'd had them for months, stored under his tie clasps in a small box on his dresser. Lotte and her mother followed him through the crowd and up a winding staircase.

The theater was scaled to Lilliputians. Its descending rows of red plush seats looked tiny from above, but—Lotte marveled yearly at the trick of perspective—were magically enveloping for adults. The stage belonged in a rich child's playhouse: a quarter of the size of the real thing, but perfectly proportioned, with red velveteen curtains swagged in gold. The Luckscheins knew enough to sit in a middle row instead of toward the front. Farther back, it was easier to preserve the illusion.

Most years, waiting for the play to begin was the part of the evening that Lotte liked best. She had never lost her early awe of this moment of anticipation, when the stage was veiled, its delights sheathed. But tonight she felt as restless as the children who twisted in their seats, asking, "When does it start?" Jane and Roberta had said that she must let them know by tomorrow, or they would have to advertise. There was—Mr. Luckschein had seen it immediately—the matter of the rent. Jane had been characteristically brash about it. "It's your birthday," she said. "A good time to grow up." Lotte had not bargained on bringing up the subject twice. She was trying out phrases in her head when the lights darkened.

They were in the courtyard again with Mary, who was so absorbed in her garden that she never heard the slow and steady pumping of the angel's wings, never saw him land lightly on one toe like a ballerina. From this precarious position, he told her in rhyming Middle English that she was full of grace. She threw up her long tapered hands, flinching, but in the same motion turned and sank into a curtsy— so gracefully, said Lotte's mother; so realistically, said Lotte's father—and declared herself to be the handmaid of the Lord.

The sky turned matte black, stars sprouting in it like wildflowers. Here came the donkey with his obstinate head swinging up and down and his Balaam's Ass-worth of wit— the only philosopher in the story, Mr. Luckschein always said. The children cheered and shouted, but Lotte's mother put her hand to her mouth, mindful of the donkey's precious cargo and the anxious husband plodding along in front. Then the shepherds, ungainly Pinocchios, and the stately procession of the Magi, Mrs. Luckschein's favorites because they were so well dressed. "Every stitch hand-sewn!" she whispered in Lotte's ear, as she did every year.

All of these travelers met at the manger, their paths converging at the humble trough where straw had been turned into gold. At first only the Holy Family could be seen, circled in a single light: Mary's enfolding arm—from year to year an amazement, so natural was its curve—meeting Joseph's to make a scrolled knot around the baby. The circle widened to reveal a halo of beasts; widened farther to lasso the gawking shepherds. Now the light rayed outward to include the Three Kings, stationed symmetrically along the rim of the group of worshipers like jewels in the prongs of a crown. The darkness at the margins slipped back and disappeared altogether. The stage was bathed in layers of light, as if gold leaf had been painted on a gold background. Lotte's mother caught her breath, her face uplifted like an elderly child's. Lotte glanced at her father and saw that his features had stiffened into the rigid mask he always wore in the grip of sentimentality.

The Magi came forward to present gifts wrapped in gracious speeches. The first two kings gave gold and sweet spices, but the third moved slowly toward the infant with a twig in his hand. He was tall and gaunt, turbaned in black, a prophet as unwelcome as a bad fairy at a baptism. The voice that spoke through him was low and full of echoes.

Hail to thee, long-expected Lord!
I bring thee myrrh for mortality . . .

A shadow was stretching on the wall behind the golden cameo. It grew branches, achieved arms. Lotte could feel on either side of her the tremors of small shock, her parents' habitual tightening in the face of change. For this was new. Some misguided director, made bold, perhaps, by actors of wood, had collaborated with his lighting technicians to create a special effect. And their combined efforts had produced nothing more than a caricature, the fallen head a fungal knob, the upraised arms bulging like a weightlifter's. The silhouette of the crucified loomed above his swaddled infant self, dwarfing the parents who still hovered over the baby, unaware. He looked as if he were holding up the crossbar, Lotte planned on telling Jane and Roberta, instead of hanging from it.

"It will end in tears," Lotte's mother would say if she knew, but she is inside the apartment, talking to the mother of the little girl who owns the skates. Lotte has strapped them on over her brown oxfords and she is teetering in place, her arms making circles in the air. "Go

*ahead!" says the little girl, who is not such a nice friend for Lotte.
"Go ahead if you're going!" She plants her hands in the center of
Lotte's back and gives her a tremendous shove. Lotte is flying, her feet
splaying over the uneven sidewalk, down the street that slopes like a
hill. She is going too fast to stop, her hair blowing in her face so she
can hardly see, her dress flat against her legs. She starts to fall but
catches herself. Her knees bend and find the balance and she is moving with the wind, a light Lotte who will stop for no one, not even the
dark shape ahead of her whose arms stretch out at the sides just like
hers, a mocking shadow who turns into her father at the moment she
plows into him, losing all her breath as she hits, his black overcoat
swallowing her up.*

The light contracted again around the Holy Family, who
seemed to huddle even closer to warm themselves in what little was left. Against the darkness the cross reappeared, phos-
phorescent now, its outline wavering as if it could not quite
hold its own substance. It had sucked all the other stars out
of the sky, and now it hung alone like an ominous constella-
tion. The chorus swelled with "O Come, All Ye Faithful,"
and the play was over.

The marionettes bowed to halfhearted applause. All
around the Luckscheins, people put on wraps and nudged
drowsing children into their jackets. Mr. Luckschein usually
reminded his wife and daughter that there was no need to get
trampled on because they were in no hurry, but tonight he
sat quietly, looking down at his hands.

Lotte watched the children being led out of the theater,
the smaller ones draped limply over their parents' shoulders. "I don't think people enjoyed it as much this year," she
said.

"Shocking," said Mrs. Luckschein. Her hands clasped and unclasped on the polished leather of her handbag. "To upset the little ones with crucifixions. Do children need to know such things? Why could they not leave the story alone?" She opened the bag, and, taking out a lace-edged handkerchief, began to dab at her eyes. "So beautiful it was, nothing to give bad dreams. Your father will write a letter to the authorities."

"To whom should I write?" said Mr. Luckschein without looking up. "To the puppet in the box office? 'Dear Mr. To-Whom-It-May-Concern, My wife and I, two enlightened Jews, would like to lodge a complaint about the Christian symbolism in your Nativity play . . .'" He coughed into his fist and cleared his throat. "Maybe someone can explain to me what is so compelling about this juvenilia that we come back every year. I myself lost interest a long time ago." He glanced at his wife and then at Lotte. "Who knows?" he said heavily. "Perhaps next year we will see something new."

Lotte and her parents sat staring at the stage while the theater emptied around them. They continued to sit, as if mesmerized by a final act that only they could see, while the ushers checked the seats and collected abandoned programs.

"Well," Lotte said at last, "we had better be going before they lock us in." She gathered her coat around her and stood, her parents rising with her like the pans of a scale. They stayed close to her sides as she made her way up the aisle and through the deserted lobby and out the narrow door, into the glacial night.

Camping In

By the time Craig comes home, Laura has been staring at the interiors of bears' cottages for over an hour. Four children's books are open on the easel: two clipped to the top and two balanced on the ledge. She has been studying the illustrations, hoping to find some point of entry for her own drawing. Each cottage has the same elements: fireplace, rocking chair, child-sized bed, round table for two, corner cupboard filled with sturdy crockery. Cozy one-room dwellings with everything a small animal would need.

The slamming of the back door startles her, although she's far from absorbed. "In the studio," she calls, and listens to the rhythm he plays on the banister as he clips upstairs.

"You're early," she says. "Weren't there any sick people today?"

"Two cancellations. Both in the afternoon. Very considerate." His earnest wire-rims descend toward her ear. He smells scrubbed, as if he were just leaving for work instead of finishing a long day. If she were drawing him, she would put him in the body of a tall, solemn bird with a black bag on one wing. Dr. Crane.

He glances at the easel. "I see you're doing some heavy reading."

"Actually, I'm looking for inspiration. The muse has been eluding me lately." She tries to keep the stiffness out of her voice. He never openly criticizes her, but his brisk efficiency makes her feel lax. "I only sat down a little while ago. Becky didn't even yawn until three-thirty."

"Isn't she getting too old for naps?" Craig pauses, suddenly careful, and lowers himself onto the futon she uses as a daybed. Becky will turn three in the same month that Laura turns thirty. The specter of a second child is already looming between them. "There's absolutely no hurry. You need to push that book out first," he tells her, but last week she caught him charting her cycle on graph paper.

"Something came up today that might interest you," he says, loosening his tie. "Lyle Beatty was in about his back."

"Oh. I suppose that's moderately interesting. Did he get soused again and trip over his rake?"

"Not this time—just general deterioration and too much bending. If you live like he does, you get old fast. He was telling me his daughter is looking for a job after school, so I mentioned we might need someone to do Becky-watching and light housekeeping. To free you up, like we talked about."

"One of the Beattys? I'm not sure that's a great idea." The Beatty kids are always spoken of collectively, as if they were a tribe. Laura has a vague image of lank-haired urchins scattering in all directions like spores.

"She's fifteen. From Lyle's first marriage. There's an older brother who's been stealing cars since he was twelve. Bad blood, Lyle says, whose he doesn't specify. But he went on and on about the girl. What a good student she is, how hard she works. 'Con-see-enshus' was the word he used. Earned the money for her own sewing machine and makes most of her clothes. Plenty of experience with kids—it sounds like she's pretty much brought up his four by Pauline."

"What's the matter with their mother?"

"Nothing that a little character wouldn't cure. High-strung. The woman spends half her life in bed."

"I don't know," Laura says. She hates being put in this position. "Can anything good come out of Lyle Beatty?"

She's been in Hartshorne, Vermont, long enough to hear the Lyle stories, all of which end, "He can fix anything when he isn't drinking." People speak of him with dismissive affection, like a wayward pet. For years he's walked, unsteadily, the line between village character and white trash. Whenever Laura takes the back road out of town his house leers at her, its purple paint job—whose whim was that? she wonders—blotched like a child's watercolor. Daisy pinwheels make a brave show in the front yard among car parts that appear and disappear like perennial plants. And always the interchangeable children, gaping out at the road. Once or twice, when Laura's looked their way, they've waved.

"Guess what her name is," says Craig, as if hearing it will clinch the deal. "Mercedes."

"Like the car?"

"Nope. Accent on the first syllable. As in 'Lord, have

mercedes on me.'" He grins and unfolds his long frame
from the futon. Laura sees his hand lift instinctively, riding
the waves of this small pleasantry to dismiss another patient.

"A friend is coming to visit us today," Laura tells Becky, "so
we have to make our house look pretty for her."

    Cleaning for the cleaning lady. Who would have thought
it? After years of rebellion, she's turning into a good *bour-
geoise.* All day she's been compulsively picking up after herself—doing the dishes she usually leaves till after dinner,
scouring toilets, gathering Becky's toys and stowing them in
the basket. Her efforts are less for her pride than for the sake
of the house. It deserves to be admired, and she knows so few
people in this forlorn town that even a deprived teenager will
do. Over months spent scraping layers of paper from the
walls and black paint from the staircase, she has decided that
the place has the allure of a miniature. It is a grand house
built on a small scale. Some romantic from the age of
Longfellow lavished extravagant detail on its modest frame.
The moldings have been elaborately carved, with shell motifs
in the corners; the living-room windows are bowed with
built-in seats; the proportions of each room are as precise
and elegant as cut jewels. She is eager to show it off, eager—
she can just about admit this to herself—for a little company.
The days are getting shorter now that fall is setting in, and
she's been feeling isolated.

    The house is the only reason Laura agreed to settle in
Hartshorne. When she married Craig, she'd known that he
intended to look for a rural practice after his residency. In
theory the idea seemed adventurous, a bold statement, like a
year in the Peace Corps or the Bronx. "We have no intention

of coming back to Connecticut," she informed her father, a Darien lawyer eager to use his connections on their behalf. "Craig didn't spend all those years in medical school so he could take care of pampered suburbanites on the Gold Coast."

But the reality of Hartshorne shocked her. It had been a prosperous mill town in the nineteenth century, and a few of its streets were still lined with stately houses where the mill owners and gentry had lived. Several of the more imposing places had been spruced up with new paint and converted to funeral homes and insurance agencies; others, divided into apartments, clung to frayed respectability like spurned women grown used to their fate. Downtown was pocked with blank storefronts. The marquee of an old movie theater advertised, apparently for eternity, the last film it had ever shown, a disaster flick released over a decade before.

The realtor, a garrulous, perfumed blonde, had an unsettling habit of implying Laura's ownership of everything she showed her. "Now here you've got your wall-to-wall in a nice, neutral shade," she'd say. "Now here you've got your lovely deck, just added on last summer." When they pulled up to the small Victorian, its sloping lawn rimmed by a wrought-iron gate, the woman took Laura's silence for disinterest. "This one needs a ton of work," she said accusingly. "I'm only showing it to you because you said you like old houses."

Laura has had a year to analyze the emotional transaction that took place at that moment. The experience, she has more than once told Craig, is the closest she has ever come to love at first sight. The realtor could stand there like one of the Fates, auguring disaster from antiquated plumbing and an unimproved kitchen, from ceilings impracticably high, from long windows that let all the heat out. But there is a destiny to this kind of love. It does not admit impediments.

At 3:15 exactly, the bell rings. Laura opens the door to a child.

"Mercedes?" Already she's pronouncing it wrong. The girl nods, but makes no move to come in. She is the size of a ten-year-old, wearing a man's hooded nylon jacket that makes her look even smaller. Her forehead is high and wide, a dreamer's brow, and Laura thinks immediately, That's her mother in her. But farther down, the face dwindles to Lyle's narrow jaw, his tight slit of a mouth.

"Welcome!" Laura is aware that her voice is too bright. "Did you have any trouble finding the house? Becky's so excited about meeting you that she couldn't settle down for a nap, so we made cookies, which I'm ashamed to say I haven't done in ages. . . ." Becky steps out from behind Laura's leg, and the girl squints at her through the screen of Laura's chatter. When Laura reaches over to take her jacket, Mercedes bends her shoulders submissively. The hood falls away. Her hair, a rich chestnut brown, has been pulled back, braided, and twisted into an elaborate coronet that cinches her head like a hard halo. The effect seems deliberately satirical, as if a fancy feathered hat had been plumped down over the plain little face.

"What lovely hair," Laura says. "It must be very long."

The girl's eyes come to life. "I can sit on it," she says, and closes down again. Her voice is brushed with hoarseness, deeper than Laura expected from such a small person.

Mercedes says "No, thank you" to Laura's offer of a snack,

and seems perplexed by Laura's suggestion that she get to know Becky. "Do you have a rag and some oil?" she asks, as if provisioning for a long journey.

She follows Laura through the house, staring at each room with fierce concentration. In the nursery, Laura points out the white iron bed—"it's painted, so just a light dusting, no polish"—and the spacious old rocker they call the Story Chair. Mercedes' eyes lock on the dollhouse. "Don't bother with that," Laura tells her. "It was my grandmother's, and it's there just to be looked at. We keep it on that table so Becky can't reach it."

Mercedes nods curtly. She reaches into the pocket of her jeans and pulls out a red bandanna. "You dust, too," she says to Becky. Laura realizes that she has been dismissed.

Today the easel has only one book on it, Becky's favorite, the one about the little rabbit saying goodnight to its room. Becky knows the text by heart and they often recite it together, Laura prompting a little, Becky chanting the goodnights until the repetition lulls her to sleep. Laura sees now that the illustrations are as mesmerizing as the words. Echoes are everywhere. The square of knitting on the nanny's apron is the fraternal twin of the triangle of blanket folded at the foot of the bed. The cow jumping over the slice of moon in the picture above the fireplace seems to be aiming to land on the white sphere framed in a window. The lamp on the night table is like the waist of an hourglass, its light coning upward to illuminate the murky ceiling and down over the bed. A child would feel completely safe in this room, Laura thinks. The night outside the window would be just another layer of warmth, a dark comforter.

She unclips the book and confronts the blank paper. If she starts with the animal, maybe the house will grow around it. Nothing banal, though. Children's literature is overpopulated with furry animals. Has anyone done anteaters yet, or possums with their whimsical tails? What about hedgehogs? She could make it literal—a pig in greenery, leaves sprouting from its quills, carrying its house on its back like a turtle. She picks up a crayon, realizes she isn't sure what an actual hedgehog looks like, glances at her watch. Four-thirty already, and she hasn't checked on Becky or offered cookies.

A smell of lemon oil hangs in the silent hallway. Laura stands outside the nursery, taking in the perfectly composed scene. Becky is asleep in the playhouse she's ignored for over a year, a thumb in her mouth and the bandanna under her head like a pillow. Mercedes seems to be arranging the jumble on the dresser top into a mosaic. One of the porcelain Seven Dwarves is in her hand and she is rubbing it with the cloth. Her eyes are half-closed, her mouth soft and loose.

Laura hesitates in the doorway. She would tell Mercedes not to waste time on knickknacks, but the entire room is pristine. The plastic necklaces have been untangled from their snakes' nest on top of the toy shelf and strung on the neck of a wall lamp. The Story Chair has been polished so deeply that its carving stands out in relief. How many years has it been since Laura noticed the two eagles whose talons form the backrest? She presses forward on her toes like a tourist leaning against a velvet rope. The floor creaks.

Mercedes turns quickly. The blouse she's wearing over her jeans is as demure as a child's party dress—pale blue, with pearl buttons at the cuffs and intricate needlework around the neck. One of her own creations, Laura suspects; the smocking alone must have taken hours. She is oddly moved that the girl has dressed up to dust in her house.

"You've made everything so pretty! It looks like a still life," says Laura. When Mercedes does not respond, she adds, "A picture."

"Thank you," Mercedes says to the floor.

In the kitchen Laura pours cider and arranges cookies on a flowered plate. She sees Mercedes' mouth prune to a No, thank you, and on impulse lifts the plate to the girl's nose. Mercedes' hand shoots out like a pickpocket's. She nibbles around the edge of the cookie, sipping cider after each tiny bite. Poor thing, Laura thinks. She's too shy to let me see her chew.

Aloud she says, "I hope it won't be too much for you, looking after Becky on top of helping with your brothers and sisters."

Mercedes wipes her mouth carefully. "Pauline can take care of the kids. They're her kids." It is a statement of fact, made, as far as Laura can tell, without resentment.

She offers a ride home, but Mercedes has already arranged to meet her brother at the gas station where he works.

Upstairs, Becky is awake, singing to herself.

Mercedes collects her bookbag and jacket. "She can keep the kerchief," she says at the door.

Craig walks into the kitchen and whistles. "Come kiss me, lady, 'cause I found you a treasure. Little Miss Clean."

"Mercedes—excuse me, *Mercedes*—is certainly thorough," Laura says. "And quick. I was thinking she'd do a room or two, but she went through the whole house like lightning." She hands the salad spinner to Becky to crank.

"You don't sound thrilled."

Laura turns away from the sink. "I know I ought to be. It's just—she's kind of odd. I wasn't expecting this pinched little thing who does her hair like Simonetta Vespucci. And she didn't say two words in a row the whole time she was here. All she wanted to do was work."

"Simonetta who? Give the kid a chance. It's a big leap from her lifestyle to ours. She'll relax once she gets used to you. Besides, she's not here to make conversation."

"I wasn't expecting deep thoughts. Elemental communication would be nice." She dumps the lettuce leaves into a bowl. "This is not your average teenager. How many fifteen-year-olds live to clean? I went to Becky's room to check on her and she was polishing the Seven Dwarves. The look on her face—I swear, it was like watching someone masturbate." Grabbing the salad spoon, she mimes Mercedes' dreamy massage.

Craig's expression is so severe that for a second she thinks she's gone too far. He has a Boy Scout streak; there are things one doesn't speak of in the presence of children. Then a broad grin spreads over his face. "Dwarfophilia! Omigod, I haven't seen a case in years. One thing I know— no dwarfophile is going to come near *my* daughter."

Laura giggles. For all his seriousness, he has a way of defusing her anxieties with humor.

Craig picks Becky up and sets her in her raised seat.

"What do you think, Beckster? Did you have fun with Mercedes today?"

Becky flattens her hand on the bandanna, which is bound to replace the blanket she's just been weaned from, and rubs it back and forth across the table. "Dust," she says. "Dust."

With charcoal Laura makes a light line across the center of the paper. She writes "Ceiling-Sky" above the line and "Floor-Earth" below it. In the white space at the top, she jots down the ingredients of a recipe:

> Bring outside inside—
> Stars on wallpaper
> Moon on night table
> Planets in picture frames—
> Camping in!!

A room of her own, finally, but who will live in it? Animals to whom enclosure comes naturally—moles or hibernating bears who pass the long winter decorating the cave? Or should the house be in a human child's head, a dream? How about a group of children confined indoors because of a snowstorm, having a picnic on a blanket from the bed? She hears a distant rumbling and thinks, Definitely a storm, but thunder instead of snow, before the noise becomes a vacuum cleaner.

Mercedes is in the hall, wielding the hose. When Laura opens the door, she narrows her small eyes.

"You don't have to vacuum every day," Laura says. The girl has been coming for almost two weeks now, and the house shines. "Honestly, I'd rather you just played with Becky."

"She's sleeping. Went down right away." Over the roar of the vacuum, Laura thinks she picks up a lilt of superiority. She steps on the button herself.

In the sudden silence, Mercedes says, "The hall is dusty. It'll get in the other rooms." Something about the way she purses her mouth sparks a memory of the Madonna of the Revulsion. That was what Laura's professor had called the Annunciation, hoping to rouse the students drowsing in the overheated lecture hall with a little comic relief. The painter—was he Flemish or Italian?—had captured the angel's wide-winged glory as it swooped down to bestow glad tidings, but his Mary was all prim refusal, recoiling with a grimace, her hands flung up to fend off the attacker. For days Laura has been trying to pin down who Mercedes reminds her of, and now she knows. The hair skinned back from the high forehead. The invisible eyebrows. That curdled expression, as if her first instinct is always to say no.

"I'm working," she says. "The noise disturbs me." The girl's face doesn't give away much, but Laura is certain that she catches a fleeting look of irony. Or is it frustrated longing? Mercedes is gazing past her into the one room she isn't allowed to clean, taking in the crumpled quilt on the futon and the books and discarded sketches on the floor. The paper on the easel is in full view, with its single wavery line, its scribbles that look as if they belong on a telephone pad. The exclamation points give Laura particular pain—the hyped-up hopefulness of them. "I'm developing a book for children," she adds, unable to stop herself.

"A book. About what?" Mercedes squints at the paper, perhaps expecting an image to come gradually into focus.

"Well, I'm not sure yet. That's what I'm trying to find out."

Mercedes absorbs this information silently, then bends to pull the plug. Today the coronet is smaller and a ponytail spurts from the center of it.

After the girl goes home Laura walks slowly through the house, pausing at the entrance of each room. The living room has the studied perfection of a magazine photo. Chairs have been subtly shifted to stand a measured distance from the fireplace. Each piece of brass is polished, and the casual pillows on the couch have been fluffed up and propped in the corners. The room is like the pattern on the Oriental rug: ordered, glowing, discreet.

Becky is still napping; how will they ever get her to sleep tonight? She lies on her back in the middle of the bed, breathing evenly, a rosy princess under a spell. The perfect centerpiece, Laura thinks. Even the child has been put in its place. But she can't resist stepping backward toward the door to get a view of the whole room. Her eye skims smoothly over the harmonious collage of whites and brights before snagging on the bookcase. The stuffed kangaroos stand in a smart row on top, but one of them has an empty pouch.

That evening, a Friday, they have a late dinner in the dining room. It is the last room to be finished, and the most elegant. They've been planning to inaugurate it with a big family feast on Thanksgiving, but Craig doesn't want to wait. "Let's enjoy what we have," he tells her.

They sit across from each other, the long mahogany table gleaming like a dark lake between them. Off-duty Fridays are Laura's oasis. Once Becky is asleep, the two of them have time for a leisurely meal and uninterrupted conversation. Craig is usually full of stories about his practice; he revels in the folksy, human side of medicine, and he's a surprisingly good mimic. But tonight they're both subdued. The room's formality imposes a reticence, a sense of being observed and overheard. Laura thinks of the servants in BBC dramas standing poker-faced behind the bickering master and mistress, waiting to change the plates. *Pas devant les domestiques*.

Clearly this is not the moment to bring up a triviality like a missing toy. The smell of polish rises faintly from old wood. Laura's ancestral aunt looks down on them from the wall above the mahogany sideboard that once was hers, lips set in a thin smile. Mercedes buffed the piece to a high sheen today, but she's put both silver candlesticks on the right instead of placing one at either end. Laura is halfway out of her seat when she notices the branched candelabrum just behind her aunt in the portrait. The painted silver makes an interesting counterpoint to the muted shine of the real. She gets up and moves the candlesticks anyway.

"I find these little *compositions* all over the house," Laura says, sitting. "Things grouped together. Things set just so."

"I assume you mean Mercedes. Whatever she does, I like it. The place is looking great." He begins to carve the chicken, severing the legs and wings in his precise, efficient way and shaving thin slices from the breast.

Every inch the lord of the manor, Laura thinks. In spite of his populist sympathies, he's more dazzled by her possessions than she is. He didn't grow up in the kind of home where you take beauty for granted. Before Mercedes, they were always having rows about her casual treatment of "the antiques"—never "the furniture," and she can always hear the capital A.

"I have to admit this girl has an eye," she says. "Untrained, of course, but pretty amazing, considering where she grew up. I do find it slightly weird that she takes it upon herself to rearrange our furniture. Pushy. She makes me feel like a guest in my own house."

Craig smiles. "Don't chase her away too fast. Maybe she's that muse you keep waiting for." He reaches for her plate. "Here's a chance for you to do a little mentoring. Compliment her on her good work, but suggest she rechannel some of that energy, take an art class or something. She's probably in awe of you. A real artist."

"God, you're such a romantic! Mentor? I don't think she even likes me. She'll tolerate Becky, as long as the poor baby doesn't get in the way of her everlasting cleaning. Her idea of play is the two of them dusting together. This whole nap thing is regressive—I'm beginning to wonder if Mercedes orders her to sleep so she can have the house to herself."

"I thought you were worried that Becky wasn't napping enough." He pauses, tools in hand. "This is a case of a three-year-old looking up to a big kid. Monkey see, monkey do. The other day she was swishing around her scarf, looking important. 'I'm Mercetee,' she said."

Craig has turned the chicken over to get at the nugget of meat behind the wing. He lifts it out whole and sets it on

Laura's plate. "Oyster for you, ma'am. You're the only one who's unhappy."

On Saturday morning the house is hers again. She walks from room to room, messing pillows, scattering books. She brings a bunch of toys into the living room and dumps them on the rug. "You can play in here for a change," she tells Becky.

The child looks at her sternly. "Pick it up," she says in a commanding voice.

Craig has offered to take Becky to the playground so Laura can draw for a couple of hours. "When do I get to see your work-in-progress?" he asks.

"It's still pretty rough." If she tells him she's struggling, he'll come up with five practical things she can do. "This is not like making cookies, unfortunately."

"Or diagnosing flu," Craig says. He hoists Becky onto his shoulders. "I may not know a lot about art, but I do know that."

In the studio, Laura's attention keeps wandering from the easel to the walls. She'd had the paint specially mixed: white with an undertone of yellow, to capture the sun. At this hour of the early afternoon the room is a bowl of light. Surrounded by such radiance she should be playing with shapes and colors, but she is restless and distracted. Something keeps nagging at her, intruding between the images in her head and the paper.

She gets up and walks into the hall, pausing for a second as if gauging the direction of the wind. Then she heads purposefully for Becky's room. As soon as she steps over the threshold, her pulse quickens. She looks around once, nervously, at the groupings of dolls and stuffed animals, rummages briefly in the toy chest, and, with a sharp intake of breath, goes to the dollhouse.

Kneeling, Laura squints into the little rooms, trying to match what she sees with some half-forgotten inventory from her childhood. At the dining room she pauses, gawking like Gulliver at the doll family in their evening finery, seated in rigid splendor around the table. The plaster turkey is there, and the minute silverware, and the Blue Willow plates that look so handsome on the square of lace her mother gave her for a tablecloth. Vaguely disappointed, she glances at the china cabinet in the corner and lets her breath out slowly. Where is the teapot? The best Blue Willow piece of all, miraculously unbroken through three generations. And the cups and saucers—weren't there six? She could have sworn there was one for each member of the family. She counts them twice. Five. Laura remembers unwrapping the set, along with all the other dollhouse furniture, on the day Becky's room was finally finished. She would have noticed then if anything were missing.

That night, when Laura feels Craig's hand, gentle and insistent under the sheets, she pushes it away.

"Is something bothering you?" he asks. "All through dinner you were lost in space."

"Just because it's Saturday," Laura begins, sliding into the old argument about the predictability of their lovemaking. She stops herself. "Really, it's nothing to do with you, but I'm just not in the mood."

"Is everything okay? You seem so edgy lately."

"It's nothing. I think Mercedes might be taking things. That's all."

"Mercedes again." He sighs and pulls his pillow up against the headboard. "Okay. What's missing?"

"China from the dollhouse is the most serious thing. Those pieces are heirlooms, my mother would die if she knew. And a baby kangaroo, and—I think—some charms from the plastic necklaces."

"For God's sake, Laura, don't tell me you're losing sleep over this. You know how toys get misplaced."

"Not now!" She is surprised at the shrill triumph in her voice, as if they've been playing verbal chess for hours and she has checkmated him. "Not since Mercedes they don't. Everything's so damn neat!"

He sags back against the pillow. "Well, it isn't exactly stealing the silver, is it? What we have here is a hardworking kid from a deprived background who may or may not have taken a few toys. I'm not condoning theft. But you don't have to seem so gleeful. You could look at the situation with a little compassion."

"Oh. So now I'm the villain. This is so typical of you. You always have to take the moral high road."

But hadn't she signed on to walk it with him? He is the son of a policeman, the only one of four brothers to make it to college, the only person she knows who worked his way straight through medical school. When he was courting her, his idealism had seemed better than brilliance, deeper than the wit and flash of her Ivy League boyfriends. She had seen it as a quality she could trust her life to.

"I'm just not finding it easy to share my space with her," she says. "Even two hours a day."

"Look, here's what I recommend." His voice has taken on the weary calm that he uses when anxious patients call at night. "Watchful waiting for a week or two. Keep an eye on her, but at the same time try to get to know her, get her to talk. I wouldn't be surprised if these so-called thefts are a bid for attention, in which case, a little communication may clear up the problem. If not, well, we'll cross that bridge when we come to it."

"You don't understand." Laura's combativeness has seeped away, leaving her on the edge of tears, a child cornered by adult logic. "Having her around is like having a bat hanging from the rafters. It's quiet. Maybe it doesn't do any real harm. But you always know it's there."

On Monday afternoon Laura unlocks the corner cupboard and takes out two porcelain cups and saucers—the grown-up equivalent of the Blue Willow, part of a set passed on to the eldest daughters in her mother's family. Laura imagines what her aristocratic ancestor would say if she knew that the delicate china was about to be tainted by the lips of a servant. You managed the help in those days; you didn't try to understand them. She wonders how her own mother would react to the care she's taking with the table—the place mats, the vase of dried flowers. But she's in no position to feel virtuous. She is about to use the cups as bait.

The day is raw and rainy. When Mercedes appears at the door, slightly late, she looks as if she has been blown the whole way by wet gusts. Her hair is plastered to her head, but the design of it—twined with a scarf and skewered with two chopsticks at the back—is intact. She drops her sodden jacket and bookbag on the kitchen floor.

"I made tea," Laura says quickly, and nudges her to the table. She lifts the pot and pours into Mercedes' cup, watching to see whether her expression changes. The girl's face is as inscrutable as ever. Humble as she seems to be, there is a matter-of-fact acceptance of the bounty that comes her way. Not exactly arrogance, Laura thinks, but a kind of entitlement. How did she ever acquire that, growing up in the purple house?

Mercedes' fingers are as milky-blue as the cup she holds in both hands. She brings her mouth to the rim and touches it lightly with her lips, tasting the porcelain instead of the tea. The steam from the hot liquid teases a few stray hairs on her forehead.

"I was wondering . . ." Laura starts. She has been rehearsing all afternoon the phrase she will use to introduce, obliquely, the subject of the missing toys. But the words transform on her tongue. "I was wondering if Mercedes was your mother's name."

The girl sets her cup carefully back in the saucer. "My mother." She pauses, biting her lip, as if the word were a concept instead of a person. "No, her name was Ruth. She named me, though. Mercedes Renée."

"Do you remember her at all?" Laura feels as if she is reading from a script that has suddenly appeared in front of her.

"She died when I was born." The girl looks up for the first time and meets Laura's gaze straight on. "Bled to death. They had hospitals from four counties looking for her blood type." She says this in the same tone of shy pride that she had used when talking about the length of her hair.

"How awful!" Laura says. "What a tragedy for you and your family. I'm sure she was a wonderful person."

"My dad misses her. My brother, too." Mercedes is still looking at her, her face engaged and expectant.

"You must think about your mother a lot," says Laura. "Have a picture in your mind of what she was like."

The girl's eyes take on an unfocused intensity. "I know what she was like," she says softly. A smile trembles at the corners of her mouth.

I found the key, Laura thinks. Now she's going to open up.

But Mercedes shakes her head like a wet dog, picks up the cup in her two-handed grip, and drains her tea in one draught. Before Laura can form another question, she has taken possession of the vacuum cleaner and is lugging it upstairs.

The watercolor has been finished for two days now. Laura gets up and moves away from the easel, walks back toward it slowly. From any vantage point, the pastel interior is fixed in perfection. The problem is that only the inanimate objects have any life—the wing chair in the corner almost dances on its squat wooden legs, but the fire in the hearth looks frozen. Her outside-inside idea, so vivid when she wrote it down, never gets beyond decoration: the stars are a tasteful wallpaper pattern, the moon-lamp a plastic replica, the planets paper cutouts in gold frames instead of the celestial family portraits she intended. "Who's going to camp here?" she whispers. "Who will move in?"

From a bedroom she hears the muted rumble of the vacuum cleaner, and Becky's shrill descant: "My turn! Let me!" Apparently her daughter has graduated from dusting. Laura doesn't have to look too far for the answer to her question.

The three bears have come home, but Goldilocks isn't leaving. And she never, ever breaks anything.

She puts the painting aside and props the sketchpad on the easel. Another white page, another icy tundra that she has no energy to cross. Making marks on paper strikes her as a ridiculous occupation. Still, she picks up a pencil. Her hand moves hesitantly at first, then so quickly that her understanding lags behind. She watches as the black line rises, levels, lurches to make a stovepipe chimney, nose-dives toward a sagging porch. The daisy pinwheels loom like trees, larger than life. She blocks in a couple of car bodies in the yard, and a smudge with legs that could be either a dog or a child. Barely pausing, she flips the page over.

The kitchen. Jars of mayo and ketchup uncapped on a table covered with oilcloth. The bulging front of the refrigerator, the old gas stove with a pan on it. She knows just how the room would smell from that time she went with her mother to Bridgeport to pick up Bernice, the cleaning woman. Kerosene and the stale odor of fried food. She fills in the white space with kids—a nosepicker, a thumbsucker, an open mouth.

The living room doubles as a bedroom, Pauline's refuge from her brood. She spends most of the day on the sleep sofa, one arm across her eyes. The TV, on, as always. Laundry spilling from a hamper. Lyle comes here after work to eat, away from the chaos of the kitchen. A low table with beer cans, cigarette stubs on a plate.

The bad-blood brother would sleep alone when he's home, which isn't often. Limp jeans splayed across the mattress, his shape still in them. The back seat of a van pushed against a wall. Heavy metal posters. A swastika.

Mercedes shares a room with the little girls. A bed and a couple of cots, neatly made up. A scratched bureau with a doily on top and a jam jar of lilies-of-the-valley. In the corner, her great prize: the sewing machine. She's made an altar of it: a cover like a tea cozy and a ruffled skirt around the legs of the table it sits on. Laura's pencil is poised like a divining rod above the dressing-table flounces. Underneath is where the toys would be, in a shoebox, taped shut and hidden in the sheltering dark under the only property Mercedes owns. Laura draws her on the floor, crouched over the box like a squirrel protecting its hoard. Quickly, furtively, prying open the tape with her small fingers.

Laura puts the pencil down. Her hand is shaking from the intensity of its nonstop tour. She can hear Craig moving around downstairs, the sound of his voice rising as if a radio has been turned up. Mercedes must be gone, then. In the bathroom she splashes cold water on her face, remembering how, when she was in school and painting every day, she used to dread these transitions to ordinary life. How long has it been since she felt this exhilaration after working?

Becky is already in her seat at the kitchen table, bibbed and chewing on a carrot, while Craig spoons peas and diced chicken onto her Peter Rabbit plate.

"Are you feeling all right?" he asks Laura. "You're all glassy-eyed."

"I completely lost track of time. My God, Becky wasn't left on her own, was she? Mercedes never let me know she was leaving."

"I finally met the young lady," he says. "I agree, she's not Miss Personality, but she was nice enough to stay until I got home. Said you were working and she didn't want to disturb you." He pulls out a chair for Laura. "You know, you've got to get out more. You really don't look well."

Becky gives Laura an orange smile. In one fist she holds the carrot, in the other a baby kangaroo.

"You're not going to find anything in Hartshorne," Kathy Duncan is saying. "But Feltsville Montessori is just five miles down the road. And then there's Little Hands in Brattleboro—very artsy-craftsy, aging hippie, if you know what I mean. Or you could go the church school route, it's mostly nonsectarian now. St. Anne's Episcopal has a wonderful program; Hayley didn't want to leave."

Laura dutifully takes notes. She is enjoying herself, although Craig practically had to twist her arm to get her to call. Kathy is the wife of a colleague of his, a pediatrician at the local hospital. She's a bright-faced woman with bangs cut straight across her brow, and she talks so fast that Laura feels like a dullard, trying to keep up with the flow.

"The preschool dilemma," Laura sighs, as if she's been agonizing about early education for months. It feels so pleasant, so normal to be sipping coffee at Kathy Duncan's kitchen table as the children's voices float in from the family room. Kathy has two daughters, and the youngest is just a little older than Becky. The woman might not be a soulmate, but she comes from a world that Laura recognizes. Her sunny kitchen, with its litter of school projects and hanging herbs, its clay handprints above the sink and crayon drawings on the refrigerator, is a temple of well-being. No wonder Laura is gripped by the urge to tell her about Mercedes, to receive absolution from this lively former teacher, to be assured that she's a good person and not the least bit crazy.

But Kathy speaks first. "I think it's so exciting that you're an illustrator. I've been trying to get up the courage to ask you—we have this little discussion group going about children's books, nothing too formal, just a few of us who are concerned about the quality of what our kids read. It'd probably be a busman's holiday for you, but the rest of us could learn so much from someone who works in the field. We sit around the fireplace and drink wine, and chat and laugh and vent. Girls' Night Out, twice a month, no commitment necessary. Would you be interested?"

Ordinarily, this is the sort of thing that would send Laura scuttling in the opposite direction. The art student in her is already savoring the details: oversized bottle of Chardonnay; tub of dense hummus from the whole-foods store; small talk fermenting into gossip as the wine kicks in, followed by earnest discussion of What Johnny—or Hayley or Cammy or Madison—Should Read. But even as she angles for an excuse, she's drawn toward the campfire warmth, the undemanding fellowship. What polar region has she retreated to this year, that she should have this primal need for bodies around her?

"Why not?" she tells Kathy. "I guess I can tear myself away from the drawing board."

At the door, Kathy holds Laura's coat to her shoulders as Becky clutches her knees, bawling. She does not want to go home. "I wanted to ask you over before," Kathy says, "but I was kind of intimidated. This place is always such a mess." She gestures toward the congenial clutter of her living room. "I hear your house is amazing."

"You take care of it," Craig had said. After telling her that he would certainly think twice about doing her another favor. After telling her he was tired of having Mercedes for breakfast and lunch and dinner, and, yes, in bed. They had argued for an hour, and it had gotten ugly. She had accused him of identifying with Mercedes' hard-luck roots. He had all but called her a spoiled rich girl. Words had been flung: Selfish! Bleeding heart! Elitist! Do-gooder! And then the absurdity of the situation hit them.

"Lord, take Mercedes—" she began.

"Out of my life!" he hooted. "Remove her! Excise her! A man can only endure so much." They had collapsed on the bed, giddy with released tension and the idea of this particular girl coming between them, this anti-nymphet with dust-cloth rampant and vacuum hose brandished like a sword. Then they made love urgently, and it was only Tuesday.

So Laura is taking care of it. "We're going to have a Ladies' Day," she tells Becky on the way to Brattleboro. It's the second week of November, and already the air smells like snow. After parking the car, they head first to the bakery to set the seal of celebration. She chooses a table by the window and sips cappuccino from a paper cup while Becky disembowels a chocolate croissant.

I do not have to feel guilty, Laura tells herself. I have good reasons for doing what I'm about to do. The girl will be all right. She's hardworking and ambitious, a real survivor. Being exposed to another way of life has given her something to aim toward. But she can't have my house. She'll have to build her own.

They make their leisurely way up Main Street, stopping at a toy store and browsing in the children's section of a bookshop. Laura lets Becky pick a book, and chooses a couple that she thinks might interest Kathy and her group. She imagines how she will introduce her selections—assured but unpretentious, wearing her knowledge lightly.

"Now it's time to find a present for Mercedes," she says. "To say thank you and bye-bye."

"Where is she going?" Becky wants to know, but before Laura can answer, Becky announces, "It's her birthday!"

The fabric store in Brattleboro had been a food co-op before its wide aisles were transformed into the stalls of a bazaar. The walls and ceiling are draped with African and Indian cottons; silks and printed velvets pour out of old trunks. Laura loves the clash of patterns, the mix of hippie chic and Oriental splendor.

They circle tables covered with roll after roll of bright cloth. It's Becky, clingy and in need of a nap, who flops down by the trunk filled with bolts of flowered silk, and refuses to look any further. "Your little girl has good taste," the clerk says. "That's our finest. Imported from Thailand." All the patterns are striking, but one entices Laura's eye: wildflowers, peach and red and purple, on a field of dark green, reminding her of the meadow that the Three Graces danced on in Botticelli's painting of spring.

The clerk rings up four yards' worth on an old scrolled cash register. I could have bought her a coat for what this is costing me, Laura thinks, but a coat wouldn't be the same.

"Could you add in some lace edging?" she asks the woman. "Just enough to tie it up with, please."

This is not a Japanese tea ceremony, Laura reminds herself. It only seems like one, each detail laden with meaning and refined over time. Why has it taken her two days to decide whether to box the silk or present it plain? Why has she been hovering in the studio for a full hour when she could have said her exit speech when the girl came in, presented the gift, and been done with it?

She takes the silk off the shelf. Folded into a square and loosely bound with lace, it makes an elegant packet. She balances it on the palms of her hands like a ringbearer's pillow.

Mercedes is polishing the brass knobs on Becky's bed. She has managed to French-braid all of her hair tightly to her skull, and her neck looks even more fragile beneath this helmet. She doesn't look up when Laura comes in. On the floor in front of the bookcase, Becky busily arranges plastic animals into rows. It's good that she's awake, Laura thinks. She can watch Mercedes accept the gift. That's a positive way for her to separate.

Laura takes a deep breath and addresses the girl's sheathed head. "Mercedes," she says, "I've been talking things over with my husband and we've decided that we probably won't need any extra help after this week. Becky's getting to an age when she needs to be with other children, so we'll be putting her in preschool."

Mercedes turns slowly, rotating her heels but keeping her eyes on the floor. "I didn't have time to do the living room yesterday," she says. "I was going to do it today."

"Oh, no, it's nothing like that. You do a beautiful job. It's just that I can manage the house for now, with Becky in school and all. Not as perfectly as you did, of course. Craig and I are very grateful, and Becky will miss you so much. We wanted you to have a little something to remember us by."

She offers the silk, but Mercedes seems not to see it. "I can come all day in the summer," the girl says. "After June twenty-first."

"You won't have any trouble finding another job. We'd be happy to recommend you." Laura extends the gift a little more insistently. "I know you like to sew. . . ."

Mercedes looks at the silk; then at Laura. Her eyes harden into pebbles. She pleats her lips. "No. No, thank you."

"Take it," Laura says. "It's for you." She raises the packet to the girl's face as she once held the plate of cookies.

"I don't want that." Mercedes' voice is so flat that she might be refusing a second helping. The polishing cloth has fallen from her hands. As if to emphasize her words, she takes hold of Laura's wrists and thrusts the packet back against her bosom. The lace bow that Laura fussed with for fifteen minutes loses its hold. Both of them watch, transfixed, as the silk unfurls between them and slithers languidly to the floor. Laura realizes with distant surprise that her eyes are flooding. She punches the air to shake Mercedes off. The girl is clinging to her wrists like a climber grasping at plant roots.

"Get away from me!" Laura's throat is tight, her arms are trembling, but adrenaline is coursing through her now, and she has the advantage of height. Bracing herself, she pushes as hard as she can. "Go home! Just go home!"

Mercedes staggers and falls backward against the foot of the bed. It is impossible to tell whether the words or the shove caused her to lose her grip, but her hands are still curled. She stares up at Laura in a kind of frozen wonder, eyes wide open for once, the irises, liquid brown, filling the lids to the brim. Laura feels herself fall into that gaze and come up sucking air—fish-eyed, flailing in an amber sea.

At that moment she notices her daughter. Becky's face is as stunned and white as Mercedes'. She has no way to process what she's seen, no niche in her small universe for such a mother. She doesn't know whether to laugh or cry; the neutral O of her mouth is just beginning to quiver. This will print, Laura thinks. This is the picture that will come to her when she's alone or frightened, when she closes her eyes at night, when she reaches out to a lover for comfort. She won't remember. She'll think it's a dream.

Inspiration is a whore, her professor used to say. What else do they call it? A fickle mistress. A reluctant muse. A wild child who comes bearing gifts, but comes when it will. How does Laura know to put her arm around Mercedes, half-drag her to the rocking chair, and sit, folding the girl into her lap? She is so quick, the choreography so deft, that no resistance is possible; still, Laura has to conquer her own. Mercedes is so close. Laura can smell the clean sweat of her, the faint, sharp odor of her hair beneath the sweet-smelling goo she uses to keep it in place. She is stiff as a mannequin, all the force in her small body clenched at Laura's middle.

But the encircling arm is seductive, the warm weight does its work. Laura can feel in her own muscles the exact moment Mercedes surrenders to it. She remembers how it was when Becky was nursing. That first audible sigh after the milk floods in, the sudden languor of the limbs. *At last.*

Becky comes, then, armed with her book, to claim her share of lap. Whenever the three of them lean back, the rocker makes a sound between a whimper and a bleat. The old chair cries out so poignantly that Laura is sure it will break apart under their combined weight. But after a few pages, even the creaking seems like part of the story, a children's chorus wailing its ritual protest each time she says goodnight.

Villaclaudia

Years ago the hotel had been open all summer, but now the DeNuccis only took in guests for three weeks in July, mostly friends from their old neighborhood in Queens who came to the wilds of New Jersey to escape the heat.

"They beat us," Dominic exulted. "Every year they come a little earlier." He jumped out of the station wagon and opened the back door for Angie and me. "Ladies, welcome to Villa Claudia!" he said, as if he had created it with a wave of his wand for our pleasure. The way he spoke it, the name had a cloud at its center instead of a claw.

Renata, Angie's mother, was still in the front seat. Only her flat, indented coil of hair could be seen as she bent to pick up her knitting from where it had fallen on the floor. When I was little and the bun was pure black, I'd believed it had a life of its own. I tried to bite it once to see if it squealed, a story that got told every year at the DeNuccis' New Year's Eve open house.

Dominic rapped on the window. "Are you staying in there all day?"

It was no secret that Renata had been urging Dominic to sell the hotel. Just the week before I had heard her talking about it to my mother, her fingers crumbling the dry, lemony cake she always served with coffee. "The place swallows up money," she had said. "Money and time. Each winter it dies a little. And the cleaning! I break my back and it still smells like the inside of a tomb. For what? A dream he had after the war? Even the regulars don't come anymore. One of these summers no one but Gino will show up. My escarole soup reminds him of his mother."

Dominic circled around to the back of the wagon and opened the trunk. In the country quiet the yawning sound was like a starting pistol, summoning guests from different parts of the grounds. I recognized most of them from the other Fourths of July I'd spent at the hotel. Rocco and Pasquale, old friends of Dominic's father in Sardinia, were the official greeters. With their square faces and neckless bodies, they reminded me of nutcrackers. The boccie court was their territory. When Angie and I played there, they muttered in Italian and swatted at us with bulky veined forearms, as if we were flies to shoo away.

"*Paisans!*" Dominic shouted. My father liked to say that Dominic was a professional Italian. I wasn't sure what that meant, but as I watched the three of them go into a huddle, hugging and slapping each other on the back, I had a feeling they were all putting on an act for the rest of us. Chattering in Italian, they began to lift cartons of food and wine out of the trunk.

The Guicciardis were back again, and the Fantos, from the DeNuccis' old neighborhood in Queens. This year the Fantos had brought their son, Nick, and his wife and baby. Nick's wife, Diane, didn't look happy. She stood apart from the group, gripping the handle of the stroller as if she intended to wheel it straight back to the city. I saw the place through her eyes: a sprawling old wooden house with shingles missing from the roof, paint cracked all over, a long sinking porch. Stalks of caning stuck out from the seats of the peeling green rockers. When we set our feet on the porch steps, the chairs moved back and forth in a stunned, groggy way like old people nodding out of a sleep.

Renata was out of the car by now, carrying her carpetbag of knitting over one arm. She headed straight for the baby. *"Bellina,"* she crooned, kneeling before the stroller. She smiled up at Diane. "What a long trip to make with a little one. At least it's cooler here than in the city."

After the first burst of conversation, the guests stood around awkwardly. Dominic clapped his hands. "Only three-thirty. Who's joining me for a swim before dinner?"

"Let people get settled in their rooms first," said Renata. "You haven't even unlocked the front door."

"You think I need to be told? Fourteen years I'm doing this! I meant for later! For later!" Right away he was angry, his voice shrill, his eyes bugging out. He laughed his mirthless hyena's laugh. "Never marry a schoolteacher. They think they know everything."

The women glanced at each other and the men looked down at the ground. Angie tugged at my arm. "Let's go play." Although she had grown up with Dominic's mood changes—

and I'd grown up next door to them—they were always alarm-
ing. People were constantly tamping him down, pressing the
lid back on him before too much steam escaped. Once
Renata came to our house crying, holding a handkerchief to
her cheek. My mother took her into the bedroom, and the
sound of their low, urgent talking had filtered through the
closed door.

"Where's Gino?" Mrs. Fanto's brisk voice broke the
silence. "Don't tell me he's not coming this year."

"He'll be here before supper," Renata said. "He was nice
enough to stop at the bus station in Dover to pick up Elvira."

"Oooh," said Mrs. Guicciardi. The old men made fists
and punched mechanically into their palms. Angie and I
exchanged looks of disgust. One of the stories the grown-
ups told was that Gino and Elvira were having a romance.
Each year the women invented errands for them to do
together, or plotted to strand them in corners where they
had no choice but to flounder for conversation. We couldn't
imagine why anyone bothered. It was clear to us that Gino
and Elvira would never love each other, or anyone else. They
were drab and ordinary. They were not beautiful.

"He'd better come, that eggplant-head," said Dominic.
"He's bringing the firecrackers."

He turned the key in the big green door and the dank
smell hit us.

No matter how hot it was, the meals at Villa Claudia always
started with soup. That evening it was bland and yellow, thick
as porridge. I ate two bites and stood my spoon up in it like
a rifle in sand, a sign of surrender. Gino was starting his second helping. He bent close to the bowl and sucked the soup

in through puckered lips, whipping it to his mouth in a steady stream. He was the only person I knew who hummed while he ate. When the bowl ran dry he looked up, flushed and smiling.

"Delicious, Renata," he said. "Almost as good as the escarole. You cook from the heart."

Renata went on collecting plates. I could tell from her eyes that she was pleased; she ate little herself, but loved to feed others. Back in West Orange, she sent me home at least once a week with fresh-baked rolls or a jar of red sauce that she called "gravy." My father claimed it was the best spaghetti sauce he'd ever tasted, and even used it on hamburgers instead of ketchup. But at the hotel her cooking lost all its neighborliness. She stewed bitter greens and napped them in smoky oil, tainted the pasta with sharp, smelly cheese. Angie and I lived on hot dogs, but no one else complained. Like good children, they ate whatever she set before them.

We sat around a long wooden table covered with white cloths, an arrangement that made me think of the etching of the charity school in my copy of *Jane Eyre*. The dishes were white and thick, covered with hairline cracks beneath the surface. The adults drank wine out of squat glasses. Renata had set tureens and covered casseroles in a row down the middle of the table and, at either end, baskets of sliced, hard-crusted bread that were emptied as soon as they were filled. "Family-style," she called it, which meant that people reached for what they wanted.

"Once upon a time only the best society stayed at Villa Claudia," Dominic said. "Aristocrats. Diplomats." He was talking to Diane, gesturing with his fork the way he did when he got excited. "The old sweetheart was a glamour girl once.

You don't see woodwork like this anymore. The family that built her brought in craftsmen from Italy."

Diane lifted her eyes from her plate and took one quick look at the wood trim painted a liverish rose to match the flowers in the faded wallpaper. She glanced sideways at Nick. The rest of us looked around, too, as though we'd never seen the walls before.

"My problem is, I got no assets. The construction business is up and down, these days mostly down." Dominic layered his fork with meat, beans, potatoes, talking through the mouthful. "Whatever I make goes into the funnel. *La famiglia.*" He scanned our faces for mockery. "My dream is to bring her back," he said.

I didn't have to wait to bring my own Villaclaudia back. She had come to me three years ago on my first visit to the hotel. Angie and I were only eight then; I had never been away from home before and the sound of my voice was a comfort to me. Now we waited all year to return to her homeland, stoking ourselves through the endless gray winters with thoughts of the Gothic terrors lurking on the third floor. I could conjure her right now, sitting alone at the head of an oval table whose high polish mirrored her evening finery. Tonight her gown was red velvet, cut low, and her hair was parted into two black wings that swooped upward to show the diamond teardrops in her ears. A string of rubies circled her throat ("like droplets of blood," I would tell Angie later), spilling a single pendant diamond into the cleft between her breasts. She sighed deeply, causing her jewels to shiver. In came her servant, the stumplike Rosa, bearing a shallow china bowl of consommé. I had never seen consommé, but I imagined it to be clear and golden, like my grandmother's chicken soup without the fat. Villaclaudia skimmed the ethereal broth with her spoon. Rosa hovered. Once she would have uttered one of the choice phrases I picked up from the DeNucci table—*"Mangia! Mangia bene!"*—but over the years she had evolved into a mute. Now she could only gesture feverishly while her eyes rolled in her large head. This evening she was an acrobat of anxious care, but her efforts were in vain. Villaclaudia had no appetite. *"Something is in the garden,"* she whispered. *"The darkness is alive!"* Rosa wrung her hands.

"What are you telling me?" Dominic thundered. "That I don't care about my kid?"

"Would I ever say such a thing?" Renata stood by the table holding an empty platter. She looked nervously over her shoulder toward the kitchen. "All I said was, how can we pour money into the hotel when we have to worry about putting a child through college?"

"Don't you think I know that? Who supports this family by the sweat of his brow? Who? Who?" He jerked his head from face to face, taking a poll. "This woman, she lives off the fat of the land. She has no understanding."

In the silence, Renata fled to the kitchen. Elvira got up and went after her. She was a bookkeeper who had been Renata's roommate in her schoolteaching days, a skimpy little woman with tightly curled hair. At the door she turned and shook her head, her fallen cheeks pulled into a mask of tragedy.

Dominic looked around again. He laughed. "Hey, what is this? Serious faces? It's nothing, a little family disagreement. And I thank God I'm among my family."

"If you ask me," said Mr. Guicciardi, "the best society still stays here." A few people chuckled. Everyone relaxed.

"And we got the best cook," said Gino, as Renata and Elvira came in with dessert.

After dinner we drifted outside. Although it was almost eight, the midsummer night was still bright. The men stood around the lawn in little pools of shadow, smoking. On the porch, the women rocked and talked. For once, Angie and I didn't have to be reminded that it was time for bed. Renata stopped us before we began the perilous journey to the third floor.

"Sleep as late as you want," she told me. "Tomorrow we go to Mass, but you can stay with the men like last year. Dominic will make sure you get breakfast."

"Oh, I want to go to church," I said. "I'm interested in other religions." Lately, the low-key Jewish God who went so well with our beige drapes and built-in bookcases had not been enough for me. I had a secret desire to peek into this dark room in my neighbors' lives, to smell the incense and whisper the incantations, to look into the idolatrous wooden faces of the Son of God and his Mother. I had watched Angie tick Hail Marys off the amber beads of her rosary. I had even asked her to pray for me.

Renata hesitated. "It's all in Latin, you know. And your parents . . ."

"I packed a dress," I said quickly. "A white one."

Renata smiled and put her hand to her mouth. She had grown up in a convent school and had a way of veiling her face when she was about to say something daring. "What will your mother think if we make a Catholic of you?" she asked.

I shrugged. I knew exactly what my mother would think. The DeNuccis' religion was an Italian thing, *talenisheh*, like the dolls with crocheted skirts that sat stiffly in the corners of Renata's couch, or the plush teddy bears I used to get from them at Christmas. Renata and Dominic had hearts of gold, my mother often told me, but they were different from us. Different also from Dr. Giardella, who played chess with my father on Wednesdays, and whose daughter, the impeccable Elise, wore cashmere sweater sets to school each day. Apparently there were grades of Italian, just as there were grades of meat. My father would make a joke of it. He'd put his arms around our shoulders. Hey, he'd say, do you know what *talenisheh* is? *Goyisheh* with Parmesan cheese on it.

"I suppose there's no harm in it," Renata said. "Just don't talk all night. You have to get up early tomorrow."

When Dominic showed people around the hotel, he always called the stairway "curved." I myself had once likened it to a swan's neck when Villaclaudia, dressed in diaphanous night-clothes, had tripped on it. The truth was that the swan's neck was broken in three places. To get to the family quarters on the third floor we had to climb up three separate flights of steps, whose landings were overlooked by small octagons of stained glass that cast the ghosts of colors over us. It was part of our game to prepare ourselves for the story by leaving the hall lights off as long as we dared. Tonight we had pledged to make it to the top, even though we moved deeper into darkness with each step we took. At the end of the first flight we held hands. At the end of the second flight we sang.

Twelve bottles of beer on the wall,
Twelve bottles of b-e-e-e-r,
If one of those bottles should happen to fall—

Night had blotted out the third floor. The air was dense and smelled of dry rot. Still holding hands, we groped frantically for the light switch, and then the hall appeared: cream-colored walls darkened to a muddy tan, magenta runner bunched in inchworm humps over the floorboards.

The door to Angie's room was open. She turned on the light and we ran for the big iron bed. Everything was the same as last year and the year before. The old metal bed frame still clanked beneath our weight. The chenille bedspread had lost so many tufts that its daisy design was etched in pinpricks. The same three teddy bears lolled against the headboard, purple, pink, and turquoise, their plump bellies making up for the flatness of the pillows. Our suitcases stood neatly at the foot of the bed. My mother had instructed me to hang up my good dress as soon as I arrived, but I wasn't sure I'd have the courage to open the tall, dark armoire. For last summer's chapter, I had summoned bats to fly out of it and circle Villaclaudia's head like honeybees.

We changed into pajamas and unrolled the old wool blankets that lay across the bottom of the bed. Even on humid nights, we always began the story under a tent.

"Where is she now?" Angie whispered.

"In the bathtub. Trying to stay calm. Rosa put in the musk-and-roses bath oil, and she has little soaps that look like flowers, but turn into cream on her skin. Her hair is pinned up on her head with an alabaster comb. She hears a bump against the window. The sound gives her goose pimples all over. *Bump. Bump. Bump.*"

A triangle of light sliced into the room. "Go to sleep now, girls," Renata said. The darkness was whole again.

"Suddenly she sees a clump of white flowers against the pane." All the flowers in the garden were white, the better to set off Villaclaudia's raven hair. "Somebody is throwing gardenias to get her attention, but she tries to ignore it. 'Rosa!' she cries. The faithful servant rushes in with Villaclaudia's white chiffon negligee and leads her through the dark hall by the light of a candle. She makes sure that her mistress is tucked safely into her canopy bed before closing the bedcurtains. Villaclaudia reaches for the glass of apricot brandy that Rosa always leaves on her night table to help her sleep. No sooner does she take a sip of the golden nectar than she hears . . . *Bump. Bump. Bump.* She parts the curtains and creeps silently to the window. Some mysterious power is telling her to open it, and she cannot refuse. And . . ."

"Go on!" Angie was all the way under the covers now. I could feel her heavy breathing on my elbow.

" . . . all this fog drifts in. Villaclaudia tries to resist, but the fog is pulling her toward the garden. She has to be very quiet stepping over Rosa, who's sleeping right outside the room. Like most dumb people, her hearing is very sharp—"

"That's *blind.*"

"Anyway, Villaclaudia grabs a candle from the hall and floats down the spiral stairway like she's in a dream. The French doors open. On their own. In the garden, fog is everywhere and flowers are swirling around like confetti. She thinks she hears a voice calling her name—*Villaclaudia, come to me!*—but the wind blows her candle out. She couldn't see at all if it weren't for the dim light coming from the gold cross on her bosom. Her mother's prayers are in it that she prayed just before she died—"

"What's out there?" hissed Angie. She had no patience with mysticism.

At this point the story always bogged down. In the beginning there had been vampires and werewolves and villains with dark beards and scarred faces, but they'd all gone the way of Rosa's speech. They were too substantial, and after a while, they got in the way. For some time now I had been looking for a replacement. Meanwhile, Villaclaudia's pursuer had become as vaporous as the fog that shrouded him whenever he was about to reveal himself.

"It's not exactly a 'what,'" I stalled. "It's everywhere. Like a spirit."

"Oh!" said Angie, yawning. "The Holy Ghost!"

Immediately I felt superior to her, but also resentful, the way I did when she talked about the Pope. "Not a *Catholic* ghost. I mean a Force of Nature." My parents always declaimed the term grandly, whether describing a hurricane or my Uncle Arnie, the comedian. "Villaclaudia can feel its icy fingers reaching out for her. She runs and runs, but her legs have turned to jelly and her eyes are getting heavy. She is sleepy, very sleepy, and soon"—I paused, flattening out my voice—"she swoons onto a bench and passes into oblivion."

The words worked like a spell. Angie had inched her head out of the cocoon she'd made of the blankets and into the crotch of the turquoise bear. After a minute or two her eyelids fluttered. Her mouth opened, and she began to breathe through it in little sputtering snorts.

I leaned back against my pillow. Angie had adenoids the way grown-ups had migraines or heartburn. I hated her for them, just as I hated her for the childish way she slid into sleep, leaving me alone to decode the noises of a strange house. This night, as on all other nights I had spent at the hotel, I lay on my side of the sagging mattress with my eyes wide open, listening to snores that hovered in the air like smoke rings while homesickness clamped me in its damp fist.

Renata's knock woke me on Sunday morning. It felt like the middle of the night. The room was dark, and beneath the cracked window shade a thin gray rain was falling. I could hear plinking on the roof.

Gingerly I put my feet on the cold floor. I must have slept, but my eyes were dry and scratchy and my bones ached from the mattress. Angie was still asleep, flat on her back in the crevice in the middle of the bed. As usual, she had won the war for the covers. I decided not to wake her until I had finished dressing.

My white dress lay folded in a rectangle on top of my other clothes, its discreet frills tucked under. When I shook it out, parchmentlike creases were etched in the delicate cotton, just as my mother had warned. I put on a white slip and underwear, the sort I imagined a nun would wear, and the white stockings and flats I'd gotten for my Cousin Eric's bar mitzvah. Last of all, I raised my arms and let the dress float over me. In the fogged glass of the old mirror above the bureau, I sucked in my cheeks, parted my lips, and let my eyes widen slowly, the way Pier Angeli's had when she saw the Risen Christ.

"Your slip's showing!" Angie was sitting up in bed, tousled and bright-eyed. "Want me to do your zipper?"

The adults weren't allowed to eat before Mass, so Angie and I had breakfast by ourselves at the scarred table in the kitchen. Renata told us that we were eating like real Italians: hard rolls, fruit in a wooden bowl, warm milk with a little of last night's coffee mixed in. Stimulating beverages were forbidden at home. Dunking my bread in the flavored milk made me feel hushed, as if I had already been initiated into the mysteries of the church. Rain streaked the windows. Renata had switched on the overhead light, but the yellow glare that cheered us at night seemed unnatural, even on a morning as dark as this one.

We gathered in the hall while Gino brought the station wagon around to the front door. The rest of the men had chosen to sleep in, and Nick's wife didn't go to church. I realized that I had already bumbled by failing to bring a hat. A doily sat on Mrs. Guicciardi's boulder of teased blond hair like a sudden fall of snow on a mountaintop. Mrs. Fanto, a no-nonsense woman, snapped open her purse, took out a handkerchief, and stapled it to her head with a couple of large black bobby pins. Elvira was nowhere to be seen, but appeared at last in a stiff-brimmed straw hat with hard little berries twined around the crown. "In this weather I can't even get a comb through my hair," she said, poking at her curls with thin, nervous fingers.

When Renata reached the landing, we all looked up as if she were a bride descending. She was wearing a mantilla of black lace that transformed her dark cotton dress into the stark garb of a Spanish widow. The veil deepened the shad-

ows under her broad cheekbones and softened her jaw. My
mother always said that Renata's face was like the map of
Italy, and as I looked now at its familiar lines, I saw her for
the first time as exotic, an inhabitant of a country that was
strange to me.

"Isn't that a lovely piece of material!" said Mrs. Guicciardi.

Gino opened the door. "Your limousine is waiting," he
announced, flourishing a big black umbrella. When he saw
Renata he made a little bow, as fat raindrops skidded off the
half-closed umbrella onto his suit. "I can't believe my eyes,"
he said. "I think I'm seeing a contessa from the Old World."

Renata blushed. "My sister sent this from her last trip.
Such an impractical thing, but I hate to waste it."

Turning to me, she said, as if she had read my thoughts,
"Don't worry about a hat. You look very nice all in white. Just
like a Communion girl."

Gino parked the car across the street from the church so we
wouldn't have to walk far in the rain. I had imagined a cathe-
dral with soaring Gothic arches, but this building looked like
our Carnegie library at home, a red-brick square with a
small white bell tower on top. A sign on the front lawn read,
Church of the Immaculate Conception. Although I didn't
know what it meant, I liked the sound of it: shadowy but official, a secret password.

Gino held the door open for us as we filed into the fra-
grant murk of the church. An organ was booming from some
unseen place over our heads, the mournful music mingling
with the burnt-perfume smell of incense. I knew that
Catholics had holy water. Was there such a thing as holy air?

The walls on either side of us were decorated with pictures of Jesus dragging his cross on his back while people spat and pointed and beat him with sticks. He seemed to be making his way up the aisle along with us. When we reached the front row I saw that he had arrived, too. His body was lifelike but he had been painted with glossy enamel that gleamed like china, and a real starched diaper was slung around his hips. Renata and the others bowed and touched their foreheads and chests. I wasn't sure what I should do. I bobbed my head and pushed my bangs back from my brow, in case anyone was looking.

We filled the front-row pew. From my seat on the aisle I had a good view of the altar. Other statues huddled in the corners: the Virgin Mary dressed in blue and a bearded man who I thought must be her husband, Joseph. Jesus' parents didn't seem to care that their son was bleeding. They looked away from him, gazing sternly over the almost empty church as if they were taking attendance. But then, maybe he wasn't really in pain. His eyes were closed and his lips set in a private smile. He might have been having a good dream that floated him miles above the holes in his hands and feet.

The organ stopped in mid-tune and started again, louder. Down the aisle came two boys dressed in white robes over black. The priest who followed them was as disappointing as the outside of the church: a short, doughy man whose steel-rimmed glasses rested on the pouches of his cheeks. His praying hands were half-hidden in the gaping sleeves of his gown. When he stepped up to the altar, I could see the worn-down heels on his black shoes.

The boys lit candles with tall crooks, and the priest began to chant in a high, toneless voice. As the Latin droned on, my attention began to wander to the statue of Jesus. Above his head was a word I had never seen before: INRI. I shaped the syllables with my lips, tasting a wistful neigh, the cry of a trapped animal. Maybe the word was something Jesus had cried out while he was hanging there, a Latin *oy* like the frozen yelps in cartoon bubbles.

Angie had explained to me about the bread and wine transforming into the body and blood of Christ. I'd vowed to follow every movement of the priest's hands, but how could I have known that his back would be turned to us? It was understandable that whatever magic he performed would be concealed from the audience. Still, I felt cheated. At least I could keep an eye on his sleeves.

Everyone in our row was standing. I started to rise, too, but Renata put a hand on my arm and shook her head. Soon they were all kneeling at the rail in front of the altar. I slid to the end of the pew, leaning forward as far as I could. One by one people opened their mouths, and I saw, with some shock, that they stuck their tongues out as the priest approached them. With a brief, brisk pressure, he patted a small disk onto the tip of each tongue. No one seemed to chew. Did Jesus dissolve right away, I wondered, or did he expand inside them like the water flowers that blossomed in jelly jars on my night table?

I leaned back against the smooth wood of the pew, suddenly queasy. Other people were lining up now, their faces empty and preoccupied. I couldn't understand how they could open their mouths so blandly, so matter-of-factly, like infants waiting for the next spoonful of cereal. And the priest—didn't it bother him to touch the pink fleshiness of other people's mouths?

"Are you all right?" Renata whispered, slipping into the space beside me. She was looking at me with concern while the priest rattled on in plain English about Bingo Night and the Ladies' Auxiliary.

"I think the coffee made me nervous," I said.

🍐

By the time we pulled into the hotel driveway, a milky sun was filtering through the clouds. Mrs. Fanto and Mrs. Guicciardi went upstairs to change into something cooler. The rest of us walked to the kitchen entrance where Dominic waited, his hands full of weeds. "A bouquet for my beautiful wife," he said, thrusting the stalks in Renata's face. "Smell that! Wild herbs growing right outside our back door. You can use them to stuff the *porchetta*." He was jubilant, practically dancing.

"What are you talking about?" Renata brushed the herbs aside, her nose wrinkling for a sneeze.

"At the farmers' market this morning Martelli was selling two baby pigs, fresh-killed. I would have taken both, but one was spoken for. All the way home I could taste the meat melting in my mouth."

"You bought a pig? What foolishness! Who would take a chance eating pork in the middle of summer?"

"You could get trixie-nosis," Elvira chimed in in her tinny voice.

"That's how much you don't know!" Dominic said. "It happens to be a tradition in Sardinia, a *festa*. For a whole week in July you can smell the pigs roasting. I remember!" He stabbed with his forefinger at the patch of black hair that filled his open collar. We all knew that he had left Italy when he was a baby, but he was always telling stories about his village.

"Where did you put the thing? The refrigerator is packed." Renata shook her head.

"In the big roasting pan in the pantry. You think every Italian has a Kelvinator?"

"I can't look." Elvira shielded her eyes with her hands and fled to the porch. We followed Dominic into the dark coolness of the kitchen. He came out of the pantry clutching the big speckled pot by the handles, and set it on the kitchen table. With ceremony, he removed the lid.

The piglet's eyes were squinched shut. Its ears curled delicately like new leaves. I would have thought it was sleeping, except for the way its lower jaw collapsed under the weight of its snout.

"Not a mark on it," Dominic said. "Martelli told me they kill the weak ones by throwing them against a wall."

Angie and I made gagging noises. Renata clutched the mantilla that she had folded on top of her missal and held it to her mouth. "You expect me to cook that?" she said. "I could never bring myself to touch it."

"I agree with you, Renata," said Gino. "It looks just like a baby human." He ran a fruit and vegetable stand in the city, an occupation the other men regarded as slightly sissy.

Dominic's laugh skidded dangerously. "Little dainty souls! Little white hands, good for nothing but squeezing the breast. I'll do the cooking myself, with the help of my *paisans*. Pasquale already went looking for a tree branch to make the spit."

After lunch Angie and I sprawled listlessly on the front lawn. The sun was out in full force now, an orange oven dispensing a steady heat. We were tired from too little sleep, cranky with each other. Already I was rediscovering what I learned each summer and forgot by the time the weather turned cold: Angie at the hotel was not the same as Angie next door. At home she was eager to please, following my lead as unquestioningly as the altar boys had served the priest. I was the golden goose. I had the words. But in the country she lost no time reminding me that she was the princess of this small domain. I heard the command in her tone when she blew at me through a piece of grass and said, "Tell the story."

I didn't feel like it. I wanted to find a cool indoor space where I could be by myself and think about Jesus on the Cross, Holy Communion, and the dead pig.

"She's in the garden," Angie prompted. "She was running and she fainted, remember?"

Like a record prodded by a relentless needle, I began to spin out my tale. "When Villaclaudia wakes up, she doesn't know where she is. Funny, she could have sworn that somebody called her name again. The air's all gray and smoky, and she's freezing cold. When she tries to move, she realizes that the fog is coiled around her like a gigantic snake, and it's dragging her to the tree in the middle of the garden. She can hardly get a word out, but with her last breath she cries, 'INRI! INRI!'"

"What?"

"It's Latin for 'Help.' This holy language travels faster than time. The word cuts right through Rosa's snores, and in a second she's downstairs. But what's this? The French doors have closed again, and now they're locked! Rosa throws her shoulder against them and pushes with all her might, but in vain. Finally she grabs an umbrella from the umbrella stand and breaks the glass. When she climbs through, she sees . . ."

"Go on!" Angie's apathy was all gone, and I was getting excited myself. I had no idea what I would say next.

". . . Villaclaudia, her beloved mistress, spread out against the trunk of the great tree. Her long black hair is whipping around her face and her negligee is in shreds. Rosa can just make out her words above the roar of the wind. 'Go to the castle! Get the Du-u-u-ke or I am lost! Tell him . . .' "

I was not proud of having brought in the Duke. He was a dull, faceless fellow, useful mostly for filling in cracks in the story, like the grouting my father pressed around the bathroom sink. But Angie didn't seem to mind. "Go on! Tell him what?"

"'. . . that if he doesn't come, I will suffer . . . I will suffer the Immaculate Conception!'" The words had leaped from some half-closed drawer in my head onto my tongue.

Angie's face closed off as if I had spat at her. "I'm telling my mother you made fun of our religion," she said. "That's not very nice. You're our guest."

"I did not! I don't even know what it means."

She looked at me warily. "Well, it's . . . The Blessed Virgin Mary was born without sin and she had a baby without sin."

"Why is it a sin to have a baby? My mother says Catholics are supposed to have babies."

Angie opened her mouth, closed it, opened it again. "Mary, Our Lady, she had the Baby Jesus a different way. It—He—got into her a different way. By the Holy Ghost."

My parents had given me a book about the facts of life, but its poetic phrasing and horticultural images had left certain connections unclear. I thought of the little catechism with the gold cross on the cover that lay on Angie's dresser, next to her brush and comb. It looked like a diary without a lock, and I had always suspected that it contained classified information.

"Does it tell in your red book," I wavered, whispering out of caution, ". . . how?"

"Little girls!" Gino was gazing down on us as if we were an interesting species of mushroom. We looked up at his thin white legs sticking out of baggy swimming trunks. Elvira stood a few feet behind him, clutching the straw Bermuda bag that she carried everywhere, even to meals. "How about coming with us for a nice boat ride?"

They both looked relieved when we shuffled to our feet without hesitating. This wasn't the first time we'd been recruited to accompany them. Sometimes it seemed as if they were communicating through us, bouncing questions and comments off our indifferent heads.

The rowboat had collected an inch or two of water from the morning's rain. We helped Gino bail it out with a child's pail. He held the boat steady while Angie and I got in and settled ourselves in the back. Elvira threw us her straw tote for ballast and climbed gingerly over the side and into the seat in front, squealing when the boat rocked. She was wearing pedal pushers and pink flats with soles that looked as if they were made of cardboard. After maneuvering her bottom into the exact middle of the seat, she foraged in her bag for a scarf for her hair.

Gino hauled in the rope, jumped in, and took hold of the oars. With a few strokes he brought us out into the lake. "Look at this water," he said. "It's smooth like a bowl of soup." He began to hum. His legs had fallen apart, and where the maroon strip of his trunks ended, a mesh pouch bulged. I couldn't take my eyes off it. It had a heavy, inert look, like the bag of fish Dominic had brought us last year. I remembered how he had tossed the packet carelessly so that it hit the kitchen counter with a soft, complicated plop, how it had settled into stillness, and how, just as he was telling us to fry the fish in olive oil while they were still fresh, the bag had suddenly moved.

I looked at Angie. She was staring straight ahead with a blank expression, scratching a mosquito bite on her knee. That was the way it was with Catholics. They stuck their tongues out at priests and swallowed the body of God, but were blind to what was right in front of them.

At breakfast the next morning only Rocco showed up, planting himself at the kitchen table and drinking black coffee out of a cup as big as a cereal bowl while Renata filled thick white mugs for him to take to the others. *"Furria furria,"* he rasped, making a turning motion with one hand. Renata muttered about taking special orders on this day of all days, but she made up a nice tray for them. The women were already gathered in the kitchen, cutting, grating, frying for the Fourth of July feast. They were making a special dish with eggplants that Gino had brought from his stand. Gino hovered over the carton of shiny purple fruit, picking up one, then another, weighing them in his hand like a boy with a new football. "Wait'll you taste this, little girls," he said. "More tender than any meat. My mother, God rest her soul, used to prefer it to veal."

Angie and I had gone our separate ways last night: I'd

retreated to the living room with a book while she played cards with the women. We went to bed silently, without mentioning the story. I didn't really think she had told on me. Still, as I ate my toast, I kept glancing at Renata, looking for the print of my blasphemy in her distracted face.

Outside, the sweetish, gamy odor of roasting meat hung in the heavy air. I sensed that Angie was as grateful for it as I was. Following the trail of the pig was a thing we could do together without having to talk. When we came near enough to see smoke, I started to drag my feet. "I don't really like looking at dead things," I said.

"I've seen six dead *people*," said Angie. Her voice swaggered, but she slowed down to keep pace with me.

Mr. Fanto and Mr. Guicciardi were standing in front of the brick barbecue, smoking and talking out of the sides of their mouths like spectators at a boxing match. Dominic was emoting for them, gesturing with both arms. He waved when he saw us. "Step right up, ladies! The show started a long time ago."

We approached shyly with our hands behind our backs. Rocco and Pasquale stopped turning the spit and swabbed their faces with big handkerchiefs. They must have been doing all the work; their sleeveless undershirts were wet with sweat. They passed a bottle of wine back and forth, tilting their heads back to drink.

The pig looked longer and thinner on the spit than it had in the pot. Its skin was singed, but pink rawness still showed under the patchy crust. Its front feet were tied together, which made it look as if it were praying or pleading. Dominic poked it with a two-pronged fork. He grinned. "What do you think, ladies?" he said.

"Disgusting," Angie pronounced. She looked at the pig clinically with her clear, uncluttered gaze. I had always envied her ability to know exactly what she felt while she was feeling it.

I was fascinated by how the pig had changed. The stick that passed through its mouth and out its backside had stretched it from a plump baby into something lean and shriveled and ancient. It seemed to have grown old overnight. Pasquale started to turn the spit again. *Furria furria.* I watched fat drip off the pig and spatter on the coals below. When it hit the fire, tiny sparks flew up. Little by little, the pig's roundness was melting away. What was left would be cut in pieces and eaten with appreciative grunts by people who would never give a thought to the recently living thing they were swallowing. The men would suck the bones—under all that flesh, pigs must have skeletons like turkeys did—and wipe their greasy hands and faces. The thought made me sway where I stood.

Angie was regarding me with the same level stare that she had applied to the pig. She took my arm. "Let's go," she said. Firmly but gently she led me off, as if I were a little sister put in her charge for the afternoon. "Now we can play on the boccie court."

On the way we passed Nick and Diane. He wheeled the stroller this time, his shoulders hunched over the handles in a defeated way. The two of them were walking quickly, their heads turned toward each other so that they never even noticed us.

"We could've gone to Atlantic City," she was saying. "We could've had a real vacation for a change."

"I can't hurt my family. My mother—"

"Always your mother! You should be married to your mother."

The metal balls were scattered at one end of the boccie court. It took both of my hands to pick one up, and when I threw it, the ball wobbled weakly for a couple of feet and veered off to the side. Angie swatted at hers with an old croquet mallet that we had found on the lawn.

"I bet Diane dyes her hair," she said. "And did you see how tight her shorts were?"

"Yeah, the elastic on her panties showed." I hadn't really seen anything, but I wanted to keep the conversation going.

"She isn't Catholic, you know," Angie said. "I mean, she wasn't born Catholic but she had to become Catholic when she married Nick." She had corraled all the balls together, and now she nudged the neat cluster with her stick. "Of course, the baby is being raised Catholic."

There was nothing provocative in her tone. I knew her well enough to know that she was only repeating her family's supper conversation. Yet, for a minute, I throbbed with the urge to fling sharp words into the placid pond of her face. *Jesus wasn't a Catholic! He was Jewish like me!* I imagined the air between us rippling with the current of my anger. But when I actually spoke, my voice was quenched and humble.

"Do you want me to tell the story?" I asked.

Angie swung the mallet like a golf club. "Oh, I don't know," she said. "It's getting kind of boring. Nothing ever happens."

I looked down at the ground, where the boccie balls glimmered moistly like giant fish eggs.

A mood of ominous festivity hovered over the hotel. The men carried the thick-legged kitchen table out to the lawn, and Renata covered its battered surface with a red-checked oilcloth. Dominic had decreed that we eat in the open air, as they did during summer festivals in Italy. He wanted the meal to be formal, no paper plates or old bedspreads on the ground. He had even hung Chinese lanterns from nearby trees.

I'd spent all day being cold to Angie, pretending I didn't hear when she asked me to do something, conversing decorously with Mrs. Fanto and Mrs. Guicciardi while she splashed in the lake. At first Angie followed me around, frowning in a puzzled way, but after a while she gave up. Maybe she was secretly relieved that I was going home tomorrow. Arrangements had been made. Nick and Diane were leaving early and had agreed to drop me off on their way back to the city. On the phone my mother was dryly amused, reminding me that I always insisted on packing for a week although I never lasted more than three days. She'd laughed when I asked if we could go to a Chinese restaurant to celebrate my return. "You'd think you were marooned on a desert island," she said, "instead of enjoying Renata's delicious cooking."

It was late afternoon before we were ready to eat. Renata arranged vegetables and fruits in a basket and set the summer cornucopia in the center of the table. She and Gino carried out big platters of eggplant, along with corn, potato salad, olives, and tossed greens. The eggplant looked like molten pizza, cheese and tomatoes sizzling in juice over velvety slabs. I had resolved to sample it out of loyalty to Renata, but as I inhaled its rich tang, I felt my martyrdom seep away. People gathered around the table by twos, the men in printed sport shirts and the women in bright cottons. Angie and I still wore our shorts, and Renata hadn't had time to change.

"What a mess I am," she said, pushing loose strands back from her forehead.

There were candles and real wineglasses and cloth napkins that Mrs. Guicciardi had folded to look like swans. Only the host and his *paisans* were missing. We waited awkwardly around the laden table until Renata said, "We might as well start. In five minutes the eggplant will taste like leather." As if her words were a cue, we heard singing.

The song was Italian, chunky syllables punctuated by frequent crescendos. Each time one of the ragged verses came to an end, the old men would swig red wine from their bottles and Dominic, the pig-bearer, would lift the silver tray above his head. He had changed into a green silk shirt, and whenever he raised the pig, large patches of sweat showed under his arms. At the head of the table, all three singers joined in a quavering high note. Dominic stretched his arms up with a jerk, like a strongman giving a final heft to a barbell, and the pig slid onto the grass. It fell in a graceful, almost leisurely way, as if he'd choreographed the move in advance. A tremor passed over Renata's set mouth.

We watched in silence as Dominic picked the pig up, tenderly brushed it off, and arranged it on the tray. He took one of Gino's tomatoes from the centerpiece and put it into the pig's mouth. "How do you like my love apple?" he asked.

Rocco clanked the utensils together, but Dominic took the carving knife away from him. Bronzed, with the tomato in its mouth, the pig looked as if it had died a long time ago and been preserved. It was so well done that its meat seemed to fall off at the lightest touch of the blade. People started to pass their plates for the pale slices. Elvira held up her hand, claiming that the little eyes were looking right at her. Angie and I clutched our china. "Jewish people aren't allowed to eat pork," I said. My family had enjoyed Renata's loin chops on several occasions, but I knew she wouldn't challenge me.

Gino lowered his face to his eggplant. He had tucked a napkin into his collar and his lips were shiny with oil.

"Hey, cauliflower-brain," said Dominic. "You must be ready for some man's food. After slaving over a hot stove all day, you need some protein."

Gino looked up, startled out of a trance. "Thank you, no," he said with his mouth full. "I'm happy."

Dominic swung his gaze from Rocco to Pasquale, seated on either side of him. "Did you get that?" he said. "Did you hear? He's happy." He laughed out of the same place he had sung from, deep in his throat. "And how about my lovely wife? I saved the best pieces for you."

Across the table, Renata's face was so still that it looked carved, as it had beneath the mantilla. She shook her head and went on eating.

The meal lasted for a long time. There wasn't much talking; people seemed to lose themselves in the food. The baby choked on a cracker, and Gino said to Diane, in his earnest way, "Do like my old Nonna. Chew the food first and pass it right into the mouth like you would feed a little bird."

Most of the pig was gone by the end of the meal. Even after the rest of us were having dessert, Dominic and the old men hacked at the carcass and ate the remains off the points of their knives, washing the meat down with more wine. Renata never looked at them. She cleared the table around them quietly and efficiently, stopping to chat with people as she worked. Angie and I clung to her apron strings, all but literally, as if her reassuring presence could fill the gap between us. I had decided that my parents were right about the DeNuccis being different. Angie certainly was. She had lived next door to me for so long that I'd been too used to her to notice. I had already decided to find a new best friend when I got home.

The sun was dropping rapidly. One of the men pierced the post-dinner stupor with a single word: "Fireworks!"

Dominic pulled himself up, holding onto the table, and stumbled toward Renata. Between his thumb and forefinger was a piece of crisped skin. He brought it right to her mouth.

"I want you to taste this fat," he said. "It's sweet. Like candy."

Renata's lips pressed together so tightly that the flesh around them was white. She turned, her whole body swinging, and walked to the back door.

Gino lit the rockets by the tails. After the bang, the flame leaped and stars stood out against the sky like spread fingers before drizzling slowly down. The night was murky, a bruised purplish gray, and the frail sparkles dissolved into its depths too quickly. It wasn't much of a show but we stayed to the end, hypnotized by weariness, too much food, the doubtful prospect of bed. Maybe the rockets hypnotized us—the sameness of them, bursting and dwindling.

Angie and I didn't go upstairs until almost eleven. Renata had retired early, complaining that the noise from the firecrackers gave her a headache, so there was no one to hustle us along. I submitted once again to the terrors of the bug-filled bathroom before climbing into bed beside Angie.

From distant corners of the hotel we could hear the gargle and splash of the plumbing.

"Did you see Rocco go up the stairs?" I said. "He could hardly walk. He and Pasquale were leaning on each other."

"Drunk as a skunk." Angie's face was turned toward me in the dark. "I wish I could go home, too. It gets really lonely here after the Fourth of July."

I wanted to console her, but I couldn't think of anything to say. The words that had flowed out of me in her direction since we were little children seemed to have dried up. I had a feeling that if I opened my mouth a language would pour out that was foreign to both of us.

"*Do you think I'm deaf and blind?*" Dominic's voice cut through the wall behind our headboard, as clear as if he were in the room. "*Your mouth is full of honey when you talk to him. 'Gino, what lovely vegetables!' 'Gino, have some more!' Him with his greasy face, looking at you like he could eat you.*"

"*How can you say such crazy things? This is what happens when you drink.*" Renata's low tones muffled her words. I had to strain to hear her.

"*I wish the priest could see you! I wish he could see what you're like under that fancy veil. A woman who makes nice to the fruit man and turns away from her own husband. It's a sin!*"

"*Please, be quiet. You'll wake everyone up. The children . . .*"

Their voices dropped, but the talk went on in a fast, furious stream, an occasional word leaping up.

"Tell the story?" Angie said.

This time she wasn't giving me an order. I plunged in without pausing, trawling up phrase after phrase out of the blankness of my mind.

"So Rosa's running through the enchanted forest to get the Duke. The simple creature is tripping over dead logs and getting slapped by branches, but all she can think of is her beloved mistress stuck to that tree. Finally the castle's turrets loom before her. There's the Duke, looking out of a tower window toward Villaclaudia's house, sick with love. But what can the faithful servant do? Naturally the drawbridge is up, since it's the middle of the night—and she can't swim a stroke. Rosa shuts her eyes and prays. She opens her mouth, straining every fiber of her short, thick body, and suddenly— 'HELP! HELP!' It's a miracle! The Duke dashes outside and leaps on top of his silver stallion, and off they gallop toward the moat. The horse rears, but the Duke raises his sword and the bridge clatters down at his command! They fly across the water and through the forest until they come to the great stone gate. It's bolted, but the magnificent steed sails right over it into the garden."

The other voices had stopped, and so did mine.

"Go on," Angie said. "What did he see?"

"Nothing," I whispered, speaking exactly what was left in my head. "Just . . . a white nightgown snagged on the branches of the tree."

Angie started to say something, but didn't. The quiet closed in on us, thick and dark as a wool blanket, and we breathed it in, each of us staring up at the ceiling as if fireworks were exploding in it. The creaking began then. We might have thought that the joints of the old house were groaning if the noise hadn't been so rhythmic, so purposeful. We might have convinced ourselves that a door was swinging on its hinges if each creak hadn't ended in a metallic clang: a final sound, like something being nailed down once and for all. And I knew that help had come too late. She was trapped now, with her limbs pinned and her black hair tumbling over her face. Behind my eyes a picture kept trying to form, rising up out of a cumulus of light and shadow and falling back again.

The sound went on forever, perhaps five minutes. At some point Angie gripped my hand, the way she had when we were climbing the stairs. When her fingers finally relaxed, I realized that I could, too. Neither of us moved, even though it was over.

"I was thinking," Angie said. "Maybe you could start a new story. About something real."

I didn't answer, but another sound was filtering through the wall now, so I kept holding her hand. We lay there listening to the stifled gasping, the long, shuddering breaths that grew fainter and fainter as Villaclaudia gave up the ghost at last.

The Consolations

of Art

"I'm telling you, I don't need no one," Kriensky said. "How much mess does one person make?" With the side of his hand, he herded the crumbs on his kitchen table into a neat pile.

"The question is, who can you get?" His daughter Arlene, having swiped with brief ferocity at his sink, lifted the dish drainer with two fingers and began to scrub underneath. "Ads in the paper for five days straight and only two responses. Nobody cares about the elderly these days." The first applicant had already been disqualified. A hulking boy from the local technical college, he had called Kriensky "Sir" in a crisp, military voice. He'd seemed aggressively clean-cut except for a small gold cross in one ear. Arlene's eye pounced on it like an owl swooping on a mouse. "I wouldn't leave my dog with that one," she said afterward. "God knows what he does at night."

Now they were expecting an art student who was already

fifteen minutes late. Arlene wiped the last drops of moisture from the drainer tray and tossed the sponge in the bin.

"Maybe the *artiste* won't show up at all," she said. "Maybe she's waiting for inspiration." She laughed, a dry cackle so like her mother's that Kriensky felt his dead wife's breath on the back of his neck.

From the floor beneath them came the sound of feet on the rarely used stairs, then an uncertain tapping in the hall and a sprinkling of rhythmic knocks.

"This one couldn't even find the elevator," Arlene said in a stage whisper as she opened the door.

The young woman was on the heavy side, with very white skin and hair straight and black as an Eskimo's. She wore a billowy lavender shift that resembled a summer nightgown. A long length of brightly printed material—Kriensky couldn't decide whether it was a thin shawl or a fat scarf—dangled over one breast and down her back. He saw with pity the bra strap sagging over one shoulder and the bare toes clutching worn orthopedic sandals. His pint-sized daughter would swallow her bones and all, like a sardine.

"The wretched bus! It took forty-five minutes just to get through the center of town." The girl's voice was high and sweet. "And would you believe I got lost in this building?"

Arlene opened her mouth, but before she could speak, the girl stepped forward and clasped her hand.

"How do you do?" she said. "I'm Olivia. Can you ever forgive me?" Without waiting for an answer, she pirouetted past Arlene and shook Kriensky's hand. She dropped gracefully into his other kitchen chair, her wide dress eddying around her. "You look like a very patient person. I hope I didn't ruin your afternoon."

"Who, me?" said Kriensky. His hand wandered to his mustache, left untrimmed for days. The girl's attention unsettled him; he had expected Arlene to take charge of the interview. "I'm not going anywhere. A few minutes here or there, who'll miss it?"

Olivia smiled with one side of her mouth, as if he had made a sly joke. Kriensky was thinking that this was what they meant by "moonface," a term he had never understood. Her face was as broad and smooth as a dinner plate, the mouth small but full, the dark eyes turned up slightly at the corners.

"I understand you're an artist," Arlene said. She flung the word down smartly, but it hit the air with a flat, hollow sound. Standing while they sat, she looked nervous to Kriensky, vulnerable even, as if she were the one being interviewed. He sat up straighter in his chair.

Olivia sighed. "Believe me, I'd give anything to say yes. But I don't have the divine spark. I'm just a student, worshiping at the altar. Italian Renaissance is my special love. The more naive things. Perspective does nothing for me. Give me gold leaf. Heaped angels." She favored Kriensky with another Mona Lisa smile. "I hope you enjoy looking at paintings. On the bus I was picturing us going to museums together and maybe stopping afterward for a café au lait."

"What's not to like?" said Kriensky. He was surprised at how raffish the tired old phrase sounded, as if her warmth had sparked him into wit. Never a talker, he had been a smooth dancer in his youth, and now he remembered a back bending pliantly at his cue, the pressure of his hip teasing a partner to spin out in a turn.

"I knew it!" Olivia brought her hands to her chin and

beamed as if she had hatched him. "You have a very sensitive face."

Arlene tapped on the table with the dinner ring that she had inherited from her mother. It was a large ring, clotted with tightly wedged rubies and diamonds, and it gave her hand an ecclesiastical look.

"This is all very congenial," she said, "but can we get back to business? My father needs someone to come in a couple of times a week to do light housekeeping, laundry, and shopping. There'll be some cooking, mostly casserole-type things he can heat up. Occasionally he'll need to be taken to a doctor's appointment, or maybe for a short walk in nice weather. I can't have him gallivanting all over the city. His heart is weak and he's susceptible to colds."

"Perfect for me!" Olivia glided smoothly over the possibility that museums were on Arlene's list of respiratory hazards. "I could come in two whole days and still have time for my studies."

"Now just a minute," said Arlene. "What we can pay isn't going to support your artistic endeavors. And obviously, I'll require references."

Olivia got up, sighing deeply like an older woman, and flipped the front end of her scarf over her other shoulder. All her weight was concentrated in the middle, Kriensky decided. Her legs were slender and her feet dainty. Like a ballerina on a music box, she seemed to pivot on a small base.

"I do lots of little things to stay afloat," she said, looking at Kriensky. "And now you'll be one of them! A pleasant part of my week, I'm sure. Shall we start on Friday? I'll bring the references then."

Once again, light footwork brought her past Arlene to the door. "I'll look forward to our time together," she called to Kriensky.

Arlene rolled her eyes. She looked down at the chair the girl had vacated, but did not sit. "My God," she said. "Put an ad in the paper and every nutcase in the city comes trooping to your door."

"What's the matter?" Kriensky said. "The chair is contaminated?"

"Cleanliness is the least of my worries. I couldn't get over the bag-lady clothes. And the affectation! 'Just give me gold leaf and'—what did she say?—'*piled* angels?'" Arlene let out a snort of laughter. "Needless to say, you'll keep your door locked on Friday."

"Let her come once. What harm? If she's no good, we won't pay. She's not going to work for nothing." He was talking quickly, like a conniver, as if the girl were still feeding him lines. "Look how tired you look. You don't need me to take care of, on top of the job and the boy. Maybe, for now, this is the best we can do."

Arlene sat. She took off the high heels she wore to work and wiggled her stockinged toes. Kriensky, feeling in spite of himself a shard of guilt, thought she seemed unusually subdued. Her life wasn't easy. If she was overprotective, who could blame her? She cocked her head and gave him one of her sharp looks. "You know what my mother would have said. Let trouble in the door and it fills the house like poison gas."

Kriensky didn't answer. "The balance of power" was another phrase that had always puzzled him. Now he could feel weights shifting, silently, relentlessly, all around him. Two against one, and he was no longer the one.

"My mother," Arlene always called her, as if Kriensky had no claim to his late wife.

When he met Fay he had just turned thirty and was managing a dry-cleaning place in South Boston that he would own in a few years. A bad back had kept him out of the army. Perhaps it was the scarcity of eligible young men, but the mothers in his Dorchester neighborhood considered him a modest catch.

"Watch out," warned the friend who introduced them. "She's a little thing, but she's got a mouth on her."

Fay was no beauty; still, Kriensky liked her style. She wore her hair and skirts short, and often dressed in black, like a French girl. Her lips and fingernails were painted a dark red, the color of cayenne. Her talk was peppery, too. She would look up into his face from her tiny height, hands planted on her flat hips, and sass him unmercifully. He tried to keep his remarks neutral, but her tongue honed his words to a point and threw them back at him. After a few months of this, he reminded himself of a dazed boxer or a giant dodging a mosquito. He had to laugh at the spectacle he made. She's smart as a whip, he told himself. Sharp as a tack. Next to her, the other young women in the neighborhood seemed bland and clinging. He was more than a little flattered that a girl with such strong opinions would be interested in him.

One evening, after a couple of drinks, he said to her, "You wouldn't marry me, would you?" The words jumped out of his mouth, kamikaze style, and he drew back instinctively, waiting for the full artillery to hit him. But for once, all she said was yes.

Having claimed him, Fay treated him more tenderly, fussing over his wardrobe and twitting him about his diet. But not long after their honeymoon, the old patterns returned. In bed she was a defended fortress. Her sharp knees and elbows poked at his soft parts. However gentle he tried to be, he was always hurting her, always in her way: too heavy, too clumsy, too slow, or too fast.

"You big ox!" she would shrill. "Cut those toenails before they slice me up like lox!"

Pregnancy seemed to soften her. She talked constantly about the coming event and spent hours shopping for the baby's layette. In the evening she would spread out the day's purchases on their bed. Together they would admire the little garments, which were always pink, as if she had willed herself to beget a girl. Kriensky assumed that his new status as co-producer had raised him in her sight. If they had little in common, at least they were united in mutual anticipation of the child they had made together. He planned on three offspring, a nice round number, but once Arlene was born, Fay's legs snapped shut like pruning shears. When he looked into the raisin-face of his infant daughter, Kriensky realized, too late, that his wife had longed not for a child but for a majority.

From the very beginning, Arlene was Fay's creation. It was as if Kriensky's sperm had lost its character in Fay's vinegary essence. He was not surprised to hear the piercing, nasal tones he knew so well coming out of the mouth of his four-year-old, who stared up at him, hands on hips, mouth drawn down in a scowl.

"*Ox! Big ox!*"

He spent most of his time at the store. The moving racks

of clothes were like a second skin to him. He was soothed by
the simple tasks of making clean: the rubbing out of stub-
born spots, the snipping of stray threads and tightening of
buttons, the hiss of an iron on flannel trousers. The smell of
chemicals was not unpleasant. It signified that here, at least,
he was master. A sign in his window said: Dry Cleaning,
European Style.

At home he lived the edge-clinging life of a boarder,
silent at table and early to bed, where he read the paper until
he fell asleep. Meanwhile, on center stage, Fay and Arlene
conducted their joined lives. They were small, bony women
whose hard calves curved inward in a genteel bow. Not content to look and dress alike, they even aged toward each
other. Arlene at thirty and Fay at fifty-five both looked forty.
People often mistook them for sisters.

Arlene married twice: briefly, in college, to a feckless English major who turned to drugs for solace, and again in her
late twenties, to a dentist named Rosenthal who, five years
into the marriage, fell asleep at the wheel of his car and
crashed into a tree. Arlene was able to salvage from this last
union a house in the suburbs, multiple assets and insur-
ances, and a son. But she always claimed that the aggravation
of the accident killed her mother.

Fay's sudden death surprised Kriensky as much as her
quick acceptance of his proposal. One instant she had been
railing to Arlene about the weakness of men in general, and
the somnambulistic Rosenthal in particular, and the next
she was on the kitchen floor, crumpled in a heap by the
stove. Kriensky remembered two things about the moments
after her collapse: the thin, weak wailing of his young grand-

son—a strangely apologetic sound—and the small amount of space Fay took up when she was still.

For a few days he was reeling and disoriented, as he had sometimes been after a severe lashing of her tongue. Arlene had already taken custody of him. He understood that she was working off her grief by assuming her mother's responsibilities, as if he were an old dog being passed from one owner to another. She insisted on doing his grocery shopping, filling his shelves with costly vitamin compounds and his refrigerator with fibrous vegetables that he had trouble digesting. The house was too big for him, she said. He must sell it and find an apartment. For once, he agreed with her.

Arlene wanted him to move into a modern high-rise for the elderly, but Kriensky wasn't ready. He found a one-bedroom in an old building, not far from the neighborhood he'd grown up in, and furnished it simply with a bed, a few soft chairs, and a TV. From the house he had shared with Fay, he took only an old plaid couch from the den and a Formica kitchen set that had been stored in the basement for years.

"You're going back to the ghetto," Arlene told him, but she was happy to fill her house with her mother's massive mahogany. She had taken a job as a proofreader and passed her days in a cubicle in a downtown office building, making curt blue marks on white paper. "I'm a single mother," she said, looking at Kriensky as if he were the one who had defected. "I need a decent place to raise my son."

When babysitters canceled or school ended early, Arlene had no choice but to entrust him with Dane. Kriensky looked forward to these times with his big-eyed grandson, whose

Viking name sat strangely on his tongue. From birth the boy had been small, dark, Spanish-looking. What had Arlene been thinking when she named him after a Norse warrior?

Dane was a quiet child who spent hours on the living room floor making animal sculptures out of wire hangers that Kriensky brought home from the store. Sometimes, as a special treat, they would go to Moe's for grilled cheese sandwiches and ice cream sundaes. These excursions were a shared secret because Arlene did not approve of diner food. The two of them rarely spoke. They would look into each other's eyes across the graffiti-etched table, chewing slowly and solemnly to get every bit of flavor from their scrap of snatched time.

Kriensky lived this way for years. He went less and less often to the store, and finally sold it. He told himself that he was content. His grandson, in high school by now, still came to see him. He had his routine. He had a little peace. But once in a while, as he lay in his narrow bed with his arms folded on his chest and his toes in the air, a longing would come over him for amplitude, space to spread out, a quilt of flesh to cushion him from life's small blows. Then his chest would seem to shrink inward, as if the ribs had caved in around a vacancy, and he would breathe shallowly until morning.

Olivia came on Tuesdays and Fridays, always with something in her hands. It might be a pomegranate, which she rolled on the counter to crush the seeds into juice, or a Chinese food container that yielded two goldfish, ready to be plopped into a glass bowl; she wanted to call them Giotto and Paolo Uccello, but Kriensky preferred Mutt and Jeff. In October she put three golden quince into his tunafish dish and set them in the middle of the table. "For the perfume," she said, and all week the scent of ripening fruit filled his kitchen.

She made his lunch and did the chores while he ate. He enjoyed watching her spin smoothly from the sink to the stove to the laundry basket, singing as she worked. Every other week she twisted her long dark hair into a Chinese topknot and scrubbed the kitchen floor on her hands and knees. His apartment was always neat and fresh-smelling now.

Arlene sniffed the air like a dog, ran her fingers along surfaces, and peered hungrily into corners, but could find no grounds for complaint. "The woman seems to be doing a good job," she admitted to Kriensky. "Unfortunately, you can't depend on this type. They work when they feel like it. One week she'll be here cleaning the bathtub and the next she'll be gone, like Mary Poppins. Just don't get attached."

Kriensky studied the blue swirls on the Formica table-top. The last thing he wanted Arlene to know was how much he looked forward to Olivia. "If she goes, we'll get someone else," he said, shrugging. "Meanwhile, the work gets done." Keeping his voice casual, he added, "I think she would come even a third day—if we wanted."

Arlene buttoned her jacket from the bottom up and pulled at the hem to straighten it. She snapped open her purse, took out a compact, applied a coating of red lipstick, and squared her lips to check for stains on her teeth.

"I still haven't seen any references," she said at the door.

If the weather permitted, Olivia took Kriensky on little trips, shepherding him by subway to parts of the city he hadn't visited in decades. They went to the Armenian shops in Watertown for spongy pita bread that was easy on his teeth, and to the outdoor market in the North End for melting cheeses and bags of fruit. "If the produce weren't half-rotten," Fay had always said, "they wouldn't sell it so cheap." But he couldn't resist the jewel-colored mounds that Olivia pointed out to him—ten varieties of apples alone!—and darted from one cart to another like a ravenous child, buying more than he could possibly eat.

Other excursions were a kind of make-believe. Pilgrimages, Olivia called them. Tired as he sometimes got traipsing around, he looked forward to these vacations from his ordinary life. One brisk autumn afternoon they stood outside Symphony Hall, listening to the orchestra rehearse for the evening performance. Afterward they had tea at the Old Vienna Café. Kriensky noted that the waiter, a portly man in an old-fashioned waistcoat, bowed approvingly when Olivia chose a simple Darjeeling from the long list of fancy blends on the menu.

"It's such a relief when the Season begins," she said, pouring out for him.

"What? Winter?"

"The Season! One can wear one's fur. One can see the new plays. One can dip one's toast points into caviar."

"Lucky for me I can get my tuxedo cleaned for nothing," he said, pleased to enter into her game.

He liked the way she took his elbow when they walked, cradling it in the soft nest of her arm in a manner that was respectful, yet intimate. There was a stateliness about their measured pace. When diners looked out at them from the glassed-in walls of a restaurant, he imagined that they took pleasure in a dignified old man escorting his pretty granddaughter. Once or twice, though, he was aware of something else in their stares. Did they perhaps see a sugar daddy showing off his tootsie? He heard the voice of his dead wife like a spatter of static on his telephone line.

Look at the alta kokker with his little bit of trash. At his age, he needs help to pee.

But when he caught a glimpse of his sagging cheeks and shoulders in the bathroom mirror, even Fay's taunts could not convince him he'd been mistaken for a lover. More likely, it was Olivia who drew smirks with her loose, gauzy clothing and flopping sandals. Everything she wore seemed a little too big, an apology for the body beneath. She was never what Fay and Arlene would call "pulled together." Parts of her were always escaping: a hanging bra strap, the torn hem of a slip, a crescent of black hair dipping down over her pale brow. In spite of this, he thought her exotic. She reminded him of the immigrant *maidelehs* in his mother's album, full-bosomed in their shirtwaists, broad hips swaying over neatly pointed shoes.

One morning she sang "Plaisir d'Amour" as she dusted his living room.

"You seem happy today," he said, daring. "Is there maybe a fella? A good-looking girl like you must have lots of fellas."

She turned to face him, holding the feather duster in both hands. "Oh, I've had my *affaires du coeur,*" she said. "But it all takes so much energy, and in the end you have nothing. I've learned to be satisfied with the consolations of art." She lingered over the phrase as if she were whispering to a lover.

"If I were younger—" he began, but stopped himself in time.

Art she would talk about from morning to night, but she was closemouthed about her private life. He still had no idea what street she lived on; she had never even offered him a phone number. On her days off, he paced the apartment like a lost soul, wondering about her and worrying. Halfway through November, she had taken to wearing thick athletic socks under her sandals. A nice pair of boots was what she needed. The thought quickly crystallized into a picture, which he embellished as he waited: old-fashioned boots of soft leather, such as a Victorian lady might wear to step into a sleigh; fur-tipped to show off her slender ankles and keep out drafts. If he presented them as a holiday gift, would she take it the wrong way?

"You can't get warm from paintings," he said to her as she uncoiled a series of moth-eaten shawls on a particularly blustery day. "If you don't mind my asking, do you have enough to get along?"

It was as if she walked away from him while standing still.

"I have other jobs," she said stiffly. Then her voice lightened. "But you are absolutely the nicest. Honestly, I don't think of you as a job at all, Mr. Kriensky. I think of you as . . . a sanctuary."

On a cold morning early in December, Olivia arrived at his door wearing an old muskrat coat that he hadn't seen before. A scarf of wrinkled, rust-colored silk was tied peasant-style under her chin. Her face glowed out at him from within its dark frame.

"It's Dr. Zhivago weather," she said. "I woke up this morning and I said to myself, 'I'm going to show Mr. Kriensky that you *can* get warm from paintings.'"

The sky looked like frosted glass, and as they waited for the bus, it broke into jagged fragments of hail. Kriensky pulled his gray homburg over his ears and tried to tuck his chin under his scarf, but his face stung. When Olivia offered her bulky furred arm to help him up the bus steps, he waited passively like a child immobilized in a snowsuit before remembering to pay the driver. Once they were seated, the sudden warmth of the bus made him drowsy. His head kept drifting toward the bulging shoulder of her coat. As if in a dream, he recalled his mother's beaver wrap, the hint of perfume that clung to it, the little quills at the root of the fur.

They walked half a block with the Museum of Fine Arts in sight all the way. Kriensky recalled taking the marble steps two at a time on a school trip and filing with his classmates between the same Greek columns. Not once in all these years had he thought to return. He had worked most weekends. Culture had been the department of Fay and Arlene, who attended docents' lectures instead of temple and arranged exhibit catalogs in perfect fans on the coffee table.

"I always feel like I'm coming home!" said Olivia. She spread her arms wide so the voluminous folds of her coat hung like kimono sleeves, and Kriensky, noticing the ticket-taker's stare, drew closer to her side. They were in a rotunda covered by a great dome. Looking up, Kriensky saw bands of cherubs clustered around a porthole at the very top. It seemed entirely logical to him that the light they sent down should be golden.

After Olivia checked their wraps, they moved on into a long hall filled with Greek statuary. "If only we had time to see everything," she sighed. "But since we have to choose, I'll show you what's most special to me."

She guided him up a marble stairway and through a maze of smallish rooms. Kriensky could tell from the Victorian

moldings and general dimness that they must be in the oldest part of the museum. The place was deserted except for a
guard or two and an occasional student copying a painting.

"Welcome to the fifteenth century," Olivia said. "We're
in Florence now. *Bella Firenze.*"

Kriensky looked around him and saw sheep-faced Madon-
nas, bread-dough Baby Jesuses whose limbs were contorted
like pretzels, saints smiling pleasantly as their bodies were
pierced with arrows or broken on wheels. A bunch of *goyishe
kupfs*, he thought. What Jew could get such enjoyment out of
pain?

"Nice work," he offered lamely. "Real quality. Beautiful
frames."

She seemed not to hear him. "Look at this Adoration by
Fra Lippi. He was a monk, but a very naughty one." She
lowered her eyes and giggled as if the monk's indiscretions
were hers. "See the naked boys sitting on the stone wall? If
they'd taken time to get dressed, they might have missed the
Magi. And over here, this beautiful Botticelli. He's one of
my gods."

Kriensky smiled and nodded and let her lead him from
painting to painting, relieved that she was doing enough
talking for both of them. Once in a while an image leaped
out at him, but the pictures were mostly a colored blur like
villages seen through the window of a car. All he knew was
that he enjoyed strolling with her through this ancient city,
where ivory walls sealed in their privacy and the only looks
they got were from painted eyes staring rigidly beneath
crowns of thorns or fire.

"You look dazed," Olivia said, after they had passed
through several rooms. "I'm exhausting you. But we're com-

ing to the perfect place to stop." She steered him toward a backless bench facing a wall of smaller paintings. "We might as well feed our souls while we rest our feet. I spend hours on this bench visiting my beloved Sassetta. So few people notice it, it's almost my secret. I did a paper on it once."

The gilt frame enclosed a hilly, dirt-colored landscape sprinkled with smallish trees and saints. A hairy man with the body of a horse, his hindquarters hidden behind a wildly slanting clump of poplars, seemed to be having a conversation with one of the haloed ones. At the bottom of the canvas, the two largest saints hugged beside a gaping hollow in the mountain. There was something simple and childlike about the picture. It reminded Kriensky of the fairy stories he had read to Dane when the boy was little. "I like this one," he said, sitting. "It's not so religious."

Olivia giggled. "I think I hear Sassetta turning in his grave. St. Anthony—he's the one in the pink cloak—was a holy hermit who lived alone in the desert for ages. One day he heard a voice saying, 'There is one holier than thou.' It turns out that a hermit named Paul had lived by himself for *ninety* years!"

"Must have been a world's record," said Kriensky.

"It was. So what could Anthony do but go on a long journey to find him? He met all sorts of perils and temptations along the way. That centaur in the forest was supposed to be giving Anthony directions to Paul's cave, but he tried to talk him into indulging his animal passions. I guess it didn't work. As you can see, the two saints got together in the end. Don't you love the way they embrace? As if they'd been waiting for each other all those years because no one else was good enough."

Now Kriensky realized that all the saints along the twisting road were really a single old man at different stages of his journey. The codger must have made very slow progress since he carried both a cane and a crutch. With such a limp, no wonder it had taken him so long to find his holier-than-thou. Kriensky could almost feel Anthony's relief as he collapsed into the other man's arms. "Take a load off your feet," Paul would have said. And Anthony probably dropped his sticks right on the spot.

"They lived happily ever after in Paul's cave," Olivia continued. "Every day a raven brought them a loaf of bread, and when Paul died, two lions helped Anthony bury the body."

Kriensky wondered if she had any information about who buried Anthony, but he was too weary to ask. While Olivia was in the ladies' room, he sat with his hands on his knees and his eyes closed. It seemed impossible that he would ever stand up, put on his coat and hat, go out into the cold to catch the bus. He was suspended in some clean, bare space between worlds, like a nameless star.

The snow that had fallen while they were in the museum had already frozen into a bright, hard carpet when they came out. The sun had come out, too, not, it seemed, to give warmth but to make mirrors. Every surface shone. As they walked slowly to the bus stop, ice-sheathed branches played xylophone music over their heads.

At his door, Olivia reminded him, "You have lentil soup left over from Tuesday. Just take out the pot and turn on the heat." She fumbled in the folds of her coat and brought out a manila envelope. Shyly, she thrust it at him. "A little something for the holidays. For Chanukah." She flashed him a quick smile, spun around before he had a chance to say thank you, and ran toward the stairs. At the end of the hall she turned again.

"Be careful where you put the tacks," she called. "I'm going to have it framed for your birthday."

By eight o'clock on Tuesday morning, Kriensky had cleared away his breakfast dishes and was sitting at the kitchen table waiting for the knock on the door. At ten, Olivia still had not arrived. Kriensky got up to make another cup of tea. He was nursing a cold and had begun to worry that she had caught the same, or worse. The thought of her tramping through the hard snow in her sandals made him smack his forehead. Somehow, he would have to get in touch with Dane when Arlene was out and send him to Filene's to buy boots. Olivia's gift had paved the way for his own.

Several times he jumped up, certain that he heard her in the hall. He kept tying himself into knots of thought and making knots on top of them. She was ill, he was sure of it, feverish and delirious in some lonely room, with no one to look after her. Or injured—beaten, raped, God only knew— by some shadowy boyfriend whose advances she had thwarted for the sake of art. Through it all, like a silver needle sliding through tangled threads, ideas kept coming to him about how to get her shoe size. He thought of calling up the Birkenstock store. Maybe they kept a Book of Life in their computer with the name of every owner of their eternal footgear.

Noon came and went. Kriensky heated up some soup.

He tried to concentrate on eating, but his eye kept arching toward the print Olivia had given him, propped against the salt and pepper shakers in the middle of the table. What would Arlene say when she saw Catholics on his wall? There were the saints, going about their holy business in their tilted little universe, as unaware of the trial about to befall them as they were of the laws of perspective.

Watch out, fellas, he wanted to tell them, she's got a mouth on her.

As day faded from the kitchen, he fell into a waking doze. A key scratched in the door behind him. The room flooded with light. "Sitting in the dark?" Arlene said. "Don't tell me you're trying to save on electricity."

She plunked a large bag of groceries down on the table. "I got eggs and veggies and bananas, you need the potassium. Oh, the Nova looked nice so I picked up a quarter pound for your breakfast tomorrow. A special treat."

"Special for what?" Kriensky said, blinking. Arlene never came on Tuesdays, and she hadn't done his shopping for months. An etherlike dread was rising in him. His hands and feet felt numb.

"You sound congested. I hope you haven't been out in this foul weather." Arlene unbuttoned her coat and with great vigor began to empty the bag. "What is this?" she asked, gesturing at the print with a package of frozen broccoli.

"What does it look like? A picture."

"Italian Renaissance, attributed to Mizz Anonymous, I suppose. No wonder you have it set up like a shrine. Very cute!"

She raised one eyebrow and looked upward. Kriensky knew she was sharing the joke with Fay.

"It's art!" he cried. "It's beauty! You, with your nasty mouth, always tearing down—"

Arlene sighed. "Excuse me, I was only injecting a little humor into the situation. I'm not exactly thrilled that she dragged you all the way to the museum in the middle of winter, a man your age, in your condition. This is what I was afraid of all along. While the so-called Olivia is worshiping at her altars—on your dollar, I'm sure—that nasty cold you got from the last outing could be turning into pneumonia. But if the print means so much to you, I'll be happy to buy a frame for it. It'll be a—whatchamacallit—*memento mori*."

"What are you saying?" Kriensky whispered. "She's dead?"

"Not dead, but, you could say, disposed of. I left a very specific note at her so-called alma mater, informing her that her services would no longer be required."

Kriensky rose from the table, his hands in fists. "What did you do to her? She was a doll! An angel!"

"Only someone as naive as you could believe it. I knew she was a phony. The minute she walked in the door, all my red flags went up." Arlene was removing her tight black gloves, one finger at a time, with such concentration that she seemed to be preaching reason to her hand. "But how to prove it? Forget the references, did we have an address, a phone number? Finally, it occurred to me to call Marv Kalish—you remember, the one with the ditzy wife who did rope sculpture? He's been an administrator at the College of Art for years. As soon as I described her, he knew who she was. 'Olivia!' he said. 'Is that what she's calling herself these days? Last year it was Sonya.'"

Kriensky sat down again. "You're a spy," he said. "A Mata Hari. I'm blocking my ears."

Abandoning the groceries, Arlene stationed herself in front of the refrigerator. "It seems she started out as a student, but didn't even last a year. Now she just hangs around the school. 'Groupie' was the word Marv used—only she worships artists instead of rock stars. Apparently she's taken up with quite a few, your angel." She paused, and Kriensky knew from the breathless clatter of her speech that she'd been rehearsing on the way to his apartment.

"According to Marv, she's a bit of a joke on campus, always ready to dispense her favors for a few nights in someone's studio. After her last lover threw her out, one of the instructors took pity on her and let her model for his class. So you see," Arlene finished, "we had it backwards. She's not studying art. The artists are studying her. Though why they'd want someone with so much flesh on her is a mystery to me."

"This is what a sensitive person has to do to survive," Kriensky muttered, looking at his folded hands. "Pennies they must be paying her for sitting still. She could come to me *five* days a week. At least she'd have enough to buy shoes."

"We're talking about an opportunist who was preying on a gullible old man. It would have come down to money in the end. With this type, it always does. First a few dollars to help with the rent, and then—the will! Why else would a young woman encourage such an unhealthy attachment—"

"Find her, I'm telling you." Kriensky brought his fists down hard on the tabletop. His voice rolled over his daughter's like a layer of gravel. "I need to see her right away. I'm not asking, I'm ordering!"

Dane drove slowly through a section of the city that Kriensky barely knew. Its narrow sidewalks and storefront restaurants gave it a Bohemian air. Indian, Vietnamese, Ethiopian, Afghan—all the eating places they passed were minimally furnished and harshly lit, like kitchens of the forties. The streets appeared to be populated with young Bolsheviks, hands plunged in pockets, peering intensely over their scarves.

Kriensky was exhausted. Anxiety had kept him tossing and turning most of the night before, trying to generate enough body heat to keep warm under his blankets. Just before dawn, he'd dropped into a fitful sleep and dreamed that he was one of hundreds of antlike saints crawling over a gigantic female torso. That mountain in the background, how could he not have noticed that it was a breast? And that cave where all the saints seemed to be headed, eyes to the ground, planting their staffs again and again— But he'd awakened then in a tangle of bedclothes. Even in his dreams, he could not follow them there.

A map of the university was spread out on his tweed-covered lap. Arlene had drawn a trail with purple marker between the outlines of the buildings, culminating in a large X over the winged rectangle of the art college. But when Dane turned into the gate at the entrance of the campus, all the neat shapes disappeared. It seemed to Kriensky that they had entered another city, whose gray buildings and bare, snow-patched grounds reminded him of the Soviet enclave his parents had fled.

"I'll drop you off here, Grandpa," Dane said, stopping at a modern building. "Don't worry, I'll be in as soon as I find parking. God, I hope I don't need a sticker." He was a new driver, and nervous, hunching over the wheel as he had hunched over the handles of his bicycle years before.

Kriensky, fighting for his balance on salt-strewn ice,

waved jauntily at the receding car, but as soon as Dane was out of sight, desolation filled him. Everywhere he looked, students were hanging out in clumps, draped over each other in pairs, walking purposefully from one building to another. He alone had no place here, no idea where he was going. He was an exile in this city of the young.

He passed through the entrance at the heels of a boy and girl in matching combat boots. Once in, he stood in the center of the hall as students detoured around him, breathing a smell so familiar that he was transported back to his grade school in Dorchester. The odor must be in the paint on the walls, he decided: that universal green, still the color of crushed lima beans. While this irrelevance passed through his mind, he took note of a stairway and many doors. Until now, his only thought had been to reclaim Olivia. He had imagined a single sweeping gesture out of a silent movie—a cloaking in his coat, a spiriting away. The building that held her had been nothing more than a sordid fate out of which he would cleanly pluck her. He had never considered that there would be more than one door.

"Can I help you?" The young woman's face was pierced in vulnerable places, as the saint's torso had been, but like him, she smiled agreeably.

"Could you tell me, please, where I can find Figure Painting 202?"

It seemed to him that she gave him a look, but she said only, "Go up the stairs one flight and to your right. You want Studio Five." All the way up he felt her eyes on his back.

The door was shut, probably locked also, to prevent such intrusions as he was about to commit. Voices drifted through, along with the smell of oil paint. Still panting from the climb, Kriensky put his hand on the knob to test it and was startled to find that it turned. He opened the door a crack, waited until his breathing quieted, and slipped in, closing it noiselessly behind him.

He stood at the rear of a large room, facing the backs of the students of art. Before he saw Olivia, he saw what they were making of her: square breasts, purple shadows, her face a salmon-colored smear, her whiteness a bruise. His eye passed quickly over these gargoyle images and swung toward the platform at the center of the room, single-minded as the lens of a telescope.

She was sitting on an Oriental rug, one leg folded beneath her, an arm resting casually on the opposite knee. Dreamily she gazed at some distant point beyond the students and their botched canvases. Her face was soft and calm, one side of her mouth lifted in the Mona Lisa smile he knew so well. What struck him first was the contrast she made: black hair falling over white shoulders and bosom. The breasts themselves, large but buoyant, reminded him of a phrase from the Song of Solomon—he and the other bar mitzvah boys had snickered over it—about climbing the palm tree to take hold of its fruit. And then the weight of her—not loose or flabby but solid as stone, if stone could give out light. Who could have guessed that beneath her baggy dresses lived such marble poise?

Kriensky knew, even as he fed on the sight, that he had no business looking. He might as well be hovering outside the window of one of the paint-spattered lofts where she spent her nights, clutching his pitiful offering of romantic boots. But he was helpless to turn away. Something had begun to stir in him that had nothing to do with him, rear-ing up lazily out of its primeval thicket, and soon it would be bucking, its shaggy throat pulsing with unearthly yips and whinnies, its horny hooves pawing the air. Lowering his eyes, he put all his strength into bringing it down.

"How did you get in here? Are you aware that a class is in progress?" The tall man in the smock spoke quietly, but his voice was tight with anger. Kriensky knew that this must be the instructor.

The students of art had turned away from their work and were gawking in his direction. From their easels, a ragtag army of body parts and bilious colors lunged forward, advancing on him. Kriensky felt dizzy and sick, but stood his ground. Olivia, too, was staring at him. Despite his disoriented state, he could see how she had changed. Her arms were crossed awkwardly in front of her body; she was bending over, hiding herself. Her hair had tumbled over her face, and with her mouth open and working, she looked almost savage. Like a cavewoman, Kriensky thought. A lump of clay that God had shaped in a hurry before going on to better things.

"Enough already!" he cried out to her. "This you don't need, pearls before swine—"

Words and laughter swirled around him. Someone shouted that Security was on the way—could such a thing be summoned?—and even before the men in uniform arrived, Kriensky was dimly aware of the Plutolike planet of Dane behind him, gesturing, explaining.

Then all the activity receded, or perhaps it was he who backed away. Dane's hand was on his arm, leading him out the door, and still he couldn't take his eyes off Olivia. She had wrapped herself in a faded chenille robe and was looking down at her lap.

"I don't know why you're so upset," said Arlene. "In some circles it's considered quite a respectable profession—certainly a step above striptease."

She had insisted that Kriensky spend the night at her house, and now she was making up the bottom bunk of Dane's bed. The sheets were patterned with different kinds of airplanes. Like everything else in the room, they were relics of Dane's early boyhood.

Kriensky sat in a low chair at the little desk, looking at a mobile of wire hanger birds that twisted in the warm breath of the heating vent. Dane rummaged through bureau drawers in search of some nightwear for his grandfather.

"If the pajamas won't fit, maybe you could find a large T-shirt," Arlene suggested. She gave a final pat to the blanket and looked around as if she hoped for some response from them. "This is a typical case of kill-the-messenger," she said at last. "I don't expect thanks for protecting your interests, but a little understanding would be nice. Believe me, it's no picnic bearing all the responsibility for this family. Not a day passes that I don't wish my mother were alive." She shut the door on their silence.

"Grandpa," Dane whispered. "She doesn't know I have this." From the back of a drawer he took out a striped bundle rolled like a sleeping bag. "My father's nightshirt. I sneaked it out of his dresser before she got rid of his things. When I was a kid, I used to sleep with it under my pillow."

Rosenthal had been a robust man, not tall but broad. The red-and-white stripes hung straight down from Kriensky's shrunken shoulders to his calves. It seemed fitting that, tonight of all nights, he would wear the dentist's cheerful camouflage for a wounded heart.

Dane put one leg on the ladder and swung himself into the top bunk.

"I'm not taking your bed, I hope," Kriensky said with effort.

"I always sleep high up," Dane said. "My dreams are more interesting from here. I don't know, maybe I just like to lord it over everyone."

Neither of them laughed. Dane pulled the string of the ceiling light.

"Goodnight, Grandpa," he said. In the darkness the words seemed to shimmer, tremulous with shared sorrow.

Kriensky lay on his back with his eyes shut. His breath came sparsely, but he tried to control the rasping until Dane was asleep. The room was stuffy. He felt as if he were in a box with the upper bunk pressing down on him like a lid. Rhythmically, he pulled in the sluggish air and eased it out, trying to hold it in his nostrils as it left him. With each breath he seemed to be chasing after oxygen that grew thinner. After a few minutes of struggle, he realized that he was climbing a hill.

When he reached the top he stood for a moment, gasping, letting his two sticks take his weight. The brown landscape spread out around him, interrupted only by groves of feather-shaped trees. He could just make out the path he had to follow, a jagged spiral a little paler than the surrounding earth, like a scar on a leg. He had a long way to go, but at least it was downhill.

Grunting, he started to walk again. His armpit ached with the dull persistence of an old war wound where the crutch prodded it. The dust of the road had gotten into his eyes and mouth and turned the white stripes of his nightshirt gray. He wanted a drink, but who knew where there was water? Who knew what he was doing in the middle of a desert in the first place? One foot followed another.

Halfway down, he looked out over the land falling away beneath him and glimpsed through the trees a small figure. It vanished in a curve of the road and, just when he was convinced he had imagined it, appeared again, luminous against a dark opening in the mountain. The whiteness of the figure made him wonder about man-headed horses. When he saw that it was two-legged, a woman, his heart began to thrum.

He tried to speed up his pace, but his feet were like scales weighted equally with all the years he had lived. Slowly and more slowly he struggled to reach her, inclining forward as if fighting a strong wind, certain that he must be moving in place. After endless minutes he came near enough to admire her dress, a loose, moon-colored gown with flowing sleeves. Kriensky was relieved to see that this bridal finery had slipped off one shoulder, and that the blazing tiara circling her head was slightly crooked. Her feet, as usual, were bare.

At last, he stood before her.

Smiling, she opened her arms, the wide sleeves falling back. He shut his eyes, suffused with shyness even here, but she did not embrace him. Instead, she bent her head and lit him like a candle.

He felt a sputtering at the top of his head as the flame flickered and caught. Brightness orbited his brow. For one millisecond their crowns mingled, gold on gold, before light turned to heat and sizzled toward his chest.

The Palm Tree of
Dilys Cathcart

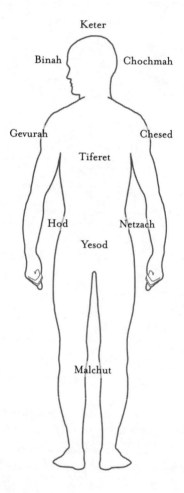

Forty-one has no character. It lacks the bracing shock of thirty, the gentle droop of thirty-five, the planted feet and thrust-out chin of forty. It leaves one in a kind of Limbo. It is no age to be at all.

These thoughts came to Dilys Cathcart with the rhythm of marching steps as she walked home from Grace Episcopal, her hymnal and Book of Common Prayer in a worn leather binder under her arm. She had been the church's organist for twelve years now, and had seen three rectors swept away in greater or lesser squalls, but she, Dilys, had ridden the waves. The fact that she was English was an asset in the job. Her accent; her rosy, slightly wilted, prettiness; her lace-collared florals and Easter hats that evoked images of Diana in the days before the late princess acquired chic—these counted as refinement in the Southern California city where she lived.

On last Sunday's walk, she'd reflected that her life had been ruled by tepid adjectives, and had counted them off one by one. Nice. Pleasant. Agreeable. Cheerful. Neat. Anywhere else such meditations would be depressing, but in San Diego on a bright weekend morning they seemed merely a mental percussion, background music for her forthright stride. "The sun," Alan had told her. "It takes the sting out of everything. You have no idea what a difference good weather makes." It had been true fifteen years ago and was true now. One couldn't really be depressed here. Frustrated, perhaps. Thwarted, yes. But liquid gold was always pouring from the sky, gilding the top of the head, inducing giddiness. She lifted her face to drink it in. If no one was looking, she would have raised her arms like a pagan.

She and Alan had been married so briefly that Dilys thought of their union as a literal rite of passage. If she had not run off with him back there—he had been man-of-all-work at her parents' guesthouse in Yorkshire—she would never have ended up here. He was the first Yank they had ever hired, a refugee from a small college in the Midwest. It was a gamble, her father warned; you couldn't be sure of these fast talkers, but the young man did seem to have a lot of "go" in him. That, precisely, was what Alan had. He stayed with them for half a chill spring and a rainy summer, learning quickly, managing the place like the business it was supposed to be, a godsend. And when the serious cold set in he bolted, luring her away with him to California and Oleander Court.

The apartments were new when they moved in. She had cried out when she saw them with a spontaneous delight that seemed precociously American, though she'd only been in the States for a week. The tiled roofs! The clusters of red and white flowers!—poisonous, Alan said, but still so lovely, so Mediterranean, the way they twined up the stucco. Even their cramped one-bedroom was a revelation; the walls, though thin, were a pristine white, and the faucets gleamed. "I'm never going to leave!" she'd told Alan, not imagining how faithfully she would keep her vow.

Oleander Court was a melting pot now, a first home for refugees of a different sort. Rounding the corner, she saw the Thai children playing in the meager courtyard and Ana Melendez waiting to tell her about the latest tyrannies of her silent sister.

"Dil-eez!" Ana was a short, round woman who always dressed for Mass in widow's black, although she never mentioned a husband. She pointed at Dilys's white Reeboks and giggled.

"Honestly, Ana," Dilys said. "I do keep a respectable pair of shoes at the church."

"So funny, with the dress." Ana spoke often of her wealthy family in Mexico, who had endowed her with a strong sense of propriety. "Listen, I have to hurry and make lunch. She sleeps all morning and goes to late Mass. Then she comes at me like a fiend if the food isn't ready the minute she gets back. I just wanted to tell you that the Jew came to your door."

"Oh, dear, what can he want? Do you suppose the piano students are disturbing him, or his poor wife?"

Once there had been a number of Jews at Oleander Court, mostly young families with one or two children. The Orthodox synagogue was only a few blocks away, and on Friday evenings she would see the fathers walking to services, holding the hands of tiny sons whose shoulders were prematurely rounded, as if the skullcaps they wore were made of stone. But they had all moved on to larger quarters in newer subdivisions, and now only one couple was left: a hulking, bearded man and his wheelchair-bound wife. They lived in the ground-floor apartment beneath hers, but Dilys rarely saw them. One Saturday she had glimpsed them from the window as the man wheeled his wife across the courtyard. The woman, in spite of her infirmity, was as bright a figure as her husband was somber, wearing a long, patterned dress and a Gypsyish scarf over her hair. Intrigued, Dilys had watched until they were out of sight, thinking for some reason of Mimi in *La Bohème* and her lingering, romantic, tuneful death.

"Maybe they have a law against music," Ana said. "These Kosher Jews have laws against everything in the world. Well, if they don't like it, let them stay among their own kind. You have to make a living."

Dilys half-expected the bearded man to be lurking in the shadows as she unlocked her door, but the hall was empty. Her living room was untidy, scattered with empty cups and sheet music. As always the piano loomed, a brooding presence from a damp climate; her parents had shipped it at great expense when it became clear that she wasn't returning to England. She had taken the gesture for a form of disinheritance. A more flamboyant family might have resorted to phone calls, threats, tearful confrontations, baroque declamations. But Dilys came from a long line of humble clerics, suppliants at the gates of life. Resignation was ingrained in them. There had been letters full of crabbed phrases with key words capitalized in eighteenth-century style—"I never imagined," her mother wrote, "that a daughter of mine would be a Concubine"—and then the piano.

She picked up the cups and put them in the sink. Usually she grabbed Sunday lunch on the run before Ryan Rodriguez arrived at two to pummel Chopin, but he was away with his family on midwinter break. As if winter had any meaning here, she thought, opening the fridge. And yet, February was February, one had all of the emotions and none of the excuses. She almost wished for heavy-handed Ryan. Why was it that days *gaped* so this time of year?

Leftover salad and half a fish taco—limp remnants of a single woman's larder. A twinge of self-pity caught her unawares, threatening to turn into something else. She set the salad on the table beside the Sunday paper and began to eat right out of the container, forking up the wilted lettuce briskly to forestall what was coming. The Style section was a good antidote, with its breezy mix of food and fashion, decorating hints, and celebrity gossip. "Moorish Influence Seen in Bedroom," she read, but no, it was too late, already her eyes were filling and the familiar pinch of salt was in her nostrils. She was having an attack of Colin and Emma.

Alan's defection no longer pained her. Some part of her had always known he would move on. But she was haunted by two small ghosts who ambushed her on weekends, perversely refusing to fade, seeming to grow more tangible with the passing years. Tanned, athletic, rambunctious little Americans—*visits were trying, her parents were not used to the noise, but how well the children looked in their filigreed frames on the mantel. "That Colin!" her father exclaimed, fond from a safe distance. "Quite a ball player he is, always* with a bat in his hand." "That Emma," chorused her mother. "A beautiful thing to see her dance. A little Pavlova." For her sins she owed them these two splendid grandchildren. And she had failed to provide.

Tears were coursing down her cheeks now. "Silly woman," she hissed to herself. "Silly, foolish cow." Pressing a napkin to her face, she staggered to the piano. "Where e'er You Walk" was on the stand, but she didn't want Handel, she needed something sunny and lilting. Mozart. *The Marriage of Figaro*. Without pausing to look for the music, she plunged in.

> *Se vuol ballare,*
> *Signor Contino,*
> *Se vuol ballare,*
> *Signor Contino,*
> *Il chitarrino*
> *Le suonerò . . .*

Extraordinary how physical the lifting was. As if she were a light-boned child and some jolly uncle had swept her up in his arms and waltzed her around the room. Her fingers hit the exclamation points of the last notes and she started in again, singing this time. She had just raised her hands from the keys before launching into *"Voi che sapete"* when she heard a knock.

Damn, she thought, this is all I need. Probably Ana had been right, there was some sort of law. She would have to be kind but firm. Dilys smoothed her hair with her hands. "Yes. Who is it?"

"Mendel Krakauer. From downstairs." The voice, low and

hollow, seemed to have bounced off mountain peaks to reach her.

As she opened the door, the Jew stepped back from it. In spite of his retreat, he filled the small hall. He was taller even than he had appeared from her window, broad-bellied but not fat. A black felt hat sat squarely on his head, making an odd contrast to his open-collared shirt and baggy cotton trousers.

"How do you do, Mr. Krakauer. Dilys Cathcart." She offered her hand in the frank American way she'd taken so long to get used to, and was startled when he drew back even farther. Perhaps there was a law against touching, too? "If this is about the music, I really am terribly sorry. I'll try to play more softly myself, but my pupils—most of them don't have the control, you see. No little Vladimir Horowitzes, alas. Perhaps I could make some adjustments in my schedule, if there are times you and your wife don't want to be disturbed."

Oh, God, what was she doing? Apologizing, accommodating herself. Why hadn't she waited until Krakauer told her what he wanted? And why had she mentioned Horowitz? Surely he would see that she was trying to ingratiate herself by naming a Jew, she could just as well have said Van Cliburn. One of her blushes was rising like mercury from her chest to her neck.

Mendel Krakauer appeared to be meditating on her. Breath swished loudly in and out of his nostrils. "The music?" he said at last. "The music we like. My wife in particular, home all day, it makes a change for her. The music, in fact, is why I am here."

"Oh, are you thinking of taking lessons? I've had several adult pupils. No one at the moment, though." The last had been Lloyd Pillbeam, whose bony thigh had edged closer and closer to hers on the piano bench.

"Lessons, no. What I am wanting is more in the nature of . . . you could say, translation. Excuse me, this is very difficult to explain."

"Well, then, would you like to come in?" After the attempt at handshaking, Dilys knew to stand aside. Still, Krakauer hesitated, taking a long, sonorous breath before stepping over the threshold. When she reached behind him to shut the door, he froze. "Leave it open. Please!"

Unsettled, Dilys gestured toward the only chair that looked large enough to hold his bulk. Could the man believe she had designs on him? She must be very businesslike, then. "Translation, you were saying . . ."

To her immense relief, Krakauer sat. "I'm grabbing at straws with that name, I don't know what else to call it. I'm a butcher, not a scholar. But where is it written that a butcher should think only about meat?"

"Nowhere, I'm sure!" she said. He really did look most extraordinary, sitting with his hat on at the edge of the orange barrel chair she'd rescued from the recycling. There was a heaviness to his presence that she associated with age, but the skin above his beard was fresh, and his lips amid the dark whiskers were as red and curved as a woman's. A butcher's lips, she thought: the blood so close to the surface.

"I work at the Kosher market, Lipschutz's, also known as the Three Block Market because it's three blocks from the shul. Maybe you know it, maybe not. My day is long, and the work—what can I say, it puts food on the table but it doesn't nourish my soul. So, when I have a few minutes, I sit on a stool in the corner of the locker and I study. A few months ago I found this in Weisgal's." He reached into his pocket and brought out a small blue book. "To be honest, the title caught my eye because my wife's name was in it. *Tomer Devorah.* In English, *The Palm Tree of Deborah.* By Reb Moshe Cordovero, Ramak for short."

"Deborah." Dilys flipped frantically through mental file cards to the Bible studies of her youth. "Wasn't she the one who lopped off some fellow's head?"

The butcher smiled, revealing a space between his front teeth. "You're thinking of Judith. Devorah was a judge. She sat under the palm tree and the people of Israel came to her to settle their disagreements. The funny thing is, the book has nothing to do with her. It's about the attributes of the Holy One, Blessed Be He."

"Attributes?"

"Qualities. What God is like, the little we can know of Him. Twice I read it before I understood. Ramak is saying that if we imitate the Holy One we will be sitting in the shade of the palm, refreshing ourselves with the sweet dates. Even if we happen to be in a meat locker, with carcasses all around us and the smell of death in our nose."

A glaze of misgiving spread over Dilys. Jews didn't proselytize, did they? She had always respected them for that. They didn't go from door to door like Mormons or Jehovah's Witnesses, with their large black Bibles and their tracts. She shot a furtive glance at the blue book. "Forgive me, Mr. Krakauer, but I don't understand what this has to do with music."

"Patience, please. The difficult part is coming. How can I explain to you what I can't even explain to myself?" He

sighed noisily and leaned so far forward that the barrel
chair's back legs left the floor. "A month ago, maybe, I was
beginning again with the *sefirot,* excuse me, the attributes I
mentioned. I had gotten no further than the first one—there
are ten, each one a part of the body, together a suit of flesh
covering what God in His greatness conceals—when suddenly
I hear melody. Not a little tune but a whole chorus, the
music is carrying me away. Where, who knows, I'm all ears,
the rest of me is sleeping. I wake up in the locker with the
music in my head. Since then, every week another concert.
My problem is how to preserve what I heard. I never studied.
I don't know notes. This is where you come in."

"You want me to 'translate,' as you say, the music that is
in your head?" Keep your voice calm, she told herself. The
man is quite mad, but probably harmless.

"I'm no singer, but I'll do my best, and you'll take down.
What could be more simple? You don't have to understand
what the music is about, only which note is which. I'll pay, of
course. Whatever the not-Horowitzes pay, more if you ask.
I'm not a rich man, but how often does the Master of the
Universe sing to a butcher?"

Dilys realized with a shock that Krakauer saw her as the
missionaries of her childhood had seen the African basket-
makers featured in their slide shows—pagan, even primitive,
but endowed by the Creator with a useful manual dexterity.
She was a technician to him, nothing more. The thought
amused her. "I'm afraid it's a bit more complicated than
that," she said. "Surely the most sensible thing would be to
go to your cantor."

He put up a hand, thick and raw-looking, to stop her.
"What am I to the cantor? To any of them? A nothing. A

Philistine. Good for pouring salt on meat. Such gifts are not supposed to come to men like me."

"I'm sure that isn't true—" she started to say, but he took no notice of her.

"When we came here from New York, my wife was already advanced with the MS, it was for the climate that we came. In the beginning I thought California was the Holy Land—fruit and flowers, what's not to like, and on my days off I could wheel my wife by the ocean. The shul is friendly, but soon I see what's behind the sunshine. Hypocrisy, backbiting. The women would come to visit my wife while I was at work, bringing their children and their covered dishes. A *mitzvah*, they called it. A good deed. For a while it's a contest who can earn most points on the butcher's wife. They're sitting in her living room, talking over her head—who's doing this, who's wearing that—and she's looking at the children, a knife twisting in her heart. I saw what it was doing to her and put a stop to it. That they didn't appreciate."

Dilys listened quietly. Hadn't she experienced the same when her father lost his church? The machinations of the vestry. The women of the parish bringing casseroles and condescension when the family made the move into the guesthouse, their curiosity masked under a veneer of sympathy. These things, apparently, had no denomination.

"I'd be happy to help, if I can," she told him. "Shall we give it a try next Sunday? At three?"

After Krakauer left, Dilys went again to the piano and rested her hands lightly on the keys. How strange to have an audience, unseen but attentive. She felt almost like a missionary herself, sending notes down to the musically deprived. The butcher's presence still emanated from the chair behind her. A Philistine, he had said. Not that, but not lute-playing King David, either. More like one of the rough foot soldiers who'd done the dirty work. She remembered giggling with the deacon's daughter, Margaret, over the marriage present that Saul had required of David. The two of them had made a skipping rhyme of it,

> *One hundred Philistine foreskins*
> *One hundred Philistine foreskins*
> *One hundred Philistine foreskins*
> *All in a pile!*

their reedy voices getting higher and higher as they jumped, until they'd collapsed on the ground in a tangle of ropes, orgasmic with hilarity. Naughty girls they had been, irreverant as only the children of the church can be. Thinking of it now she blushed again, imagining at her back Krakauer's palm held up like a policeman's, the thick fingers spread.

KETER

It had not been a good week. On Monday there had been the notice from her landlord about the rise in rent, and Mrs. Rodriguez had called, as if on cue, with the news that Ryan would not be continuing with lessons because they interfered with soccer practice. Then the letter from Aunt Esme, who only wrote at Christmas: Dilys's father wasn't well, her mother was losing her memory; they ought to be in a nursing home, but who would pay for that? she wondered. And only yesterday Dilys had been creaming her face when a dark speck appeared in the white—a tiny irregular blemish on her right temple. Fear had pierced her so quickly that she'd clutched the edge of the sink for support. How often had the doctor warned about sunscreen and hats?

All the way home from church, the litany of anxieties repeated like a fugue in her head. She rushed right past the Melendez sisters as they chatted on the courtyard's single bench (could the neat, composed Silvia really be the demon that Ana had described?), giving a vague wave in answer to the question Ana called after her: "What did the Jew want, Dil-eez?"

What, indeed? Often, during the week, she had looked out the window hoping to catch a glimpse of Krakauer and his wife. As the hard realities overtook her, last Sunday's visit seemed more and more fantastical, Krakauer himself like an apparition, too exotic for her mild Anglican dreams. Yet whenever she glanced at the orange chair a physicality arose from it, invisible but potent, and she felt the butcher's weighty presence, heard his metronomic breathing marking time as she bustled around the flat.

Probably he wouldn't even show up. Dilys arrived at that conclusion as she rushed through lunch, straightened up the apartment, exchanged her sneakers for a pair of dressy sandals that could be worn over hose. Naked toes—would they be considered provocative? Such a strange new world, with its own laws and customs. And he must find her equally outlandish. Who could blame him for having second thoughts about sharing his musical revelations with a gentile?

At 2:45 she went to the piano, and began to play, for lack of inspiration, the waltz she had been working on with Ryan. Once, twice, three times she went through it—the tinkly melody, the parchment-and-tea-rose quality her mother had loved—before checking her watch. 3:05. She had been right, then, he had reconsidered. Well, so much for that. Another pupil would have to be found to fill Ryan's slot, but for now she might as well take the Volks down to Mission Beach, treat herself to a gelato. Her thoughts moved along briskly but her limbs refused to budge. She sat with her head bowed, hands in her lap, staring at the keys.

How long she held that pose she didn't know—no more than fifteen or twenty minutes, but long enough that the knock, when it came, made her jump.

Mendel Krakauer stood in the doorway. "Last week was better," he said.

"Last week? What do you mean?" She felt fogged, as if she'd been awakened from a sound sleep.

"The music. This we didn't like so much. Too brittle, my wife said. Like a spoon against a glass."

"Yes, well, it is Chopin, he really is quite good, you know." The accuracy of the comment irritated her as much as his certainty of tone. "The fact is, you're late, Mr. Krakauer. I—I have a schedule to keep."

"My apologies. This afternoon my mother-in-law arrived from New York. For Devorah Leah, to give her some help while I'm at work. Up all night on the red-eye, right away she wants to know where everything goes, how it works. Talking, talking, I couldn't get away. Believe me, I was looking forward . . ." He stopped, as if he had said too much.

Devorah Leah. The name sounded like an endearment one might croon to a fretting child. "Of course. Completely understandable," she said. "I'm quite free today, actually, so no harm done. Shall we get started?"

Although Dilys was careful to leave the door open, Krakauer appeared nervous once he was inside. He headed first for the orange chair, paused, and moved stiffly to the piano, where he stood at attention as if awaiting the lifting of a baton.

"Why don't you just sing it through?" Dilys said, circling around him to the bench. "I'll use the tape recorder, if you don't mind, and then I can start plinking it out on the piano." She smiled at him encouragingly as she smiled at her students.

The butcher licked his red lips. "Could I have, please, a little water?"

Water. Neutral, therefore safe even from dietary laws. Testing the waters indeed—if he could accept this, perhaps she could offer a cup of tea. But when she tried to hand him the glass, his fingers recoiled as if from fire. In the tips of her own fingers she felt a charge, brief but unmistakable. She set the glass on top of the piano, and watched as he picked it up and drained it, tilting the bottom to get the last drops as her father had tilted his nightly glass of whiskey.

"*Keter*," Krakauer said. "Crown of attributes, highest of the high. In terms of the human body, the skull. A shell only, you think, but inside is the whole brain. God in His compassion bends His head to listen to us. From Him we learn to bow. We learn humility." He gazed downward, clasped his hands as if praying, and began to sing in a faltering tenor that was nothing like his speaking voice. The melody emerged in a thin stream, hoarse and halting at first, then stronger, fuller, his throat opening as his eyes closed. Vaguely Middle Eastern, she thought, that sinuous curving line that reminded her of the swaying of charmed snakes or the belly dancer's churning hips. Krakauer had begun to sway himself, his upper body gently oscillating above his planted feet. He reached for the upper registers, rising higher than she would have thought possible. The music soared, reverberating in his throat, an ululation. Dropped to a low keening and dwindled to nothing.

In the silence, neither of them spoke. Dilys's mind was empty, for once, of its store of polite phrases. Krakauer, still standing by the piano with his eyes shut, appeared to be in a trance. Dilys listened to his breathing and imagined that her own made a delicate counterpoint.

"Remarkable," she said at last, "that you've remembered so exactly."

"It's like it's printed. Burned in." His voice was hollow again, as if the marrow had been scooped out.

"I never would have thought 'humility' if you hadn't told me. The music is so triumphant. In England, being humble is something you're born to—a kind of destiny, if you know what I mean. Of course, things aren't quite so rigid now."

A picture came to her of her mother bending over the guests' tables to remove the plates. "Was it nice?" she always asked in the baa-ing tone she used when talking to her betters, both pleading and restrained. The food itself, in its blandness, its softness, could not evoke anything so radical as pleasure. It had been prepared to pass smoothly through the digestive system without calling attention to itself. And yet her mother had waited for the murmured "Very nice," as if it were an exoneration. However low she had fallen—the husband with the little problem, the demotion from pastor's wife to innkeeper—she could still set a refined table. Her cooking did not give offense.

Krakauer lumbered to the orange chair and dropped into it. "Here is not so different. When I first asked to marry my wife, what a furor! Not only from her family—they were making other arrangements, that I could understand—but my own parents. Who did I think I was, a butcher, the son of a butcher, to aspire to a girl like that? To see her dance was an experience. A brightness like a flame. Every eye was on her. She could have had an educated man, a scholar. Even I thought I had a nerve."

"But you triumphed, didn't you?" Dilys could hear the music reach and soar. "The meek shall inherit the earth."

"Meek? I was crafty, a serpent. Her other suitors were all over her. I held my feelings in, concealed myself like God, and in the end she came to me. The humility was all hers—a man like me, from what height could I lower myself? But the Holy One, Blessed Be He, brought justice out of it. She was stricken, and now . . . I stoop, I carry, I serve."

The last words were barely audible. The butcher had sunk so deep into himself that Dilys could contemplate him openly. Now she knew what she had felt when their fingers almost touched, what she had sensed emanating from the chair in his absence. *The force of what he held back.* All the passion that had been set free in the music was boxed and bound in the man; the little that escaped infused the atmosphere like steam. She remembered reading, years ago, about athletes in ancient Greece who withheld their semen until the competitions were over for fear of dissipating their power. Krakauer was like that, she decided. Devorah Leah—the fiery, the vivid—must have sensed it, too.

Already the afternoon sun was fading from the room. Not even half past four, and she would have to turn on some lights. "Perhaps we should begin to review," she said softly. "Your family will be expecting you back soon, and we have so much to do."

Krakauer stood, immediately attentive. "What am I talking? The music loosened my tongue."

CHOCHMAH, BINAH

The worst part was explaining the bandage. "A nasty little mole," Dilys said when people asked. "Skin cancer, in all probability," the doctor had pronounced, after slicing it from her numbed face to send to the lab. "But not the bad kind, I don't think. Consider it a warning." Strange to see the black speck disembodied, floating in a vial. If only all our troubles could be so easily removed, Dilys thought. Still, the fragment with its waving tentacles of tissue seemed ominous. She'd left the office feeling like puff pastry, an assemblage of fragile layers.

At choir practice on Wednesday evening, the Lenten music suited her mood. They had begun rehearsing for the annual Easter concert, but she was not up to glorious risings. Passiontide was as high as she could get tonight, that hoisting up and stapling to the Tree of Life. The directions for "O sacred head, sore wounded" read *Solemnly, but not too slow.* As if in mockery, the choir dragged along at a funereal pace, turning the piece into a dirge. She cut them off in the middle of a phrase. "He isn't *dead* yet, you know. Where's the passion, you people? This is God hanging here—do try to feel it!"

You people. She sounded as shrill and querulous as an

Old Testament prophet trying to goose the indifferent masses. The choristers looked back at her, reproachful. They had given up their Wednesday nights for this; they could have been watching *The West Wing*. But she thought she saw a glimmer in Lloyd Pillbeam's eye. "Still waters," he had said once, winking, all but accusing her of turbulent depths.

Back home, Dilys glanced at the TV but went instead to the piano, where staff paper was spread out "like a patient etherised upon a table," she thought. The line, retrieved from a youthful flirtation with Eliot, was suddenly in her head again. All week she had been looking at notes and seeing bodies. The butcher had told her that each attribute corresponded to a part of the human form. As she added to the pages of chicken-scratch, listening to a section of the recording and painstakingly searching out the notes, a fancy had come to her that she was molding a face on a skull, gently palpating its features into existence.

She thought of how Krakauer's face had contorted when he was reaching for a high note. The sight of his twisted features had stirred her so deeply that she'd flushed and looked away, Now, looking at his music on the page, Dilys remembered the first time she and Alan made love. It had been her first time with anyone. Having finally succeeded in sneaking her into his room at the guesthouse, Alan was laboring away at her when his face seized up in a teeth-baring grimace, and he gasped. Dilys had been so frightened that she forgot her aching legs and the drama unfolding between them. "What is the matter?" she'd cried. "Are you all right? Is it something I've done?" She would never know if the deep groan that issued from him was triggered by laughter or rage, only that its substance was liquid and warm and that it flooded her until she spilled over. "God, you really don't know anything, do you?" Alan had said afterward. She'd felt such a fool that she wept, and he was kind then, cradling her in his arms and explaining how the pleasure was so intense that it was like pain. But whenever they had a disagreement, he would put on a mincing falsetto and ask, "Is it something I've done?"

Heat crept up her neck again. Wasn't this what love had been for her—a deep embarrassment tinged with excitement? For all her naïveté, she had been thrilled to see competent, masterful Alan in the grip of a force larger than himself. And Ken, the biology teacher who'd discoursed so knowledgeably on the mysteries of the pituitary gland, and Harvey, the accountant who'd helped with her taxes. A barbed tenderness had swelled in her to see these able men rendered helpless as babes, and to know that it was, after all, something she'd done. She'd said good-bye to all that long ago, renounced the messy bed for the pure sensuality of music. Until Krakauer, bodies and notes had been separate realms in her life, as neatly segregated as the beds of flowers in her mother's garden. The butcher was certainly no Don Giovanni, but Dilys knew that he had been transported to a place of agonized ecstasy, and music had carried him there.

The notations blurred before her eyes. She was tired, ready for bed. All these thoughts of passion, God's and man's, had exhausted her. Instead of getting up, she rested her fingers on the piano keys and waited for the anticipatory vibration that she sometimes felt before pressing down. Everything was in the music, her teacher had taught her. One need only become skillful enough to draw it out.

Sunday, the first of March, brought a barely discernible softening of the air. All the seasons were subtle here. Over the years Dilys had become attuned to the gentle hints that signaled change: the drier heat of summer, the modest fall of leaves from trees that never turned color, and now, after the mildest of winters, new bloom. In the shower she anointed herself with lavender bath oil and decided to wear linen—the long robin's-egg dress from two Easters ago and the wide-brimmed straw hat that went with it.

"Well, aren't you a picture!" the rector's wife said. "Blue Girl. That's who you remind me of." The choir was in fine voice after their dismal rehearsal, and Dilys was aware of admiring glances from several of the men. Women, too. She was grateful that her sexuality was of the unthreatening variety, no heavy musk but a delicate herbaceous aura, pleasing to all. With each motion of her arms, the fragrance of the lavender wafted up, faintly sweet and desiccated, like the scent that was said to arise from the bodies of the saints.

A grace seemed to be over all her movements. At the coffee hour she worked the room deftly, lighting just long enough to exchange pleasantries and ask sensitive questions, but avoiding conversational gulches. Martin Runyon, a banker recently separated from his wife, chatted her up about the dearth of chamber music in the area and hinted in his hearty way that they ought to "take in" a concert one day. She caught Lloyd Pillbeam eyeing her, ready to pounce, but managed to elude him with a wave, a smile, and a hasty exit.

There hadn't been time to change to trainers for the walk back. No matter, heels were more suitable today. She would move with the wind as nature intended her to, tall and swaying like the palm tree, stately as the biblical Devorah. For once, not a thought was in her head. The spring breeze had blown away the intensity of the last few days. She was aware of her body within the loose linen tube: the discreet bounce of her small breasts, the inflection of her waist, the easy swing of her legs. Was this what it meant to be at home in one's skin?

The whole population of Oleander Court was out this afternoon. Boys careered back and forth on skateboards, mothers exposed their doughy infants to the sun, men in tank tops tossed baseballs to one another or sat in folding chairs smoking cigars. Dilys smiled on them all. Ana, occupying her bench like a large black bug, patted the seat beside her. "Can the fine lady sit a minute or is she rushing off to a party?"

"Heavens, no. Business as usual, I'm afraid."

"You look very elegant today. A pity to waste it on the little ones. Or maybe they are not so little?" Ana did some complex choreography with her eyebrows. "We heard strange sounds coming from your apartment last Sunday. Chanting. A-a-a-a-a-a-h. I didn't mind, it's not my affair, but *she* complained. 'What has Dil-eez got up there, a sick cow?' On and on she went."

A spectacle saved Dilys the necessity of answering. The butcher's wife was being wheeled through the courtyard by a slender woman in a burgundy suit, a Garboesque hat slouched over her brow. If a moment before there had been a buzz of activity, now there was only the slight whirring of the chair and the tick of the stranger's high heels as she made her way to the gate. Devorah Leah, a chic flower child in a batik print, smiled dreamily at the soft red shoes that adorned her feet.

Boots of Spanish leather. Dilys had been staring as shamelessly as anyone else, taken by the odd charm of the sight. Not until the women were outside the gate did she realize that this must be the talkative mother-in-law. She had been picturing a thick-ankled Russian type in a housedress and babushka. Who would have imagined this svelte, stylish creature who had cut through the gawking crowd like a knife through butter?

In a kind of dream herself, she said good-bye to Ana and walked slowly toward the apartment. She thought of how attentively Krakauer had bent over the wheelchair, hovering above his wife's head and looking down into her face. From the few comments he had made, she'd gotten the impression that his entire weekend was devoted to his wife. Perhaps he was relishing his free time, but she couldn't shake the feeling that he had been supplanted.

After lunch Dilys sat down at the piano, conscious that she was about to play for Krakauer alone. Her buoyant Vivaldi mood had given way to elegy. She doodled for a few minutes before settling into *Pavane for a Dead Princess,* a piece she loved as much for its evocative title as for its melody. Then she meandered into Satie's *Gymnopédies*, dropping the notes one by one like crumbs in a forest. She imagined the butcher following them to her door.

When the knock came, she had just completed one of her eloquent pauses. "Excuse me," Krakauer said. "I'm not interrupting, I hope. Every time I think it's over, you start again."

"Oh, no need to wait. I'm just amusing myself with these

little concerts, thinking out loud, so to speak. This particular piece is awfully slow, a bit of a meditation, really."

"I thought maybe one of the not-Horowitzes forgot to practice." The butcher grinned, allowing her another glimpse of the beguiling space between his teeth. A boyish thing, somehow, an aperture in his seriousness. "I came early, to make up for last week. My wife is away for the afternoon."

Dilys stepped aside to let him pass. "Yes, I saw her—with her mother, I suppose? Quite an attractive lady, not the typical mother-in-law at all, such old dragons they can be." Why, why did she babble on like this? What did she know of mothers-in-law? She had never even met her own. "I hope you haven't given up some family excursion to be here."

He gave a dry laugh. "I wasn't invited. My wife's mother calls it 'giving me a hand.' After we married, she wanted nothing to do with us. We called, she hung up the phone. Now that Devorah Leah is sick, she's the loving mother again, come to rescue her from the mistake she made, meaning yours truly. Suddenly it's the Gang of Two."

"But Devorah—your wife—must resent the intrusion."

Krakauer walked blindly to the center of the living room, almost tripping over the small glass coffee table where, earlier, Dilys had set the completed transcription at a rather self-conscious angle alongside a bunch of violets in a cream pitcher.

"She's torn! Who could blame her?" He seemed to be speaking to himself. "Devorah Leah's heart is with me, this I don't doubt, but already my mother-in-law is putting on the pressure. Come home for a couple weeks, see your friends, see the New York doctors. Two weeks turns into a month, six months, all the time they're working on her. In her mind she's thinking, if I hadn't disobeyed my parents, maybe God wouldn't have punished me." He shrugged, looking at her quickly before turning his eyes away. "The so-called dragon who's staying in my house—no wonder she's making me nervous."

"So often," Dilys said, "the things we fear never come to pass, do they?" This was such a blatant lie that she felt herself coloring up. "Perhaps—perhaps you'd like some tea?"

"Water, please. My throat is dry. Usually I don't talk so much."

She presented it on a tray like an offering, and waited at a handmaiden's respectful distance while he drank, replaced the glass, and stationed himself by the piano. The water, she saw, would be part of their ritual, a way to separate the music from their ordinary lives.

Krakauer cleared his throat. "This week is *chochmah* and *binah,* also a Gang of Two. Mind and heart. Wisdom and understanding. Right brain, left brain. Put them together you get the whole head, meaning knowledge."

"All these pairs." Dilys said. "I keep thinking of that silly song—love and marriage going together like the horse and carriage."

"Male and female is in there, too. The Holy One in His mercy shoots down His enormous thoughts that the whole universe couldn't contain, we open ourselves to receive. Without this arrangement, we would be lumps of clay like Adam started out. Slabs of meat, if you'll excuse a professional reference. How much can we take in? A particle. A micromillimeter. But even that little is enough to plant life in us."

"What an inspiring thought!" Dilys had taken her place

on the piano bench with the tape recorder. She was aware, though it seemed sacrilegious, of the flattering light pouring in from the window behind her.

The butcher hesitated. "Since the male-female subject came up, I should say that I heard the music also in two parts. Deep voice, high voice. Braided together, so to speak. . . ." His words trailed off. "I'll sing one, then the other. It won't be the same, but what else can I do?"

"Maybe, after we've gone through the parts, I could attempt the soprano?" Dilys had used her meekest voice, but the suggestion sounded brazen. "It would be awfully rough, of course, but at least you'd have some idea of how the music sounds in the—well, in the world, if you know what I mean."

Krakauer's eye went for the first time to the papers on the coffee table, then to Dilys herself. He nodded, as if he had at last grasped an obscure connection. "Strange," he mumbled, "to see this outside of my head."

She waited for him to say more, but he began to hum instead. A low, vibrating throat-sound as cold and impersonal as the whirring of a machine. Gradually the sound moved to the front of his mouth, where it took on color. His lips trembled, then opened, and the music poured forth, hypnotic, atonal, strangely enveloping in spite of its abstraction. An image came to her of a cone widening out, entangling her in its spirals. When it ended, as abruptly as it had begun, she felt abandoned.

Krakauer stood in place with his eyes shut, his neck arched at an odd angle. They had both been left high and dry, Dilys thought. She had often heard the phrase "music of the spheres," but who could have imagined that the reality was so lonely—as if one had been spun around and around and set down, dazed, on the fissured surface of another planet. She closed her eyes, thinking to join the butcher in his solitude, and was not surprised to find tears gathering behind the lids. Minutes passed before he began to sing again, the melody creeping up on her from a distance.

A lullaby this time. Weeping tones, pulsing sweetness. A cradle song from the old lost Europe that she knew only as chunky names in her father's war stories. But who was being sung to sleep? God Himself, perhaps? She thought of a Pietà, Mary clasping the dead Christ in her arms, looking down on her son as if he still suckled at her breast. In the midst of life we are in death. *I am sorry,* the music wailed. But also, the heart-eating cry of mothers: *How could you do this to me—to me?*

Only when they united the parts, hours later, did she understand how the second attribute embraced the first, warmed and humanized it, made pure thought comprehensible by sheltering it in flesh. Krakauer turned brick-red when she began to sing *binah*. His own voice broke off, leaving her soprano to quaver amateurishly in the silence, but he joined in again—by force of will, it seemed to her. And then the music took over.

It was almost eleven when they finished. Their eyes, which had been fixed on each other while they sang, looked away with difficulty. The butcher gazed at his feet. Dilys contemplated the painted clock on the wall. A tenth-anniversary gift from the church, its face was decorated with wisteria vines, which wove in and out of the numerals in a manner that seemed to her intrusive.

"Just look at the time!" she said. "Your wife must have come back hours ago. Whatever will the poor woman think?"

"She will have heard the singing," Krakauer said. His voice was hoarse, and he looked so haggard that Dilys felt a surge of pity at the thought of what awaited him in the apartment below.

He picked up the transcription from the coffee table. Nestling it in the crook of his arm, he shambled toward the doorway, breathing audibly as if the effort cost him. In the hallway he turned.

"What happened here?" He pointed to his temple.

For a moment, Dilys had no idea what he was talking about. Slowly she reentered her body, feeling it close around her with a leaden solemnity. "Oh, that," she said. "Just a bit of skin cancer. Not the bad kind. We don't think."

Krakauer nodded. He turned again and headed for the stairs.

Dilys was so exhausted that she could barely find the strength to undress. But once in bed, a breeze massaging her from the open window, she discovered that her mind would not relax. What had it been like, singing with the butcher? An exchange of ideas, a dialogue without words. "The best sex," Alan had told her, "is a kind of talking." Rather a one-sided conversation, Dilys had thought at the time, but now she could almost understand what he meant. She put her hand to her mouth and giggled. Pairs of stick figures were passing across her tired brain—Krakauer's Gangs of Two, copulating jerkily like animated skeletons. Put them together you get knowledge, he'd said. But knowledge wasn't always a good thing, was it? Look where it had gotten Adam and Eve. There would be plenty of time to think of that tomorrow. Smiling, she slept.

CHESED, GEVURAH, TIFERET

The radio, tuned to the city's only classical station, was supposed to wake Dilys up. Instead, it furnished background music for her dream. She stood in the cloister of an ancient building, watching from behind one of the pillared arches as Devorah Leah was borne on a pallet across a medieval square. The faces of the bearers and a few mournful followers were indistinct, the butcher nowhere to be seen. Devorah Leah was as still as a figure on a tomb. Her eyes were closed, her face set in the same tranquil, bemused smile she had worn as she crossed Oleander Court with her mother. Dilys leaned out from the shadowed arcade like a predatory bird clinging to its perch. Hungry to see. Hungry.

She woke up ravenous, her nerve ends tingling. In the shower, she remembered—with a certain relief at the logic of it—that she'd had no dinner the night before.

Most mornings Dilys ate lightly, but today she took out eggs, bacon, marmalade, actual butter rather than the canola-oil margarine she'd virtuously been using. She felt the need of solid, heavy food, a real English breakfast to anchor her to earth after yesterday's singing. The dream hadn't helped matters. Even now, standing in her kitchen breaking eggs into a bowl, she could conjure up the slow procession and her own yearning curiosity. Oh, she knew what Freud would say. She was so starved for intimacy that her duet with Krakauer had led to a subconscious wish to hasten his wife's end. Vigorously she beat her denial into the eggs, along with a sprinkling of herbs. Devorah Leah was a lovely, poignant figure, and the butcher's devotion to her was part of his appeal. Not even in the secret corners of her mind could Dilys harbor such wicked thoughts.

She peeled off three strips of bacon and laid them in the hot pan. American bacon never seemed quite right to her: too delicate, nothing like the thick rashers her mother had fried for Sunday breakfast at home. Well, the smell was the thing, wasn't it? The same with coffee—why hadn't she thought of making a pot this morning? It would have served her better than tea. She turned away from the stove to slice a tomato and some bread. Behind her the bacon sputtered, filling the kitchen with its pungent aroma. She inhaled appreciatively and her gorge rose, so suddenly that her mind still registered pleasure. Dilys managed to turn the gas off before lurching to the sink, where she retched but could bring nothing up.

As soon as she felt steady enough, she opened a window. Looking away, she slid the half-cooked bacon into the garbage and filled the pan with hot, soapy water. The package, just opened, lay on the counter with its contents exposed—pink slices neatly seamed in white, a pattern she had always found pleasing. As if obeying some natural law, she pitched that away, too. She was quite well now, and still wolfishly hungry. In an absence of thought she cooked the eggs, forking them up straight from the pan, and ate two thick slices of toast without bothering with a plate.

The oddity of her behavior didn't strike her until she sat at the table, warming her clammy hands around a mug of tea. She knew that pregnant women developed aversions to foods they liked. It could be that the same symptoms prevailed at the other end of the reproductive cycle, but wasn't she awfully young for the Change? A food allergy was more likely. Or worse, some dire signal from her immune system. Instinctively, she put her hand to her temple, remembering that she would hear from the dermatologist soon.

Last night's duet was waiting in the recorder, but Dilys wasn't ready to let the genie out of the bottle just yet. She was too jumpy to sit still. Glancing at the calendar, she saw that she'd penciled in "Food Shopping" over "Emily Mott 4PM." Even as she resigned herself to a day bordered by mundane tasks—earnest Emily, whose plump fingers left sweat marks on the keys, definitely fell into that category—the white space around the scribbled letters seemed to stand out in relief. She had been meaning to get a copy of *The Palm Tree of Devorah* to guide her as she worked on the attributes. Why not drive to the bookstore that Krakauer had mentioned, then do her shopping at the Three Block Market? The Orthodox community was concentrated, he had said; the two stores were within a few blocks of each other. It would be a change. Interesting in an anthropological sort of way.

If Dilys's first impression was accurate, every business on Herrera Street had started out as something else. A dry-goods store had become Schimmel's Drugs, an old 5 & 10 was now a Kosher restaurant, Bob's Family Footwear displayed cakes in its window instead of the Buster Brown shoes hawked by the boy and dog on its faded sign. When the Jews moved in a half-century ago, they had changed the street but also preserved it in time. Every business was individually owned. The chain stores that had swept over the rest of the city in a Red Sea of progress had come to a halt here. The street itself was as plain as the stores were functional: the buildings were low and unadorned, and a few straggling palm trees

along the curb looked as if they had been thirsty for forty
years. Dilys, peering out her window at women in snoods
and long dresses and men in black hats, was transported back
to the sleepy market towns of her earliest childhood.

Weisgal the Bookseller had been a pawnbroker's once;
three golden balls were still suspended like idols over the
door of the narrow shop. As soon as Dilys stepped out of the
car, she was aware of her bare arms and Capri pants. She'd
rushed out of the house without giving a thought to appro-
priate attire. Walking toward the entrance, she saw a sepul-
chral figure—Weisgal himself?—staring at her from within
the dim interior. But when she opened the door, the pro-
prietor took no notice of her. One by one he reached for
books from a large box at his feet and checked them against
an invoice on the little counter. The shop was as crammed as
it must have been in the days when it held people's cast-off
treasures. Books covered the walls, overflowing into piles at
the bottom of each shelf. Dilys made a pretense of browsing,
but the light was bad and even the English titles were
unfamiliar.

She stationed herself in front of the counter. "I'd like
The Palm Tree of Devorah, please," she said, more crisply than
she'd intended. The man looked up at her with something
like incomprehension, as if she'd ordered a hazelnut gelato.
His face was lined and sallow, but the hair that fringed his
skullcap was as black as a boy's. "Cordovero, you know," she
added, stumbling. Wordlessly Weisgal plucked the book from
the shelf behind him. When he muttered the price, she was
startled. Such a lot of money for so few pages. Was he over-
charging her because she was gentile? Her father, for whom
the Jews were a renegade tribe, would have assumed so.

Ashamed of the thought, she offered the bills with a smile and waited for a long half-minute before remembering that he wouldn't take them from her hand.

The sun seemed especially bright after the claustrophobia of the shop. In the car Dilys almost succumbed to the temptation to flee back to her own neighborhood, but found herself turning, as if by remote control, into the market's little parking lot. The hand-painted sign on the roof over the entrance, *LIPSCHUTZ'S* in sweeping cursive, had been propped against two large wired letters, A & P, whose tops loomed above it. As she pushed open the old-fashioned swinging door, a small army came out—a woman with covered head and seven or eight children of different ages, from preteen to babe in arms. Surely they couldn't all be hers, she was far too young. The woman gave Dilys a sharp glance and looked away. The children stared openly. Again, she fought down the impulse to leave, but was drawn forward by inexorable curiosity.

At the entrance Dilys grabbed a shopping cart, grateful for something to hide behind. New markets were always a challenge—it took a while to learn the lay of the land—but here she was truly a foreigner in another country. The aisles were filled with women like the one she'd seen outside, chatting with each other as their little ones milled around. As she passed by with her cart, it seemed to her that silences descended, followed by animated bursts of talk. Determined to keep her eyes down, she couldn't help but notice that the linoleum on the floors was so worn in places that cement showed through. Dilys imagined Lipschutz and his family moving into the abandoned supermarket under cover of night, filling the dusty shelves with cans and boxes stamped with Hebrew letters. The place looked unsanitary by modern standards; still, she couldn't walk out empty-handed. On impulse she grabbed a box of soup nuts, whatever they might be—some sort of cracker, she supposed.

After years in California, Dilys had grown used to the abundance that had so dazzled her during her first weeks in San Diego. The polished heaps of produce were ravishing in their variety and perfection; she'd stared so avidly at a display of jewel-like peppers that Alan had accused her of acting like a refugee. But at the Three Block, a wartime sparseness prevailed: the bins were half-full, the fruits and vegetables pale and waxy, as anemic in their way as the bloodless slabs she'd glimpsed hurrying past the meat counter. She took two apples and moved on.

Dilys had debated whether to visit Krakauer and decided against it; he mustn't think she was invading his world. She saw now that there was little danger of that. She was weightless here—not invisible, but discounted, as if she were an alien life-form walking among beings who lacked the sensory equipment to take her in. The anonymity was strangely liberating. She stationed herself by the dairy section and pretended to deliberate over the cottage cheese while the life of the community swirled around her. "Four packages already we have in the freezer!" a stooped old man said. His wife, whose head was covered with a braided wig, sighed and said nothing but kept hold of the blintzes, reminding Dilys of her mother. There were couples, like this one, who looked as if they had come straight from the ghetto, but also young women whose hair flowed free, who carried themselves with easy confidence. Clearly, these must be the not-yet-married. One striking girl, who wore dangling earrings and a long dress that subtly revealed her curves, flirted openly with a couple of married men whose wives were attending to the groceries. The young Devorah Leah must have been like that, Dilys thought.

And soon this girl would be claimed, would cover her hair and her body, unveiling her beauty only for her husband, only at night. In a year she would have a child, and then another and another, and the little ones would flock around her as she shopped for wan vegetables and sanctified meat at the Three Block Market, and at the evening meal they would sit like olive shoots around her table, just as the Psalmist had written. Every step of her future was already inscribed in patterns as deep as ruts in a dirt road, the road itself going only one way.

It was a life—albeit stamped with Hebrew lettering—that Dilys had crossed an ocean to escape. Rules. Respectability. Predictability. Hadn't Alan saved her from all this? Why, then, was she transfixed, rooted by the dairy case with a container of cottage cheese in each hand, as if her own future depended on the choice between small curd and large curd? Why was she filled with perverse longing, which sat in her chest heavily, sweetly, like nostalgia? She wanted to go home, but home was not the place she'd just left: a one-bedroom in a run-down subdivision where no one waited but a mediocre piano student named Emily Mott.

Disorienting, then, to find herself back at Oleander Court after all. The soup nuts, in their quirky tangibility, were Dilys's proof that she had escaped to another world— picked items from the shelves, passed through the checkout line, installed her tiny bag in the back seat of the car, deposited specimens from her journey in her still-empty refrigerator.

After Emily left, she ate the cottage cheese with a large spoon, seasoning it with bites of an apple. It was a perfect supper—exactly what she wanted, with the soup nuts for dessert. Reclining on the couch, Dilys popped one after another into her mouth, partially dissolving the nuggets on her tongue and crunching what was left. They were as taste-less as sawdust but their texture was deeply satisfying, and like the loaves and fishes, they went on forever.

Rounding the corner at a jog-trot, Dilys acknowledged that the choir had never sounded worse. They were the embodi-ment of Lenten deprivation: spiritless and lagging, carni-vores deprived of meat. Dilys could not get away from Sunday service fast enough. She was, as American law enforcement tersely put it, the perp. At rehearsal on Wednesday she had given them as little as possible; she'd been distracted and indifferent, every crevice of her mind filled with the attributes. And only three weeks to Palm Sun-day. She ought to be spiffing up her arrangement of "All glory, laud, and honor" for the procession. She ought to be going over the Bach cantata for Easter. The church was still her livelihood, if nothing else.

Dilys thought she might be immune to religion—not surprising, since she'd had such a severe case as a child. Sev-eral times over the past week she'd tried to read *The Palm Tree of Devorah*, but Rabbi Cordovero's words had none of the juice and passion of the music; the text, for all its obscurity, seemed numbingly familiar. The usual thing, wasn't it? God all right. Man all wrong. Try to be more like Him. Fall on your face. Her father had done that quite literally, tripping over his vestments as he climbed the steps to the altar. He was a tall, cadaverous man whose looming height gave him an air of dignity even after he'd started tippling. When he fell, he'd sprawled like a scarecrow, robes tumbling, trousers riding up to expose his white calves. It had been the beginning—no, more like the middle—of the end, not only of his relationship with the church, but of Dilys's friendship with her longtime sidekick, Margaret. Dilys's mother had started up out of the pew and sat down again as, all around them, the congregation congealed into frozen silence. Margaret, sitting on the other side of Dilys, had laughed out loud.

"Is the Devil chasing you?" Ana appeared so suddenly that Dilys, in the headlong rush of her thoughts, would have plowed right over her.

"Oh, do forgive me! I was away with the fairies."

Ana narrowed her eyes and trained her black-marble pupils on Dilys. There was something immobilizing about her gaze, Dilys thought; if you were in her line of sight, you wriggled helplessly as if impaled on a pin.

"It's just as well you ran into me," Ana said. "I was about to leave an invitation under your door. We would like for you to be our guest at luncheon next Sunday."

Luncheon. The word conjured starched tablecloths and parish potluck. "So kind," Dilys said, "but I couldn't possibly. This is my busy season, you know, with Easter coming up."

"Lucky for you, then, that you won't have to open a can. It was *her* suggestion. Oh, we must have that lovely lady, she said to me. Just like royal blood of the Old School." Ana raised her eyebrows. "Perhaps you can explain to her about the singing. Speaking of which, such a racket was coming out of that apartment these last few days. Shouting. Weeping. Fists pounded on tables, or, God protect us, through walls. I thought of calling the police, but it is not my business."

"Really? I didn't hear anything, and my flat is right over theirs."

"Of course you didn't hear. You were away with your fairies. One o'clock?" Ana said, scurrying off before Dilys could answer.

Raspberry sherbet was all she could manage for lunch, but Dilys busied herself washing real fruit for Krakauer. Peaches, plums, apples, a banana, some lovely early strawberries. She doubted he would eat any; still, it gave her pleasure to arrange the fruit prettily on a cut-glass platter and set it on the coffee table beside *chochmah* and *binah*. Her own appetite had been dicey since the bacon incident. A pickiness had taken over, an aesthetics of the gut that rarefied her tastes; out of a newly stocked refrigerator, the sherbet had seemed the only possible choice. Her waistbands might be looser, but she felt healthy and energetic. The long cotton skirt she'd put on after church sat almost on her hips. Over it she wore a peasant blouse that Alan had bought her years ago; he had always said she looked too buttoned-up. Perhaps he had been right. She rather enjoyed the glimpse of flesh as she raised her arms to put up her hair.

Dilys wanted to play something that would soothe the butcher's frayed soul, some Hebraic melody to show him that she understood. But all she could think of was "Hava Nagila," and clearly that wouldn't do. In the end she settled on the quiet, haunting slow movement from Beethoven's

Pathétique. She had always loved the way each note seemed to rise inevitably out of the one before, as if the process of thought had been set to music. A Buddhist calm settled over her. After a volatile week, Krakauer might be in no condition to sing about God today. He might even have left the flat. That was all right. She would send down the music as a *mitzvah* for whoever was there to receive it.

A staccato rapping tore into her composure. Loud and demanding, it was the sort of knock a policeman might give before forcing the door. "I'm on my way," she called, rattled, reminding herself that she'd given the butcher permission to interrupt her.

Krakauer nodded curtly and strode in. His uncombed hair and beard stood at angles around his head, threatening to give off sparks if touched, like a Roman god's. Dark circles ringed his eyes, and he looked thinner, almost haggard, although his bulk still dominated the room.

"There's fruit," she offered. "Perhaps a little refreshment before we begin?"

"I ate already." His voice was hoarse. He went directly to his post by the piano, and she had no choice but to follow him.

"I was in your neck of the woods the other day," she said. "I got *The Palm Tree of Devorah* at Weisgal's. Fascinating!" It was a harmless fib. How could they work together when he hadn't even made eye contact with her?

Krakauer gave a dry laugh. "You think you can read such a book once and understand? It takes years. A lifetime. Music is a shortcut." He drank some of the water she had left for him and set it back on the tray with a clink. "So, to business. Here we have *chesed*"—he flung out his right arm—

"which is loving-kindness, also mercy. And *gevurah*"—he did the same with his left—"restraint and judgment. The right arm wants only to draw everyone near so it can pour out love unlimited, but the left arm pushes away the ones who are unworthy. Often associated with the verse from Song of Solomon, 'His left arm is under my head and his right arm embraces me.'" The butcher paused and took a deep, shuddering breath. He made pumping motions with his arms. "Push-pull. Push-pull. How can such a conflict be resolved? In *tiferet,* the torso, the beautiful center that brings harmony." He clapped both hands smartly to his chest and, as if he had jarred something loose, began to weep.

Dilys, still stung by the butcher's rudeness, was not primed for his tears. She sat for a few seconds in dumb amazement, at last grasping at the phrase her father had reserved for distraught parishioners: "There, there." She murmured the nursery syllables again and again, ashamed of their vapidity. If only it were possible to touch Krakauer on the shoulder or pat him on the back. Never had she felt so impotent. All she could do was run to the bathroom for a box of tissues.

Krakauer staggered to the couch and collapsed into the soft cushions, still weeping. "Excuse, please excuse," he choked. He took a giant strawberry from the platter and stuffed it whole into his mouth, chewing and swallowing quickly. If the fruit had been meant to stanch the flow, it had the opposite effect. The sweetness seemed to shatter what was left of his heart. He worked his way through a peach and a plum as tears and juice coursed down his cheeks and into his beard.

Dilys was almost crying herself. "Mr. Krakauer, do please let me know how I can help."

Krakauer grabbed a clump of tissues and blew his nose. "Help. What is there to help? All week was push-pull, push-pull, and now harmony is restored. Devorah Leah leaves with her mother on Tuesday."

"This is dreadful! Surely she's being coerced."

"My mother-in-law said things. I said things. We were like the two women arguing over the baby, only we had no King Solomon to judge, so Devorah Leah was torn in two. Finally end of week she caved in. She'll leave for a little while, she says. A vacation. Until she feels better. You understand, with such a condition as she has, the implications?" He nodded, wringing his hands. "Who can blame her? I'm away all day. She's alone in the apartment with the MS for company. No matter how much I do for her, the life I can offer is not what she's used to. With them she'll have every luxury."

"But she won't have her life's companion," Dilys said. Why hadn't she reached out to Devorah Leah herself—offered a ride or an afternoon musicale? Appalling how selfish she had been. "You're her husband, after all. I think it would be awfully difficult to go back to your parents' house after being mistress of your own. To be treated like a child again."

The butcher sighed. "Devorah Leah is in some ways a childlike person. For this I take responsibility. When we married she was like a young horse, unbroken, and I didn't want to tame her into the good Orthodox wife, it was for her spirit that I loved her. I thought with children would come maturity. But circumstances prevented, the children didn't come. And so she *became* the child." He shrugged and looked at Dilys. "You've never been married?"

"Once. Not for long. He left me for a woman who owned a vineyard in Santa Rosa. He was very ambitious, Alan was."

"A nice word for what he did, 'ambition.' I wouldn't be so polite."

"It was ages ago, and really, we weren't suited. We probably wouldn't have married at all if I hadn't needed a green card to stay in the States. I know what you mean about children, though. I was convinced we'd have them—that they'd make up for everything else. My parents had disowned me, you see, and the little ones were going to be the trophies of my triumphant new life. A boy and a girl. I've never told this to anyone, but I actually gave them names. Colin and Emma." She blushed. "Too, too pathetic."

"Aharon, Shaina, Zimron, Rahel, Shmuel . . . Devorah Leah and me, we didn't stop at two. Ten, there were." Krakauer's cheeks were still wet, but he was no longer weeping. He took another handful of tissues and swabbed his face and beard. "For each one I had to sit *shiva* in my mind. When the *sefirot* turned to music, I thought the Holy One, Blessed Be He, was giving me compensation."

A silence settled over the room, laden but peaceful. The butcher's breaths, ragged at first, began to even out. Dilys closed her eyes and allowed herself to entertain a picture of their collective unborn children flitting about like *putti*. Pleasant—consoling, too—to think of all those tiny muses hovering over the piano, shedding untapped potential.

After a few minutes, Krakauer stirred and cleared his throat. "It's finished now, I think. If I would have known I'd get so upset, I wouldn't have come. Why should I bring my mess into your afternoon?" He lifted himself carefully from the cushions and stood before her. How could she never have noticed his eyes—so large and lustrous, even in their reddened state? "I appreciate it that you listened," he said. "You have a good heart."

"Not at all," Dilys said, absurdly flattered. "I'm only glad you felt free to share your feelings. Life can be unkind, but— well, music is a comfort, isn't it? You must let me know when you're ready to sing again. Perhaps after the . . . transition is over."

"Ready? I'm ready now." He managed a crooked smile. "For what else am I here?"

Krakauer went to the piano. His hands shook as he picked up the glass and drank the rest of the water down. Dutch courage, Dilys thought. He took a deep breath. "As I was saying. *Chesed,* loving-kindness, flows down from the Almighty to us. When we are kind to each other, we give back to God what He is giving out in the first place. Present company not excepted." He gave a little nod in her direction. "This is the cosmic arrangement. Always the two-way street, et cetera unto infinity."

Krakauer shut his eyes and stood in silence, his hands balled into fists at his waist. Dilys watched the fists become cups. Slowly he started to sway, holding his hands before him like begging bowls. Seconds turned to minutes as she waited, finger poised above the recorder button, wondering what invisible manna was falling from the sky. When the bowls were full, he began to sing.

Usually he faltered when he began, but this sound was immediately warm and rich, as if his voice had been lubricated by tears. Round tones, an Italianate lushness. An aria without words, she thought, bathing in it—all high notes, all emotional peaks. It was the first thing he had ever sung that

seemed to her to have the character of a love song; no wonder he had mentioned Solomon's. For years the Song of
Songs had been the only part of the Bible that she could read
with pleasure. She and Margaret had giggled at the bold cat-
alog of body parts, but the poetry had lingered. In her teens
she had memorized whole sections, and as the butcher sang,
passages came back to her.

> *As an apple tree among the trees of the wood, so is my*
> *beloved among young men.*
> *With great delight I sat in his shadow, and his fruit was*
> *sweet to my taste.*

That was how love should be, Dilys had thought then. An
alloy of earth and heaven—grand and holy and, yes, sexy as
hell. Necks like ivory towers, thighs like jewels, arms of gold,
legs of alabaster. Bodies worshiping each other, just as the
marriage rite in the old Book of Common Prayer had
ordained. Hardly surprising that the reality had fallen short.
Romantic, high-minded young women such as she had been
were doomed to disillusionment, born to be preyed on by
cads, pragmatists, cold-blooded technicians. In her short
amatory career, she'd known them all. But the music was
transporting her back to that walled garden where she still
waited for the knock on the door, the hand on the latch.

> *He brought me to the banqueting house, and his banner*
> *over me was love.*

Dilys was so lost in reverie that she hardly noticed when
Krakauer stopped singing. She looked at him and saw that

the raw grief was gone; on his face was an expression of tender reminiscence that echoed her own feelings. The music had taken them to a similar place. His garden, she imagined, would be inhabited by the young Devorah Leah—sensual as Salome, uninhibited as Eve. She waited respectfully for him to emerge from his own dream of love.

When he spoke, it was only to say the single word "*Gevurah,*" his voice as hollow and distant as it had been the first time she met him. The character of the attribute was apparent as soon as he began to sing. If *chesed* had been an aria, *gevurah* was the recitative. He sang syllables without meaning, shards of words that struck the ear harshly, repetitively, like one side of an argument, a point made again and again. The tone was familiar to Dilys. Alan had sounded like that when he was angry; instead of raising his voice he would grow quiet, besieging her with logic, funneling his emotions through an aperture so narrow that they came out as contempt. Now, as then, she had to resist the urge to put her hands over her ears. Just as she reached the breaking point, the syllables smoothed and turned to melody. At first she heard only dissonance. Then a pattern evolved, an ordered chanting tempered by an underlying sweetness that reminded her, of all things, of plainsong. Not so odd, really. Although she had never been to a Hebrew service, she had been taught long ago that Christian chanting was derived from synagogue worship.

Dilys would never have believed that two such dissimilar pieces of music could be brought into harmony, but *tiferet* was what she and Krakauer made when they sang together late that evening. The attribute reigned in the music and between them, banishing his embarrassment, her hesitation.

There was an ease now, an instinctive blending; they might have been singing together for years. She knew that she had never been in better voice. The voluptuousness of *chesed* seemed to add pillows of flesh to her thin, sweet soprano. Krakauer let her sing alone for a while, listening intently before inserting his sharp syllables. She experienced them first as a pinging distraction—as a child she had been frustrated to the point of tears when singing rounds. But the chanting, when it came, was pure support, encircling her dulcet tones and tremulous vibrato lightly but firmly, as a sash girdles a loose gown. If *gevurah* held the abundance in, it also gave it shape.

Krakauer had moved closer to her while they sang, and he stayed near when they finished. His eyes continued to gaze into hers, ardent and unfocused, as if the music still filled the perfectly respectable space that separated them. But he is looking at *me*, she thought. Whether he realizes it or not. In the end it was Dilys who turned away, out of regard for his privacy. She had already glimpsed Krakauer's nakedness today; he would not, she knew, forgive further trespasses.

The butcher refused an offer of more fruit, but paused in the doorway. "Thank you for your hospitality," he said. "And the rest also."

"Will you be all right?" Dilys asked.

"I'll live. God willing."

"Come up anytime, if you need to talk." Brilliant. Shades of Mae West.

Krakauer put his hand up, as he had the first time she met him. Now the gesture seemed more a benediction than a prohibition. "I wouldn't trouble you," he said, with finality.

"Well, then. Next week." She nearly added "God willing," but thought better of it. After he was gone, she saw that he had left last week's notations on the coffee table.

Dilys undressed slowly in front of the full-length mirror in her bedroom, letting her peasant clothes fall to the floor. The woman in the mirror was slender, even girlish—"I wish I had your figure," the choir ladies were always telling her—but her body had an unused look. Alas, she was no Shulammite, no dark, delectable maiden to give pleasure to a king. Her breasts were too small to rest in the hand like clusters of grapes, her navel too shallow to hold wine. It was obvious that she'd neither borne nor given suck.

She ran her hands over her torso. Krakauer had called it the beautiful center—but of what? The scattered limbs. The treacherous heart. The vulnerable belly with its coiled appetites. On impulse she crossed her arms behind her back and massaged her sides. She and Margaret had done this when they were not yet in their teens: pretending that boys were groping their skinny flanks, panting and lolling their tongues in mockery of an ecstasy they had just begun to sense. The illusion had been pretty thin even then. Dilys was not prepared for the heat that flared up when her hands became the butcher's. The pads of his fingers applying just the right pressure. The practiced touch of a man accustomed to the texture of flesh, the give of it.

Later, safely shrouded in a flannel nightgown, a mug of hot milk on the night table, Dilys talked sense to herself. Was it really possible to be sexually attracted to someone who wore a hat indoors? Someone so thoroughly clothed that a glance from his naked eyes made her avert her own? She had always been drawn to lean, fair, tightly muscled men. The very idea of Krakauer was ludicrous—and yet he had stirred her pond, he had made her burn with desire.

All her life she had resisted mystical explanations. *The Lord spoke to me. The Devil made me do it.* But now her viscera were crying out, telling her fate as loudly as if they'd been spread on a shaman's altar. It's like it's printed, Krakauer had said of the music. Clearly, in her case, the attributes had gone deeper. They had pierced her like stigmata. They had gotten under her skin.

NETZACH, HOD, YESOD

"*I'm just going to do* a scrape-and-burn," the doctor said. "Trim a little more to make sure we've got it all, and then cauterize."

Dilys, lying back with a drape over her eyes, was aware of a dull pressure. Not painful, but disconcerting. Her mind knew perfectly well that the instrument doing the scraping was sharp, though it felt as blunt as a thumb. The pen that the doctor was wielding must be the burn part, applied judiciously like the lit end of a cigarette. As he worked, the nurse sucked up the smoke with a tiny vacuum. "Charred flesh doesn't smell too good," she said cheerfully. Cover it up with a bit of tape, and that was that. The smoke and mirrors of modern medicine.

"You English roses can't take too much sun," the doctor told her afterward. She thought that was rather poetic, coming from a stocky man with a grizzled crew cut whose previous conversation had been confined to words like "basal cell."

She'd been ordered to take a cab home because of the anesthetic, but managed to persuade the receptionist that she needed a bite to eat first. There was a pleasant outdoor café at the medical center, situated between the physicians' offices and the acute care facility. Dilys thought that it ought to be called the Café Limbo. She carried her latte and oversized scone to a table with an umbrella and settled down to consider the events of the day before.

On Tuesday morning she had awakened early and stationed herself by the window, hoping to observe the leave-taking of the butcher's wife. It was a drama in which she'd played a small part, she told herself, adjusting the curtains. She didn't have to wait long. At 8:15 Krakauer carried two large suitcases into the courtyard and stowed them in the trunk of his car. He went back into the building and returned with a number of smaller bags, some of which he wedged under his arms like a porter. On the third trip he wheeled Devorah Leah, muted in a moth-brown vest and taupe pants. Dilys was sure that the outfit had been chosen by her mother, who walked behind them erect as a soldier and as smartly fitted out. Krakauer, pale but stoical, lifted his wife into the front seat of the car. The mother-in-law got in the back with the collapsed wheelchair, and they were off.

The thought of Krakauer returning to his empty apartment sent Dilys back to Herrera Street to look for some token to leave at his door, some small reminder that he wasn't alone in the world. On second viewing the neighborhood was almost familiar. Weisgal nodded when she came into the bookstore. He seemed to have anticipated her request for a commentary on the *sefirot,* bringing a paperback out from under the counter as if he had been saving it for her. Encouraged, Dilys walked the whole length of the street, looking into windows and ruling out their contents. Food? Krakauer worked in a market. Flowers? Too funereal. Judaica? How would she feel if someone presumed to give her a cross or a framed picture of the Lamb of God? In the end she bought a bottle of Kosher wine and a box of note-cards featuring watery pastels of Jerusalem. And she found the shul.

She hadn't been hunting for it, as far as she knew. She'd wandered down a side street in search of more shops and dis-covered in the middle of the block a stucco building, vaguely Spanish in style, neither new nor old. Hebrew letters were inscribed over the double doors. It was exactly what one would expect of that homely sliver of a word, *shul*: not so grand as a temple or self-important as a synagogue. Unique in the neighborhood, the shul had retained its original identity. Members of the fledgling congregation must have stinted on their own storefronts to raise money for a house of prayer. She pushed on the doors, certain that they were locked, and was startled when they opened inward.

She found herself in a small anteroom, furnished only with a bookcase that held prayer books and a box of skull-caps. Not a sound could be heard. Timidly she nudged open a second pair of doors, half-expecting to see a congregation of covered heads bent in silent prayer, and felt a rush of gratitude that the sanctuary was empty. The simplicity struck her first: two banks of wooden pews; a balcony; a raised plat-form holding a desk, a table, and a few chairs. The altar was a sort of cupboard curtained in embroidered velvet, mounted on the back wall beneath a suspended light. For an Anglican, it was rather like looking at a face without eyes. She was used to the focal point of the cross and the sacramental finery surrounding it, a Magus's bounty of silver and candles. Apart from the curtain, there were few decorative touches here. The stylized candelabra sculptures on either side of the cupboard reminded her depressingly of the early sixties trappings she'd seen so often in older banks and office buildings throughout the city.

She sat at the end of a bench, a few rows from the back. The smell, at least, was familiar. Minus the incense, there was still that gallimaufry of must, furniture wax, and old book bindings, along with something else that she was aware of whenever she sat alone in a church. Call it breathed prayer. The exhalations of the faithful over time, hanging in the air like a rain cloud. One didn't have to be a believer to feel it.

The cupboard looked as if it should contain communion silver, or the Jewish equivalent. But this must be the ark—she knew that much. During services, the curtains would be drawn apart, the doors opened, and the Torah scrolls exposed, reverently, fastidiously, like a heart within a body. She had seen pictures of Jews lifting their shawls and prayer books to the Torah as it was carried past them, kissing the part that had touched the sacred text. Next door to idolatry, her father had intoned. Dilys hadn't been willing to go that far; she had merely found it comical that people could be so reverent about a roll of paper. Sitting in the shul, she sensed for the first time the magnitude of the intimacy that had been granted. Judaism seemed to her to be a religion of secrets. Each week the hidden was revealed here, but only in part, and only to a chosen few. She felt a bit the way she had as a child when her father took her along on parish calls some evenings. The lighted windows in the village, with their hints of rich life within, had filled her with poignant longing. She had yearned then—she yearned now—to be *inside*.

Some sound from above, no more than a disturbance of the air, made her look up. A bearded man stood in the balcony, his hands spread on the wooden barrier. She had no idea how long he had been observing her. In the second or two before she bolted, she had time to note that his expression was both studious and unalarmed.

If there was an actual Limbo, Dilys decided, it wouldn't be nearly as attractive as this café. Probably it would be gray and rainy like the north of England, with that creeping dampness that kept one from ever getting too comfortable. Here she sat, in this way station between diagnosis and possible death, and all she could worry about was whether crumbs were spraying out of her mouth as her numbed jaw labored over the last quarter of her scone.

Not that she was in danger of dying. Basal cell wasn't fatal, the doctor said, but it had to be controlled. "Wear that sunblock," he had exhorted, "and check in with me every six months." She ought to feel the long shadow of mortality. She ought to be asking herself what her life meant and where it was going. Instead, she gave in to cow comfort, relishing the sun and air and the taste of her coffee, turning over in her mind with a placid masticating rhythm the question of what would happen next.

After rejecting fruit (too evocative), wine (might lead to

temptation), and a few consoling words on the watery notepaper (pushing her luck), Dilys had simply rolled up the forgotten notations into a scroll, which she bound with blue satin ribbon and left outside Krakauer's door. The wine she had put in the refrigerator. Best to keep it on ice.

Dilys was going to be late for lunch at Ana's, through no fault of her own. The rector had gone on and on about how the world was quickening toward the great drama that would culminate in Easter. He had reeled off the stages of Jesus' journey like a sports announcer calling plays: "He's pausing to counsel the rich young ruler. . . . He's leaving Jericho at the head of a milling crowd, but what's this? A blind beggar by the roadside. . . . He's sending his disciples to see a man about a donkey. . . ." The congregation would follow Him every step of the way, the rector promised. They would feel the sweat on their brows and the dust on their feet.

All well and good, Dilys thought, but what about the folks responsible for the special effects? She'd arrived at church an hour early to rehearse with the choir, and spent an extra half-hour after the service with the soloists. When she'd told Ana that this was her busy season, she hadn't been hedging. Dilys had tried to call, but the Melendez sisters had an unlisted number. So now, at one o'clock, she was half-running, half-walking in the midday sun, one hand clamping her straw hat to her head, and yes, she could definitely feel the sweat on her brow. It was probably washing the sunblock away.

The Melendez flat was on the ground floor, across from Krakauer's. Dilys glanced over her shoulder at his door, trying to suppress the feeling that she was consorting with the enemy. She lifted the large brass knocker that the sisters had installed, but before she could bring it down, the door opened. Ana and Silvia stood in the entrance. They had arranged themselves—who knew how long ago?—in hieratic poses of welcome, hands clasped at their waists, heads inclined deferentially toward the visitor in the manner of the diplomatic corps.

"We thought you had forgotten," Ana said. "Although I left many notes."

The living room reminded Dilys of the hotel she and her parents had stayed in while vacationing in Spain—the only time they had visited the Continent. She recognized the carved furniture, the mirrors framed in gilt, the ornate draperies lowered to half-mast to keep out the sun. There were a number of tables, each cloaked in silky material with ball fringe around the hems. Although it was the middle of the day, all the lamps had been switched on.

"How grand!" she said. "And so immaculate. My place is like a college dormitory compared to this."

"Heirlooms," said Ana, pronouncing the H. She pointed to two small bowls on one of the tables. "We had nibbles, but now there is no time. Everything is ready."

The table was too massive for the small dining alcove, which had been designed for subsistence eating. Dilys, seated in the middle with the kitchen at her back, tried to make conversation with Silvia at one end. This sister was no less enigmatic close up than she appeared from a distance. Although clearly the younger of the two—Ana, it seemed, had been born wearing black—Silvia was dressed as Dilys's own mother might have been, with smoothly set hair, a blouse with padded shoulders, and a fitted skirt that fell below her knees. She answered Dilys's questions politely, in barely accented English, but volunteered nothing. It was as if talking itself were a discomposure, her features always eager to settle back into a sphinxlike mask. As soon as she finished speaking, her eyes wandered beyond Dilys toward the kitchen.

Ana reappeared, carrying a large platter. "The little breads were nice and puffy when I took them out of the oven. By now they are flat," she said.

"Puddings," Silvia corrected. "York-shire puddings. We thought you would enjoy a dish from your homeland."

"In our country, a pudding is soft and sweet," Ana said. She set the platter down. At its center was a chunk of ribbed meat surrounded by beige disks, looking for all the world like a ship's prow run aground on rocks.

It was almost parody, Dilys thought, sawing at the thick slice on her plate. How had they managed to capture the precise degree of overcooking, when the fiber of the beef, bereft of its juice, turns defensively to string?

Ana and Silvia were having no easier time of it than she was. They chewed deliberately, taking delicate sips of wine after each bite. They rarely spoke to one another, but glances passed between them across the table, and Dilys was certain that Ana's eloquent eyebrows had moved more than once. She was beginning to feel like one of those New World innocents from Henry James. Why had they asked her anyway? Surely not to chat about the royal family, although she was doing her best.

"And what about this Charles?" Ana asked. "Will he marry his lady friend?"

Dilys took a long drink of her wine, which was red, and

so coarse that it left a sediment on her tongue. She was very thirsty. "I don't have the faintest idea. I shouldn't think the queen would like it much if he did."

"Ah, the queen. She must be listened to. She is thinking of respectability, yes?"

"She's the only one with any left, I think. After toe-sucking and Tampax and all the divorces. Who can blame her for putting her foot down?"

Ana fixed Dilys in her hard, bright gaze. "The queen across the hall, the haughty one, she has also put down her foot. She has taken away her daughter. The Jew is alone now. Maybe you know."

Dilys, caught with a mouthful of Yorkshire pudding, said, "Mrs. Krakauer left for medical reasons, I believe. To see a doctor in New York." She smiled as coolly as she could manage with a wad in her cheek and prayed that she wasn't blushing. The biddies had probably been living with their ears to the door for weeks.

Silvia got up to collect the plates. Ana removed the platter. The two were eerily unalike; Dilys would never have guessed that they had come from the same womb, and yet their every action showed the cranky symbiotic complicity that one saw in long-married couples. Perhaps, she thought, they weren't sisters at all, but lovers who had chosen to live out an elaborate masquerade. That would explain Silvia's guarded smile, Ana's interest in the scandals of others. What fun if it were true—the idea of a hidden life somehow made them more tolerable. Quickly she checked her watch. Thank God, she could make a graceful exit soon.

Ana, returning with coffee cups and a small carafe on a tray, leaned over Dilys and whispered, "She has made you her flan. It is the only thing she cooks." She lifted her brows significantly.

The flan quivered when Silvia rested it on the table. At least it's set, Dilys thought, remembering the runny yellow custard ladled over the desserts of her youth. Silvia cut wedges and slid the pieces expertly onto glass plates. Both women watched as Dilys took the first bite.

"Delicious!" For once she could speak the truth. A subtle, melting sweetness, a hint of citrus. She shook her head when Ana offered coffee. "I hate to eat and run, but really, I must dash. I have a—a lesson, you know, at three. . . ."

A look passed from one sister to the other.

"Ah, a lesson," Silvia said. "Then you must take the rest of the flan and share it with your pupil."

Dilys followed them into the kitchen, weaving slightly from the wine. Things had gone well, considering. Easier to deal with a bit of gossip than the interrogation she'd been expecting. They were really rather dear, this odd couple. "Such a splendid lunch—" she began.

"So. This lady friend of Charles," Ana cut in. "This Camilla. Not a beauty like the poor princess, but an aristocrat of good family, married, I have read, to a handsome fellow with small ears. It would have been better for all if she had stayed home with her horses. As we say in my country, a woman has only one reputation to lose." She ripped a sheet of waxed paper off the roll and made a tent over the flan. "If you would be so kind as to return the dish?"

Krakauer was due in twenty minutes. Dilys had just enough time for a reviving shower and a change of clothes. After tossing half her wardrobe onto the bed, she threw on a caf-

tan that she'd bought long ago but never worn. White, with
blue embroidery, it had seemed too elegant to lounge in, too
exotic to wear outdoors. Krakauer would probably take one
look at her damp hair and think she was wearing a
nightgown.

At the piano, her fingers picked out random notes. She
hadn't a clue what she would play this afternoon. In spite of
the rush she felt mellow and unhurried; the shower had
washed away most of the effects of the wine but left a residue
of ease. Lately she'd been thinking more about composing—
nothing too ambitious, just a couple of short mood pieces to
start. Working on the attributes this past week, she'd been
aware of something that she could only call permission. A
sudden freedom, a playfulness. Why not embellish a little,
use her knowledge and skills to bring out the hidden riches
in the music? Until now she'd been afraid to do more than
slavishly record what Krakauer had sung. Daunting as it was
to monkey with a transmission from above—she had enough
religion left in her to see that—her field trips to Herrera
Street had given her some confidence. She was beginning to
feel more like a collaborator.

She'd been playing for about five minutes when she
heard the knock: gentle and tentative, the opposite of last
week's. Relief flooded her; he must be coping then. On the
way to the door she ran her fingers through her hair, hoping for a tousled effect.

The butcher was noticeably thinner—was it possible to
lose so much weight in a week?—but perhaps it was only the
way he was dressed. Instead of his usual shapeless clothes, he
wore a crisp white shirt and pressed pants. His hair and

beard had been trimmed, and the black hat, set atop his newly clipped head, seemed almost rakish. He clutched a string-tied box to his belly.

"Mr. Krakauer! I'm so glad you've come. I've been concerned. . . ."

"Concerned, who wouldn't be, after such a performance?" He came in and, looking around, set the package on the coffee table. "A little something from the bakery." Without being asked, he settled himself on the sofa.

"How kind. May I peek?" She slipped the string off and opened the box. Inside was a dense-looking loaf, already sliced. "A quick bread, is it? Lovely."

"Bobka. Between bread and cake. It has raisins, also walnuts. You're not allergic, I hope?"

"Oh, no. You'll have some, won't you?" After her heavy lunch, the last thing she wanted was another dessert. She must try to manage just one piece.

The bread was tasty and lighter than it looked. Krakauer made quick work of a couple of slices, but held up his hand when she offered another. "I have to be careful not to overdo. The last few days I didn't eat much."

"Of course not. How could you?"

"The food wouldn't go down. Words I could take in." He fell into a silence, and she imagined that he was reentering the week.

"Was it . . . forgive me if I'm prying, but was it very hard?"

"Very hard, yes, with the accusations, beginning Sunday night as soon as I walked in the door." The words reeled out of him in a monotone, as if he spoke under hypnosis. "She's a talker, my mother-in-law, the things that come out of her mouth, believe me, you wouldn't want to meet on a dark street. What am I doing week after week in another woman's house, a blond *shikseh* no less? What kind of music do I think I'm making? I'm bringing shame on my wife, I'm bringing shame on the whole family that I have such an honor to belong to. The door to the lady's apartment is always open, I tell her. Oh, she says, the rules have changed? Open the door and it's Kosher what happens inside?"

"Devorah Leah," Dilys said. The undulant name seemed to stick in her throat. "What does she think?"

The butcher sighed through his nose. "From the beginning my wife loved the music. She was the one that suggested I go to you. Who knows now what she believes? The last couple days she didn't leave the bedroom, on the way to the airport not a word. I'm lifting her out of the car, it's like a ghost in my arms."

"Mr. Krakauer, I'm so dreadfully sorry. That I—that the music—should be a cause of division. I had no idea."

"The idea was in another head. For this we're not responsible. As to sorry, for what?" He leaned forward. "The first night she's gone, I come home after work and there at my door is the music. Tied up with ribbon, like a package from God, special delivery. He's telling me that this is what I am left with, this is my consolation prize. With one hand He takes away, with the other He gives a present. Now I have no distractions. All week I've been studying—at work, at home. I'm eating the words, how can I be hungry?"

"And the music?"

Krakauer's eyes gleamed. "Like never before."

Dilys moved back in her chair. The blanched intensity of

his face alarmed her. Where had she seen this aggressive rapture before? A memory flitted across her mind and was gone before she could catch it.

The butcher seemed to sense her discomfort. He retreated into the cushions, and, taking a handkerchief from his pocket, mopped his forehead. "Warm today," he said. "If you don't mind, I could use some water. I think I'm dehydrated."

As Dilys opened the fridge, she could feel his eyes on her. She busied herself with ice and glasses. What if the caftan was transparent in the light? He would think she was a *shikseh* after all—was that the Hebrew word for "whore"? And in her hurry she'd grabbed any old underwear out of the drawer.

"You're wearing an angel's dress," Krakauer said.

"Hardly." She laughed, but her hands trembled as she arranged the tray. He had never alluded to her physical being, except to ask about the bandage on her temple. "It's Moroccan, actually. Pure indulgence. One of those things I should have known better than to buy."

"They sell them also in Israel. Devorah Leah got one from her cousin, she liked to wear it at night. . . ." His voice trailed off and he looked away.

Dilys put the tray back on the counter. "Speaking of indulgence, I happened to be on Herrera Street the other day and I bought a bottle of wine. So silly, I liked the picture on the label. I don't suppose you'd—well, it's a bit early, but I don't entertain much and I can hardly offer it to my pupils, though I expect they'd play better if I did. Would you care for a glass?"

"A few drops, why not?"

The wineglasses were on the top shelf of the cupboard. Alan had insisted that they buy good crystal; he had been caught up in the romance of the vine even then. Dilys wondered when she'd last used them. Harvey, was it? He always wanted to eat in because he was saving to go back to school for his MBA. He'd go on and on about tax shelters and long-range planning until she was limp with boredom, and then, in his methodical way, he'd jump her. She would not think of that.

Krakauer drank a full glass of water before sampling the wine. He pursed his lips and took it in slowly. "It tastes like it looks. The color, I mean."

He was right, she thought. The wine was almost golden, sweet but not cloying, with an aftertaste that reminded her of pears. She topped off her glass, then the butcher's, and he did not protest.

Krakauer picked up the bottle when she set it down. "Made in the Golan Heights. I see why you liked the picture."

The idyllic scene had caught Dilys's eye: a vineyard set against a backdrop of symmetrical mountains; a stucco house off to one side, a pair of minute figures at its door. "I've always loved miniatures," she said. "Little worlds in a frame. They make me feel homesick, somehow. As if I'd left that place when I was a child and never returned."

"You miss England, maybe?" This time Krakauer filled the glasses.

"That's the odd thing. Familiarity has nothing to do with it. I've never been anywhere near the Middle East, not in this life, anyway. It's the smallness, I think. Tiny, perfect worlds—they always seem so inviting. I have a feeling that if I could only go back, all would be well. I suppose any place

looks good if you see it through the wrong end of the telescope."

Krakauer nodded. "Far away makes life look simple. The
people in the winery, what do they need? Some sun, some
rain, a nice chicken to go with the wine. Close up is when the
complications begin." He startled her with a grin. "Drink a
little more, who knows, maybe we'll get a return ticket.
Speaking of which."

"Yes?"

"Not being a camel, could I use your facilities?"

He had said "we." Dilys was sure of that, although probably it meant nothing. The bathroom was in the hall between
the living room and bedroom. She went into the kitchen and
made a great show of rattling plates and running water in the
sink to give him the illusion of privacy. Still, she could hear
his restrained trickle, which seemed to last for many seconds, as if he held back even there.

She was careful not to turn until she heard him close the
bathroom door behind him. He smelled of her lavender
soap. Marooned in the middle of the room, they smiled at
one another awkwardly. We don't know how to be normal
yet, Dilys thought. We still need the piano.

Krakauer glanced at the clock. "If you're too tired to
work, I understand. It's no problem to come back another
night."

"Not a bit. I'm so eager to hear what you've . . . received
this week. Really, I couldn't be more awake." It was the truth.
The wine, instead of dulling her senses, had made her
hyper-alert. Her nerves tingled.

The butcher seemed to hesitate, but took his place by the
piano while Dilys set up the recorder. He inhaled deeply.

"*Netzach* and *hod*. Another pair, often called twins, to me more like husband and wife. The body thinks it's whole"—he ran a hand down his side—"but where can it move until it splits into right leg and left leg? *Netzach* is victory, the best foot going forward. Like a marching army, like a hero who conquers. Fences, walls, this *netzach* kicks them all down. He won't stop until the whole world is filled with the goodness of God. By which I don't mean that *hod* is second best. How far can the right leg go without the left leg? Slow down a little, *hod* is saying. Keep on the path. If you give to everyone, it's too much water in the soup, the glory is diluted. Relax, take off your boot and stay awhile with me. And the conquering hero listens because this other half is majesty, she is splendor, what is he without her, she's worth more than rubies." Krakauer's voice, which had gotten shrill and incantatory, dropped almost to a whisper. "You see what I mean. It's important to keep the balance."

"Yes, quite." Very well, then. It would be her responsibility to help him stay on course. "But there's a third attribute, isn't there? What do they make when they come together?"

Krakauer glanced up at the ceiling, as if the answer would drop from above. He seemed in such distress that Dilys wondered if she had offended him with her prompting. "*Yesod*," he said at last. "The foundation of existence. Very difficult. Very complicated. Between *netzach* and *hod* is another kind of harmony. The end of the torso, but life begins there. The sign of the Holy Covenant."

What was she to make of that? It all sounded rather smells-and-bells, the High end of Anglican. The expression in his eyes was almost pleading. She had no idea what he wanted from her, but tried to look brightly attentive.

The butcher opened his lips, ran his tongue over them. "Reproductive organs," he said.

Oh. Baby-making. She should have seen that one coming. Dilys almost smiled, but was stopped by the sight of his face, which had turned an odd, congested red. Her own blushes were no more than a momentary coloring of the skin. His stained him like dye. Something deeper than embarrassment must set them off, she thought. Something more like shame. But what had he said that was so terrible? From what she'd seen in the Kosher market, the Orthodox took literally the command to be fruitful and multiply. And it wasn't as if the words themselves could misbehave.

Krakauer closed his eyes. Last time he had waited to receive the music. Now he seemed to be struggling toward it through enemy fire, head lowered, body rigid and tensed to run. She expected that his clenched fists would open, but his foot moved first, striking the scuffed tiles with such force that she almost jumped out of her seat. Then the other foot, heel and toe, until both feet were beating out a rhythm. Was he listening to the song in his head, or doing an extended drumroll of an introduction? He lifted his legs higher and brought his feet down with greater force. His arms were crossed over his chest now, his upper body as stiff as a Cossack dancer's. The sight should have been ridiculous. Instead, it was chilling. Dilys thought of goose-stepping armies, and then of the groom grinding a glass underfoot at Jewish weddings. "They say it has to do with the destruction of the Temple, but symbolically, you know, the bride is being crushed," her father had explained, pointing out the advantages of New Covenant marriage. The raw primitivism of the image had thrilled her as a teenager. Now she felt an unease that was equally primitive, equally raw.

The song, when it finally came, seemed like an extension of the stamping. A thudding bass, a dogged rhythm pierced at intervals by shrill cries. From his description of *netzach* she had anticipated some sort of patriotic anthem. What she heard was another kind of hymn, ancient and timeless. Native American, she thought at first, visualizing a tribe of feathered warriors dancing around the fire, but the melody could be Hebrew, or even Greek. Odysseus might have sung it on the way to battle, or a hunter as he stalked his quarry. Tremendous longing was in it, but the structure was as formal as a fugue's. Desire had been ritualized. No matter how wild the cries, there was the counterpoint of the rhythmic footwork, slow at first but gradually gaining speed, voice and movement honed to a single intensity. It reached a peak and stopped.

Krakauer was sweating and breathing in spurts. He can't possibly sing anything after that, Dilys thought. Although the music had stirred her, the look in his eyes made her feel cornered. The butcher had always seemed too big for the flat, but never more than now. He had opened his mouth and let something wild into the room. He had swung a club over his head, scattering all her little niceties, her carefully preserved touches of civilization. What did she really know about him? She almost wished that he would go.

Several minutes passed before Krakauer began to slowly rock back and forth. Dilys wondered if he was praying, but as his breathing became more measured, she saw that he was creating another kind of rhythm. He closed his eyes and threw back his head. A single note came out of him. If this was a cry, it came from a deeper place than the throat-cries of *netzach*; it was the sound a cello might make as a bow was drawn across its strings. Dilys had been standing on a threshold until the rich tone lured her in, and as the melody built she found herself in a hall, grand but intimate, with walls of polished wood. The acoustics were extraordinary. She could feel in her bones every tremor of his voice, every change in pitch, as if the music were inside her. It circled and circled, a simple, plangent theme made intricate through repetition, and at the height of its intensity, it stopped.

Dilys waited in silence while Krakauer came back to himself. His face was almost ascetic now, the fleshiness melted away by grief and also, she thought, by study. He was beginning to resemble the scholars he held in such awe, who spent their days contemplating sacred texts. The irony was that he had never been so conventionally attractive. It wasn't only the pounds he had dropped, but the quite literal refinement he seemed to have undergone. The dross of ordinary life had been pressed out of him. Even the sweat that dampened his shirt seemed part of this purification. She could see the outline of his body in the limp folds, the faint pink of his skin where the cloth clung.

Krakauer's eyes opened. He wiped his forehead with the back of his hand and looked around him in a distracted way. I should never have offered him wine, Dilys thought. Not on an empty stomach. When she got up from the piano bench, he all but shrank from her.

"Mr. Krakauer, are you all right? Can I get you anything?"

"Nothing, thank you. I should leave." He stared at her as if she had the power to dismiss him. What had become of the fearsome warrior?

"You don't want to go on working? Please, tell me what's the matter."

The butcher dropped into the orange chair and cradled his head in his hands. "The bow must only be drawn when it's pointed at the right target," he muttered. "In the book it says."

"I beg your pardon?" Was it possible that he had thought of a cello, too? But no, he was speaking of a different kind of bow.

Krakauer seemed to have sunk into himself again. Dilys resisted her tendency to fill the void with nervous chatter. She felt, for once, calm and sure.

"You know that I can't do the notations properly until we put both parts together," she said. "Whatever you're feeling, I hope you'll think of the music. Please remember, we're only the instruments, you and I."

You and I. She had released them into the room as unit, couple, pair, duet. Two vowels, she thought nonsensically. They fluttered in the air like trapped birds.

Krakauer sighed into his hands. The face he raised to her was pale and strained, but composed. He lifted himself out of the chair and went to stand beside Dilys at the piano.

His bass was steadier by the time they were ready to join their voices, more purposeful than insistent. The cries, which had sounded random at first hearing, had a rhythm of their own; they were both beast and stick, the animal desire and the goad urging him forward. Krakauer nodded, and Dilys entered when the tempo quickened. Her voice was too fragile to sustain the long note, but still, it drew him in. She was Penelope in the splendid hall, an artist at waiting welcoming her lord in all his roughness. Who would have believed that the restless beat that drove him could be domesticated so soon? Who would have imagined that her quiet sonorities could be stirred up to such a wild gypsy dance? From chamber to chamber they twirled and spun and stamped until, together, they stopped.

Breathless and shaking, Dilys and Krakauer looked at one another. His face is a mirror of mine, she thought. He sees what I see. We've brought each other to the same place.

"It's such an amazement to me." Krakauer's voice was low and hoarse. "That someone not a Jew . . ."

Abruptly he wheeled around and rushed out. She hesitated for a second before snatching up last week's notations. "Mr. Krakauer!" she called from the doorway. He was already at the bottom of the stairwell. When he turned to her, half in a crouch, crossing his arms before him like a small boy caught naked, she understood why he had left so quickly.

MALCHUT

"*All those men*," Margaret had said, standing too close to Dilys, searing her with her gaze. "They were just a shadow of the real thing."

The two of them hadn't seen each other in ages. After the incident at the church they had pointed their faces in different directions, like the saved and the damned in a medieval Last Judgment. Dilys was the obedient daughter, helping her parents make the transition from church to guesthouse, practicing the piano, earning honors at school and getting her certificate from a local teacher's college. Margaret went bad. She hennaed her hair, disguised her mild features under a whore's mask of garish colors, shortened her skirts until they barely covered her rear. By the time she was thrown out of school in her last year, she had already had several lovers and an abortion. She had gone to London then, with an auto mechanic twice her age, and her scandalized parents had not tried to stop her.

At the guesthouse door that December day, Margaret looked remarkably like the child Dilys remembered. Her hair had been cropped and her scrubbed cheeks were raw from the winter wind. She had come home to make things right with her family before entering a community of Anglican nuns in the city. Yes, it was true, she had fallen in love with Jesus. Dilys must come to visit her at the Order of the Holy Parakeet, see the wonderful place for herself. "Oh, I will," said Dilys, backing away.

When Dilys told her father the news, he wagged a shaming finger at her. "Not 'Parakeet.' Para*clete*. It's another name for the Holy Spirit. Imagine a vicar's daughter not knowing that!" But Dilys preferred to think of her wild friend in an aviary, saying her prayers amid lush greenery as brightly feathered, highly verbal birds chattered from every branch.

Margaret came to mind, an avid, feverish presence, as Dilys sat cross-legged on the bed on Tuesday evening. Spread out on the duvet were books on ritual, holidays, history, conversion—instruction manuals for the seeker whose identity she had assumed over the last weeks, recently categorized as "someone not a Jew." Not that she was ready to declare herself. She'd gone to the library and Barnes & Noble instead of Weisgal's. The bookseller's melancholy eyes would have peered into her inmost parts; he would have reached under the counter for the book he had set aside for her. In a community as small as Herrera Street, word would get around. She didn't want Krakauer to see her as his mother-in-law did: the *shikseh* seductress willing to put on Jew's clothing to land her man.

But would she wear the costume if given the chance? Would she hide her hair under a scarf or wig as Margaret had hidden hers under the veil? Hide her life, for that matter? Looking through the photographs in a book on Jewish ritual, she tried to picture herself as the woman standing over the candles on Shabbat, tenting her eyes with her hands as if to shield them from the sun. The image had a visceral attraction for Dilys, as the shul and market had, but when she put herself in the woman's place, it felt like playacting. Facts must be faced. She was too old to be the fruitful vine surrounded by olive shoots. And the man she envisioned at the head of the table was married to someone else.

Scholars, she read, were obliged to fulfill their "marital duties" on the Sabbath. Did the same apply to butchers? She imagined Krakauer sawing away at his beef and his books in the gulag of the meat locker, each tedious day bringing him closer to the set table, the braided bread, the feast of Devorah Leah. How Victorian of the writer to call such pleasure a duty! Still, as Dilys's mother was fond of saying, who knew what went on behind closed doors? Whenever Krakauer spoke of his wife, Dilys detected a wistful sadness that she attributed to the illness. Once or twice she'd wondered if Devorah Leah's condition had disabled her romantically.

Of course, the problems might be more fundamental. Krakauer had dropped little hints. Childlike, he had called Devorah Leah. In the code of his stunted speech, that could mean skittish or headstrong or a tease. Circumstances prevented, he had said, when talking about the lack of children. Was it possible that the marriage had never even been consummated?

That thought was such a revelation that Dilys sat straight up and hugged her knees, causing several books to slide to the floor. If true, it explained so much. All these years Krakauer, a man of passion, had been living with banked fire, heaping on more ashes when the flames threatened to leap too high. *I stoop, I carry, I serve.* Until the music brought him to her door, he had never had an equal partner, never known the ultimate intimacy. They'd been strangers when they began to work together. Different cultures, different religions, no more than an abstraction in each other's minds. Week after week they had traveled down the body, blending their voices in a kind of mystical foreplay until, last Sunday, they had overcome separateness altogether. The two of them had teetered on the brink of ecstasy. And they had never touched. Not once.

After Krakauer had left that night, she had turned to the next chapter of *Palm Tree,* reading with an urgency usually reserved for thrillers. The final attribute was *malchut,* kingship or sovereignty. Its corresponding body part was the mouth, but according to the commentary from Weisgal's, it had also been associated with the crown of the penis. She'd had to wade through pages of lofty obscurity before grasping the idea that both seed and word existed to be released—into the woman, into the world.

Dilys smiled now, thinking of the gamut she and the butcher had run. From the crown of creation to the crown of the penis, from the lordship of the universe to man's small domain. Apparently Judaism encompassed both. If the small blue book was any indication, the cosmos was in a constant flux of attraction, arousal, and fulfillment, one attribute flowing into another. The laws, with all their restrictions, only made the coupling more intense. "You were wrong, Margaret," Dilys sang out, crowing. "Men aren't just the shadow of the real thing. They're the main event. They're quite the point, actually." As the wimpled presence receded into the distance, Dilys gave herself permission to think openly of what had bubbled beneath the surface of her thoughts for the past two days.

Years ago she had developed a theory about penises, based on the few she had acquaintance with. It seemed to her that, rather like dogs, they took on the character of their owners. How else to explain Alan's, a slender, efficient instrument that got the job done in a manner that could only be described as brisk? Ken's had been interrogative and a bit earnest, as a high school teacher's should be. "And what do *you* think?" it always seemed to be asking. With him she had felt like a nebulous cave through which he was leading his charges, flashlight held high, drawing their attention to points of interest to disguise his own fear of the dark. What a contrast to Harvey's pragmatic organ, which denied all mystery. Harvey had inserted it like an ATM card, and as he

pumped away, Dilys had imagined instructions appearing on
the screen: MAKE DEPOSIT. LET SIT FOR A WHILE. INTEREST
WILL ACCRUE.

Certainly it was an invasion to think of Krakauer that
way, but in a sense he had already revealed himself to her.
Leaning back against the pillows, she closed her eyes. This
most hidden part of him could only be conjured from what
she already knew. Red and full, then, thrusting out of a bed
of dark, curling hair as his lips bloomed from his beard.
Suffused with pent-up desire. And if that desire at last found
release, where would it carry them both? To what good,
green place? To what seventh heaven?

Before choir rehearsal on Wednesday night, the rector's wife
came up to Dilys. A new family had just joined the parish,
the Wings from Taiwan. The father was a doctor and there
were four children, including twin girls who played the
piano. "They're looking for a teacher for the girls," she said,
"so I couldn't resist bragging about our wonderful organist.
If you're not full up, do you think you could give them a listen? After the holidays, of course."

Dilys had been too distracted to think of money matters,
but the rent was due next week and Krakauer hadn't paid her
yet for the notations. "Actually, I've had a cancellation. I
might manage to see them on Friday afternoon."

The vile necessity, she thought. These days her piano
students occupied only a small corner of her mind. She had
begun to think of herself as a musician again, a practitioner
instead of a nurturer. The patience that was her stock-in-
trade eluded her now; it seemed intolerable to have to instill
passion and skill where none existed. Last week, even the

slump of Emily Mott's back as she huddled over the keys had been enough to provoke a silent tantrum. Shall these bones live? she had wanted to shout. Shall these bones *ever* live?

The Wings arrived punctually at half-past three on Friday: the mother small and neat; the girls looking younger than their nine years in sequined jeans and jackets that seemed at odds with the classic solemnity of their faces. Mrs. Wing had little English and left the talking to her daughters. The two of them sat up very straight with their hands in their laps and answered Dilys's questions with pained precision, all the while gazing at the piano. When Dilys said, "Well, now, let's see what you can do," they ran for the bench as if a spring had been released inside them.

She had thought that they would play separately, but they slid onto the bench together and launched immediately into Bizet's *Jeux d'Enfants*. What struck Dilys first was their technique, then all that went beyond it. If, in their shyness, they had seemed stiff and almost robotic, they were graceful as dancers at the keys. And the delicacy of feeling they were able to evoke amazed her; already, at such a tender age, they were little divas of controlled emotion. They followed the Bizet with another duet before ending with individual short pieces.

"Marvelous!" Dilys said when they had finished. "But really, gifts like yours should be developed by a master teacher. I can give you a few names, there's someone very fine at the university—"

Mrs. Wing stared at her, shocked. "You do not want . . . ?" The girls, sitting side by side on the other end of the couch, went rigid, as if sentence had been passed on them. They must think that she was fobbing them off. How could she make them understand?

"Of course I want . . . I would love to work with you. It's only that—" *That I don't deserve you. That I have spent my own promise on the mediocre. It's a kind of vocation, if you know what I mean. A calling.*

Dilys looked at the two pinched faces across from her. The mysteries of the split egg. Their mouths were pulled down identically, the lower lips pendulous from trembling on the brink of tears. No doubt they were complete individuals, once you got to know them; she could see it in their hair, the messages on their T-shirts, the way they'd arranged their preteen regalia. But in the realms of instinct and intuition they were alike. That was why, at the piano, they were so effortlessly attuned to one another—as though some exquisite code of etiquette were inscribed in their shared DNA. What would it take to teach this little Gang of Two, to make more of them than the sum of their parts?

"Then what day, please?" Mrs. Wing said in her silvery voice. "And how much?"

Dilys felt a stitch in her side. Apparently the universe had given her a nudge. "I—I must just check my schedule and give you a call." She turned to the twins and saw her smile reflected in the softening of their faces; already they had entrusted themselves to her. "It will be an honor to work with such wonderful pupils. It will be"—she paused, wanting to give them some bright souvenir to take home—"an *exhilaration.*"

She hadn't asked for a sign, but she had gotten one. It was not quite five when the Wings left. Time enough before sundown to toss together a potluck Shabbat.

Fortunately she'd defrosted a packet of chicken legs and wings—not the burnished bird she had in mind, but parts would have to do. When had she started eating appendages? A symptom of her helter-skelter, snack-on-the-run way of life. From now on food would be lifted up, eating itself would be a sacred rite. She basted the chicken pieces with soy sauce and honey and put them in to bake, along with a sweet potato. In the corner of the vegetable bin she found a bag of green beans, past their first youth but for tonight better than frozen.

As savory smells filled the room, she curled up on the couch and read about conversion. It wasn't easy to become a Jew. First, you had to ask three times while the powers-that-be plumbed your motives and gauged your seriousness. Then a year of study—history, festivals, life-cycle events, keeping Kosher—culminating in an oral test before a court of three rabbis. Finally, ritual immersion in the *mikveh*, the Jewish version of the baptismal tank. For Dilys, it would be a baptism-in-reverse.

Well, she'd had no choice about the first one, had she? A photo framed in silver stood on the side table by the wing chair in every house they had lived in: her father, newly ordained, his Adam's apple showing above his clerical collar; her young mother, blond and still slender in dotted swiss, holding the infant Dilys, a round penny of a face all but lost between the ruffled cap and the long white christening gown. It must have been a good time in her parents' lives, a promising time. Who could have foreseen the miscarriages or the drinking or the public fall from grace? Who could have predicted that their only child, after alienating them in so many ways, would strike the final blow by deciding that she was, in her father's term, "of the Hebrew persuasion"? Poor bewildered lambs. She thought of them almost with tenderness, as

if they were the children and she the callous grown-up about
to break their hearts again.

The timer beeped. Outside it was almost dark. The only
candles she could find had been given to her by one of her
students last Christmas. Muddy green and reeking of bayberry, they were clearly homemade, but set into china candlesticks they acquired enough dignity to preside over the
table. Dilys put bread on a plate and covered it with a doily.
The bottle of wine that she had shared with Krakauer was still
in the refrigerator. Enough was left for one more glass,
which seemed to her a benediction. She lit the candles with
a kitchen match and read the blessings as well as she could,
stumbling over the transliteration. *Baruch atah Adonai* over the
flame, the wine, the bread. With the book in one hand it was
difficult to cover her eyes, but as instructed, she waved her
free hand around the candles to draw their light and warmth
inside her. She would need these reserves if she kept the Sabbath through the next day.

As she ate her dinner in the dimming room, she watched
the moon from the window. Not quite full, with an aureole
around it. *Malchut*, she had read, was like the moon, without
light of its own but reflecting the light of the sun. Tomorrow
she would let the attributes shine through her. She would
rest, go over this week's notations one more time, perhaps
play some of the other pieces from memory. Work was forbidden, but one didn't "work" a piano, one played it. And
she wasn't a convert yet.

The candles were still burning when Dilys made her groggy
way into the kitchen the next morning. The whole apartment
smelled like Christmas. She felt hung over, not from wine,

but from lack of sleep. Her mind had refused to quiet down last night; she'd stared at the ceiling, immobile as Gulliver, as random questions pricked her one by one. Why hadn't she gotten an automatic coffeemaker? Why didn't she ask one of the Thai children next door to turn on the lights for her? How would she explain why she couldn't do it herself? Around two the rain had begun, a steady English drizzle that persisted into the new day. She wrapped her robe more tightly around her. If it weren't for the cold stove and dark kitchen she might take pleasure in this rare respite from the sun. Years in California had not effaced her genetic need for coziness, for tea and a good read beside a cheering fire. Today, though, she would have to settle for orange juice and cold cereal by the light of sputtering candles that flickered eerily in the funereal gray of the room. The bayberry was as pungent as incense by now, and as unsettling to her stomach. She snuffed the flames before sitting down to eat.

Dilys had thought of walking to the shul after the service started. Last night it had seemed like such a good idea to stand outside and listen to the chanting. She had imagined the building expanding with sound and contracting into silence, a rhythm as physical as breathing. But the rain made her less keen. Better not to rush things, she told herself as she showered. The cycle of attributes would not be completed until tomorrow. From a symbolic point of view, it was more fitting to wait until next week. And who knew how the universe might have shifted by then?

She put on an old stretched turtleneck and sweats, and settled at the table with the notations. If only she could have a hot drink to take the chill off her bones. The notes were cold, too, hieroglyphs that refused to sing for her. Black on white, they were as impenetrable as the nonsense syllables that common words sometimes turned into: "foot" or "vase" —what on earth was that? The tape was in the machine, and she was too apathetic to press the button. She didn't want to be stirred up today, taken to those heights, left quivering on that edge. She was in a mood to be soothed.

How did the Orthodox manage to fill the day? She had never been very good at feeling spiritual on cue; in her churchgoing days, no sooner did she bow her head than up would float items from a plastic jewel box of trivia that apparently occupied the lower portion of her soul. It had been the same with Oxfam fasts and meditation. She had wanted to think of the attributes today, and instead she was reviewing the British comedies that she would watch after sundown. *Fawlty Towers, Are You Being Served?*—she would have disdained them in England, but here they were slightly exotic.

The piano, then. She would let the keys meditate for her. Dilys grabbed the afghan from the back of the couch and draped it over her shoulders as she sat down. The ivories seemed to have absorbed the chill in the room; something must be wrong with the furnace, but the landlord wouldn't be bothered on a weekend. Closing her eyes, she whispered the names of the attributes one by one, invoking them to pass through her. After a few seconds her fingers began to move, picking out a melody that was vaguely familiar, and yet strange. Which attribute was it? She let the notes lead her on for another minute or two before the dots connected into "Sheep May Safely Graze."

It was a piece that had always had a soporific effect on

her. The Sabbath was for rest, anyway. Better to give in, to curl up on the couch instead of falling asleep over the keys, to unfold the afghan and wrap herself in Aunt Esme's orange, gold, and rust-colored squares, to open the Shabbat manual and read through the litany of thirty-nine forbidden acts. Plowing, sowing, reaping, sheaf-making. No danger there. Writing was listed—erasing, too—so for one day she needn't feel guilty about her unfinished letter to her aunt, a trail of crossed-out lines and emendations that meandered down the page like old railroad ties and ended just as abruptly in white space and a signature: Yours affectionately, The Prodigal Niece. Threshing, winnowing, selecting, sifting, grinding, kneading, baking, sheep-shearing . . .

The water was warm and delicious. She sank down and down, her arms loose as seaweed, her hair streaming above her. Who could have imagined that the tank was so deep? Her eyes were wide open. She could see the three rabbis outside the glass, their mouths moving in their beards. Were they praying or singing? What did it matter, it was all the same thing, wasn't it? She wasn't in the least embarrassed by the presence of men in black hats; her nakedness was as blameless as an infant's. But there were her parents, looking grim and out of place, and there was Alan. Her mother whispered to her father. Her father turned with one of his martyr's sighs to the American, as he had so often before. "If you wouldn't mind just giving us a hand . . . ?" Alan smiled his tight-lipped smile. He rolled up his sleeve and, reaching one arm into the tank, pulled her up by the hair.

Dilys couldn't have said whether the knocking awakened her, only that she heard it when she emerged into the air. She would have drifted back under, but the cold hit her as soon as she threw off the afghan. The apartment was completely dark. She switched on some lights and shuffled to the door, blinking. "Who is it, please?"

"Krakauer."

Had she slept all the way into Sunday? What would they think at church? "Just one moment, Mr. Krakauer." She ran to the bathroom to splash some water on her face and run a comb through her hair. The afghan had etched its pattern into her left cheek. Lovely.

"I'm afraid you caught me at the end of a snooze," Dilys said, opening the door.

"What else is it good for, a day like this?" The genial boom of his voice hit her like a clap on the back. He was wearing a red sweater, thick with cabling, which looked so unlike him that Dilys thought it must be a gift from his mother-in-law. But perhaps this robust, hail-fellow-well-met garment was covering up his embarrassment about last week.

She gestured for him to come in. He stepped over the threshold, but paused within a couple of feet of the doorway. "Won't you sit down?" she said, puzzled.

"I can't stay. I only wanted to tell you that I won't be able to make it tomorrow." Krakauer grinned as if he had said something clever. "I would have let you know earlier so you could make room for a not-Horowitz, but the Shabbat . . ." He sniffed deeply, his nostrils flaring. "You're planting pine trees in here now?"

It was still Saturday, then, and her amateur Sabbath was blessedly over. That was a relief, but Krakauer's manner jarred her. Given what had passed between them, she would have understood a few smothered words, or even a note shoved under the door. But he was effusing a breezy joviality that seemed completely out of character. Smiling. Rocking on his heels. Any minute he would toss his black hat in the air and break into a soft-shoe.

"What a pity," she said. "Not another crisis, I hope?"

"Crisis I wouldn't call it. My wife is coming home, her plane arrives tomorrow at one. Meanwhile I'm cleaning like a madman. You wouldn't believe the mess I made in two weeks."

Dilys couldn't speak. Gracious phrases choked her throat, ancient civilities that now seemed as atavistic as tails. She hoped that her expression conveyed pleased surprise.

Krakauer took her silence as an invitation. "Friday I got the call. She's lonely, every minute she's thinking about what she left. In her fancy room, down-filled this, silk-lined that, she misses her old chair and her old bed. None of this is mine, she said. Her parents were telling her wait a month, you just got here. But Devorah Leah said no." For a second his eyes gleamed the way they had when he spoke of the music. "She's a strong person, my wife, when she wants to be."

"My goodness, what marvelous news. I'm so happy for you." Probably she had been wrong about the marriage not being consummated. Wrong about everything.

"And that's not all. There's a bonus. My in-laws don't like the idea of Devorah Leah living in a place like this, no amenities, a not-so-nice element, if you know what I mean. Bad enough they have to swallow the butcher, at least their daughter should be with her own society. So they're buying us a house. In Happy Isles, no less. Three bedrooms, hand-icapped accessible." He shrugged theatrically, his eyebrows lifting along with his shoulders. "I didn't ask for it. But who am I to say no?"

That clownish grin. The gap between his teeth—had she

actually thought it charming? He was the picture of coarse-
ness, a caricature that her father might have summoned up,
and it was through her father's eyes that she saw him now.
The man had the right to rejoice in a little good fortune.
Still, she clung to her sense that this new well-being was fake,
that it would slip off as easily as the ridiculous sweater,
revealing the Krakauer that she knew.

"Quite Job-like, isn't it?" she said. "God has given you
back double what you lost. Will you be moving soon?"

"The house is ready. Three weeks, maybe a month."

"You'll be over your ears with packing, then. I know
how moving is. But I can't help thinking about the music.
We're so near the end now. If you could find a couple of
hours . . ."

She thought that she saw his eyes shift. "The music,
funny you should mention, I was speaking to the cantor
about it this morning. I gave him the translations. He only
had time for a quick look, but he was impressed. 'Mendel,'
he says, 'who knew you had such a talent?' He'll go over them
this week, and if he likes what he sees, he's talking maybe
professional singers, a CD. A big fund-raiser is coming up
for a new shul. It could be this is what the Holy One
intended from the beginning."

Her lips were wooden. "In that case, we'll have to get
busy with *malchut*, won't we? Grand finale and all."

For the first time she felt that she had penetrated his
façade. His smile faltered. He gave another exaggerated
shrug. "Nothing came this week," he said. "I opened the
book, it's only words. My feeling is, the music is over." He
paused. "I told the cantor about you in regard to the CD,
but . . . he's thinking a baritone and a tenor to get the full

effect. At least I can give you something for all your work. Overdue, I admit, so a little extra is in there."

He took the check from his pocket and, lacking a convenient surface to lay it down, held it by one corner as if a sudden wind would waft it to her.

All the forbearance Dilys had shown through the years, to Alan, to the others, fired her now like fuel beneath a rocket. She threw back her head and laughed—a wild, scale-climbing, mad-diva's laugh that drove Krakauer back toward the door. "So you're replacing me with a tenor. Oh, that *is* flattering. Take all the passion out of the music, drain it of its blood, and it's pure enough for the synagogue. I suppose you think of me as a sort of secretary, jotting down the precious notes from heaven as they drop from your lips. The anointed butcher sings his holy songs, and the pagan piano teacher takes dictation. Until we began to sing together, you never even looked at me. And then—and then—" She was weeping, the tears falling down her face warmly, deliciously, like the water in her dream. "Do you have any idea what I have brought to this work? How much of me is in it? And you shrug your shoulders and say it's over, as if the whole business was up to you. Well, God must have something to say about it, mustn't He? There is one more attribute. Why would He stop now?"

Krakauer had not moved under her assault, except to lower his head. When he looked up, she saw that her words had ripped away the mask of affability. His face was as raw and exposed as her own.

"The Holy One chooses to wear a fig leaf," he said. "In this, also, I imitate him."

He extended his hand—to offer her the check, she thought,

but the paper fluttered to the floor. With his forefinger he touched the patch of new skin on her temple. The pad of his finger was broad, the pressure he brought to bear just enough to indent the flesh, exactly as she had imagined.

"Stay out of the sun," he whispered, and was gone.

🍑

On Palm Sunday, Dilys Cathcart sat among vines and ferns and flowering plants in the Botanical Building, her favorite spot in Balboa Park. She was to meet Martin Runyon here and go to lunch with him at the new restaurant that had just opened near the sculpture garden. They had both agreed that leaving church together would not be wise; gossip circulated quickly at the coffee hours, and Martin's divorce was not final. Dilys liked Martin. In his banker's suits and striped ties, he was the image of what her parents would call "solid": Bond Street, but with a twinkle. He must be close to sixty, though; he had been sweetly rueful about having to spend Easter with his married daughter.

The old blind man was on his usual bench by the orchids, headphones on, Walkman in his lap. Dilys wondered why the anonymous helper who dropped him off didn't have the sense to sit him down among flowers that smelled. But perhaps that didn't matter, with the mingled fragrances of a thousand other blooms surrounding him and the music filling his head. Bach, she hoped, or Mozart. He looked today as he always did, enviably absorbed and self-sufficient. For all she knew, he might spend every waking hour breathing in this thick green air as sunlight filtered down on him through the louvered roof. The wholeness of his solitude made her feel peaceful.

The palm branch she'd waved in the procession was sticking out of the top of her carryall. Why hadn't she thought to leave it in the car? Silly to be holding on to a dead frond when exotic varieties of the tree were flourishing all around her. There was something appealingly human, she decided, about the palm's tall, slender trunk and small cap. It wasn't one of those behemoths that dwarfed the person underneath. She could understand why Devorah the Judge had chosen to hold court under one. The tree would enhance her authority without overwhelming it. The tuft of leaves would be her horsehair wig, making a crown over her as she sat on her pedestal doling out equal measures of justice and mercy to the contentious children of Israel. Dilys saw the petitioners lined up in a long queue, two by two, like creatures waiting to board the ark. Some stood quietly; others traded sharp words or violent gestures. But all, as they inched closer to their moment in the shade with the woman who would mediate between them, must have looked with longing at the clusters of dates hanging from the branches above her head: ripe, succulent, out of reach.

Acknowledgments

The Maryland State Arts Council provided welcome support during the writing of these stories. I am indebted to the MacDowell Colony for the gift of time and a beautiful place to work, and to the Wurlitzer Foundation, where, so many years ago, I began to think about Eden.

I know how much I owe to the extraordinary community of writers at Warren Wilson College. Andrea Barrett has been a wonderful and inspiring mentor, a model of grace in every way. Debra Spark's encouragement and generosity have been unstinting. I am grateful, too, to Joan Silber, and to Janet Peery for being right about a story. Margot Livesey, Peter Turchi, and Richard Russo have graciously given advice.

Abundant thanks are due to all those who have read and commented on the stories over the years, especially Christine Hale, whose insight into my work, even at its earliest stages, verges on the prophetic. Long conversational walks with a good friend and fellow writer, Ann Jensen, have sustained me through many difficult days at the desk. Alan and Wendy Regier, faithful friends and readers, have often shared their private Eden in Vermont. I am indebted to Stephen Corey of *The Georgia Review* for his comments about "Rug Weaver" and his patience with my obsessive fine-tuning, and to Molly Kleinman for her input on the musical references in "The Palm Tree of Dilys Cathcart." And I remember with gratitude a small writers' group in Peterborough, New Hampshire, that provided manna in the desert.

Members of the Kabbalistic Circle of Annapolis introduced me to *The Palm Tree of Devorah* and continue to bolster my shaky knowledge of Kabbalah. I am grateful to Ann Wilner for sharing details of her spiritual journey, and to Ellen Meyer and Debbie Renaut for feedback.

It has been my privilege to work with an editor as exceptional as Carol Houck Smith, whose perceptions about the stories have been quiet revelations. Wendy Weil not only guided me through the thickets of first publication but offered insights and encouragement.

I am fortunate in my family. My husband, Stewart, who delights in language and uses it well, has given boundless love and support. Sara, my exuberant daughter, has brought much joy, and does me the honor of being proud of me.